CRUEL
Saints

USA TODAY BESTSELLING AUTHOR
MICHELLE HEARD

Cover Designer: <u>Cormar Covers</u>

TABLE OF CONTENTS

Dedication

To my fellow authors and readers.
Thank you for the encouragement and support
while I wrote Cruel Saints.

Italian translations: Luca Brunetti.
Thank you so much, Uncle Luca & Aunt Dorothy.

———————————

Songlist

Click here - *Spotify*

Calling on Angels – J2, Natalie Major

Kingdom Fall – Claire Wyndham

Land of Confusion – Hidden Citizens

No Mercy – UNSECRET, Icetope

We All Bleed – Roenin

Paint it, Black – Ciara

Not So Bad – Yves, Ilkay Sencan, Emie

Take Me to Church – MILCK

Bad Romance – J2, SAI

Ready for War – Liv Ash

It's a Sin – Hidden Citizens

Atonement – Denmark + Winter

Never Tear Us Apart – Dia Frampton

Synopsis

Alliances are made. Loyalty is owned. Love is taken.

Little did I know my love and freedom would be taken to form a new alliance.

Brutal, possessive, and dangerous, Lucian is feared by all. Including myself.

When his father is assassinated, Lucian takes his rightful place as head of the Cotroni family. They rule the Mafia with an iron fist, and he's set his sights on my family.

Until now, we've been the only threat, but when a new one emerges, my father is forced to arrange a marriage between Lucian and myself.

He might be handsome, but he's not the kind of man who loves. He takes what he wants, and right now, it's my body.

I might belong to him in name, but the question remains – will our union be consummated in blood or love?

CRUEL SAINTS

Mafia / Organized Crime / Suspense Romance
COMPLETE STANDALONE.

If you need a warning before reading a book, then this book is not for you.

Please heed the warning.

Family Tree

Lucian Cotroni

Luca Cotroni
Father

Family Business: Mafia/Arms/Drugs/Bootlegging

Mother: Dorothy Cotroni (*Deceased*)

Aunt: Ursula Brunetti

Elena Lucas

Valentino (Tino) Lucas
Father

Family Business: Mafia/Arms

Mother: Eva Lucas (*Status Unknown*)

Personal Guard: Dante Capone

Chapter 1

ELENA

The Past - 17 Years Old.

My stomach is knotted with nerves as I glance over my shoulder before sneaking out of the house. Making sure I'm not seen, I break out into a run toward the stables.

With my father away on business, it makes it a little easier to meet Alfonso. I've been sneaking around with the stable boy for a month now. Alfonso was a pleasant surprise when he came to work here with his father, Gino, who's been in our employment since I was a little girl.

Because my father deals in arms, I don't get to live a normal life. I'm surrounded by an army of private tutors, guards, and staff who won't hesitate to tell my father if I do something wrong.

Taking one last glance back at the sprawling villa to make sure none of the staff saw me leave, I walk into the stables.

I stop to pet Brimstone, my father's favorite horse, and movement catches my eye. Turning my head, I watch as Alfonso comes out of the tack room. He's only a head taller than me, with dark brown hair and amber eyes.

"You're early," he says with a grin tugging at his lips.

As he walks toward me, I enjoy the warm expression in his eyes. It's the closest thing to love I've experienced. That's why I'm breaking all the rules to have these stolen moments with Alfonso in the stables.

To my father, I'm a bargaining chip to secure an alliance when he needs one. Just another one of his many belongings. My father has never shown me any kind of love. When I was younger, it broke my heart, and I used to spend nights crying myself to sleep. Now that I'm older, I've accepted it's the way things are. I guess he's cold and cruel because he's a part of the Mafia. No matter the reason, I'm done crying over something I can't change.

My mother left after my birth, and I have no memory of her. Whether she's dead or alive, I don't know. No one ever talks of her. The only thing I know about her is her name. Eva Lucas.

I don't blame her for leaving if that's what she did. Between my father and my personal guard and tormentor, Dante, life is nothing but endless days of suffocation.

My mouth curves up into a smile when Alfonso stops in front of me. He gave me my first kiss, and last week I gave him my virginity.

He's not the most handsome, and I don't get butterflies, but that doesn't matter. Just the thrill of sneaking around with him and having him want me is enough for me.

I also get to defy Dante. He'd probably kill Alfonso and beat me if he found us together.

"The house is suffocating," I explain why I'm early. "I needed to get out."

Alfonso walks to the wide wooden doors and glances around the property before he turns back to me. "How did you escape Dante?"

"He's having lunch."

Alfonso comes back to me, and taking hold of my hand, he leads me to the back of the stables where the tack room is. It holds all the saddles, brushes, and other equipment for the horses. It's also the only private place where Dante won't think to look for me.

Alfonso shuts the door behind us and turning to me, his gaze drifts over my face. "Run away with me," he says once again.

Honestly, the idea is tempting, but I know there's no escaping Dante. He'll find me, and his wrath will be cruel.

Lifting my hand, I rest my palm against Alfonso's chest. "It's not worth the risk. When we're found, Dante will kill you."

"When we're found? You don't think I can keep you safe?" Alfonso asks, a frown forming on his forehead.

No one can keep me safe, least of all a nineteen-year-old stable boy.

Instead of voicing the truth, I ask, "Where would we go? With what money?"

"I'll find work," he says while he places his hand over mine.

"That's not a guarantee," I argue.

Alfonso's head begins to lower, and before his mouth meets mine, he murmurs, "Let me take you away from here."

My naïve stable boy.

Not wanting to talk about something that can never be, I accept his kiss. I part my lips for his tongue to enter, and soon we're stripping each other out of our clothes. I get lost in the moment where I get to be free. Having sex with Alfonso has nothing to do with attraction but everything to do with making a choice for myself. For one blessed moment, it feels like I'm not a prisoner in my father's villa.

For a moment, I feel loved or as close to loved as I'll ever get.

I know it's selfish of me. I do feel guilty for using Alfonso, but my need to defy my constrained life drives me forward. My need to be more than just a bargaining chip makes me return his kiss.

When we're naked, and Alfonso rolls on a condom, I lean over a wooden table. Bracing my hands on it, I close my eyes as Alfonso positions himself behind me. He enters me slowly, and I bite my bottom lip from the slight pain. It's only our third time, but at least it doesn't hurt as much as the first time.

"Elena," Alfonso groans when he's all the way inside me. He grips hold of my hips and begins to move. My cheeks flame up at the slapping sounds filling the room.

I let out a soft groan, and it makes Alfonso move faster. "I love you," he grunts at my back.

I soak in his declaration, savoring it like a starved girl. Alfonso is the first ever to say those words to me, and I never knew how much I needed to hear them until now.

My eyes burn with emotional tears, but unable to return the declaration, I instead reply, "You feel so good."

Suddenly Alfonso's ripped away from me. He staggers backward and slams into a wall. Glancing over my shoulder, my eyes dart to Dante's face, and seeing his angry scowl instantly makes fear pour through my veins like acid.

Mother of God. This is bad. So, so very bad.

I grab my shirt from the floor and quickly cover myself as best I can while frantically pleading, "He didn't do anything. I forced him."

Dante's top lip curls into a sneer as his malicious glare snaps from me to Alfonso, who's climbing to his feet. My stomach churns with dread, and I swallow hard as my body begins to tremble.

"You're fucking Elena?" Dante growls while yanking his gun from behind his back.

"I'm sorry," Alfonso cries with panic tightening his features. There's no sign of the boy who wanted to run away with me. Instead, Alfonso's pale with terror, his eyes wide on the gun aimed at him.

Dread bleeds through me, making my skin prickle and my heart race wildly. "Please! Please don't," I shriek as I dart forward, grabbing hold of Dante's arm. "Don't kill him. Please."

Even though I'm pleading with Dante, I'm still surprised when he shoves Alfonso back against the wall because he's never done a single thing I've asked of him before.

I almost let out a breath of relief, but then Dante trains the gun on Alfonso again. Dante turns a dark glare on me before he backhands me hard with his free hand.

It sends me sprawling over the wooden floor. An ache spreads through my cheek, but I quickly scramble to my feet. Covering myself with the shirt, my breaths explode over my lips as my heart beats out of control. Dante's ominous chuckle fills my ears, and I know it promises nothing good. Only pain. It's always been followed by pain.

Before I was born, Dante was my father's right-hand man. He still is, but now he's stuck babysitting me, and he hates me for it. As the years passed, it only seemed to make it easier for Dante to become a vicious monster.

Dante's cruel gaze locks with mine, and then his sneer grows, making the scar on his left cheek pull. "Principessa," he growls. Shaking his head, he steps closer to me, never taking the gun off Alfonso, who's white as a ghost where he's frozen against the wall. "Tsk. Tsk."

"I'm sorry. It won't happen again," I try to reason with Dante. I should know better, though. There's no reasoning with the devil.

His eyes rove over my trembling body, and then the usual viciousness in his gaze turns to something else… something sinister. A shiver rushes down my spine, and I fist the fabric tighter against my front as I hunch my shoulders to make myself smaller.

"I'll tell my father," I try to threaten Dante, but we both know it's an empty threat. My father will always believe Dante's word instead of mine.

"Tell him what?" Dante sneers. "That I killed Alfonso for touching you?" He lets out a dark chuckle, then he shrugs. "Tell him."

He turns his attention back to Alfonso, and it has me screaming, "Don't shoot him! Please." I can't have Alfonso die because of my selfishness.

Dante's right arm darts out, and he grabs hold of my hair. My muscles tighten as I'm yanked against his body, and my mouth grows dry with fear. There are no words to argue or plead with because Dante doesn't care. Not about me. Not about anyone. He's nothing more than a soulless tormentor.

I'm shoved down to the hard floor and try to brace myself for the kicks and punches that are bound to follow.

I'll take any beating Dante wants to give me as long as it means Alfonso gets to live.

My heart hammers against my ribs, and my breaths explode over my lips as every part of me tenses. When Dante doesn't beat me, I cautiously glance up at him from where I'm on my hands and knees.

Dante's gaze snaps from a terrified Alfonso to me, then he sneers, "You think you're a woman, Principessa?"

"I'm sorry," I whimper, not knowing what else to say. When I push myself up on my knees, Dante shakes his head, and it has me freezing.

He begins to unbuckle his belt, never taking the gun off Alfonso. My heartbeat speeds up until it's nothing more than a terrifying flutter in my chest. I watch with growing dread as he unzips his pants, and raw horror bleeds through me when he frees his erection. Instantly, revulsion churns in my stomach.

"Show me you're a woman," he growls.

Shocked out of my mind, I shake my head. "N-no."

He wouldn't.

Dante's a lot of things, but he's never made any sexual advances toward me.

He won't.

Grabbing hold of my hair again, he yanks me toward him and shoves his erection in my face. The sharp smell of stale urine burns up my nostrils, and I gag from the stink alone. Feeling his erection against my lips makes bile burn up my throat.

With a murderous glare, he spits at me, "Suck my dick, or your lover dies right now."

Oh, God.

No.

My body convulses, and I swallow hard on the burning bile in my throat.

"Suck," he growls, his eyes narrowing on me with warning.

"I'll leave," Alfonso suddenly says.

My eyes snap to him, and I want to tell him to keep quiet and not make things worse, but Dante slams the gun into the side of Alfonso's face, snapping, "Shut up, or you die."

Alfonso covers his bruised jaw with a hand and trains his eyes away from us. It makes Dante focus his attention on me again. "Suck my fucking dick, or I'll paint the walls with your lover's brains."

My chin begins to tremble, and it feels like my stomach is on fire with the bile churning in it.

This is sick.

Twisted and sick.

I have two choices. Defy Dante and be responsible for Alfonso's death, or do as Dante says and...

My thoughts come to a screeching halt, unable to even think it.

My hesitation makes Dante react, and in absolute horror, I watch as he shoots Alfonso in the left shoulder. The sound of the gunshot echoes, and then it's followed by Alfonso's howls of pain.

Shock shudders through my body while Alfonso covers the wound with his hand. Blood seeps through his fingers while he tries to bite back the cries.

I want to tell him I'm sorry. I should've stayed away from him.

Dante's murderous gaze swings back to me. "The next one will be between his eyes."

Up until now, I thought Dante would just beat me like he's done countless times before. The terrifying realization that he won't kick and hit me, but instead, he's going to force me to give him a blowjob, makes me instantly cold. It feels as if my whole body is being submerged in ice.

I can't.

I can't even begin to imagine taking him in my mouth.

The stink alone is nauseating.

No.

No

Please, God.

Dante grabs hold of my hair again and yanks my face to his pelvis. His erection pushes against my lips, and as the overwhelming stench burns up my nostrils, I pinch my eyes shut. Somehow I manage to open my mouth instead of clenching my teeth like I want to.

It's either this or Alfonso's life.

Dante's erection thrusts into my mouth, brushing hard against my tongue until it slams into the back of my throat. My stomach rolls violently, and my body trembles as if it's going to shake apart into a million pieces.

I keep telling myself that Alfonso's life depends on this as Dante begins to thrust relentlessly into my mouth. I instantly gag, and a sob rippling up my throat makes it worse and harder to breathe.

I can't stop gagging as Dante keeps forcing himself into my mouth, coating my tongue with his pungent taste. I try to shut down my mind, but I can't ignore the disturbing feel of his erection rubbing over my tongue before slamming against my throat.

Disgust and degradation swallow me whole as I keep gagging. It strips me to the bone. It robs me of my rationality until all that's left is my will to survive. Hatred and rage claw at my heart. Whatever innocence I had left is desecrated until there's nothing left but traumatic shame.

Dante's thrusts become uneven, and then a slimy, bitter fluid coats my tongue and throat. He pulls away from me as my body jerks, and then I vomit at his feet.

A shot rings through the air, and a second later, Alfonso falls beside me, his eyes wide as blood trickles from his head.

Noooooooo!!!

My stomach empties itself, and I gag through the sobs tearing from my chest.

Oh, God.

No.

No.

"What…?" I hear Gino's voice, and before I can lift my head, his cry is muted by another gunshot.

Gino's body drops near his son's, and I scramble backward until I slam into one of the walls. Horrified, I can't stop staring at the two bodies. Bile dribbles down my chin, and my chest is on fire.

Dante moves, and terrified, my eyes snap to him. I watch as he tucks his flaccid dick away.

I gasp for air, my lungs burning and my throat aching. The bile rushes up again, and somehow in my traumatized state, my body knows to turn to the side so I can throw up.

When there's nothing left to vomit, I sink back on my butt, and leaning against the wall, I try to breathe through the gruesomeness surrounding me.

Gino and Alfonso's bodies. The blood staining the wood. The tainted scent of leather and steel.

It's all too much to process. It's a nightmare. A cruel and depraved nightmare.

"You will fucking stay here until I come back," Dante warns me. As he begins to shut the door, he threatens, "Try to leave, and I'll fuck you raw, Principessa."

Dante leaves me in the room with the two bodies, trembling with the fear of being raped. The air quickly grows putrid with the acidic smell from the vomit.

I sit frozen in the nightmare orchestrated by Dante. Unable to move… unable to believe what happened… unable to process anything, I just stare at the lifeless bodies.

I have no idea how long I sit like that, staring at death, my mind filled with static.

As the sun sets and the room begins to grow dark, life returns to my limbs. Slowly, I crawl to my clothes. It takes a lot of concentration to get dressed as if my mind has forgotten the simple task.

Only then do the events begin to replay in my mind, ripping a broken sob from me. I move to the other side of the room, and sitting down in a corner, I wrap my arms around my legs.

Alfonso and Gino are dead. Dante forced his erection in my mouth. He came in my mouth.

Every thought is a merciless blow to my soul. The shame bears heavily down on me as if it's trying to squeeze the very life from my body. I can still taste the bitterness of Dante's orgasm on the back of my tongue, the vomiting having done nothing to erase it.

For a moment, my eyes lock with Alfonso's lifeless ones, and it makes me cry harder.

I'm sorry.

I'm so sorry.

Please forgive me.

Chapter 2

ELENA

The Past - 20 Years Old.

I can feel Dante's cruel stare on me where I'm standing out on my balcony. The raindrops pelt my skin, chilling me to the bone.

I gaze through the curtain of rain at the grounds. The last time I left the house was when Alfonso and Gino were killed, and Dante forced himself on me for the first time.

The days following the horrendous incident, I was like a zombie. A prisoner in my own mind, plagued by the horrors that occurred.

It annoyed Dante, and when he beat me for it, the hatred and rage I felt during the incident flared to life. It was the first time I tried to fight back against him. I didn't win. Of course not. Dante's twice my size and much stronger. But it never stopped me from trying to defend myself.

It's been four years, and my nightmares keep growing. I thought my life was suffocating before the horrific incident, but compared to now, it was nothing. I was almost happy before it happened. Now, I'm a prisoner of perpetual torture and guilt, with the threat of being raped by Dante hanging over my head.

Even though I'm freezing, I stay out on the balcony as long as I can. It's the closest I get to outside. My days are now spent between the library and my room. I no longer get to walk between the manicured flower beds.

Whenever I try to leave the house, I'm rewarded with a beating from Dante. Every time he's done painting my skin with bruises, I promise myself to try harder to escape the house. It's weird. It's as if Dante torturing me is fueling me instead of breaking me. In turn, Dante seems to thrive on it when I try to fight back. It's like we're stuck in a destructive tango that will only lead to one thing – one of us dying. And unless I learn how to fight, it will probably be me.

It's only been Dante the past three years. I haven't had tutors since I finished school, and honestly, I miss the reprieve they offered. The staff and other guards have been instructed to ignore my existence, and they're too afraid to do otherwise.

I see my father occasionally when he's home from attending to business. I use the word 'see' lightly because even though Father is in the villa, it changes nothing for me. He allows Dante to do what he wants with me.

My father lives only for his business. I know he deals in the illegal trade for arms, but nothing more. I'm not trusted to know more.

Sometimes I wonder who's the bigger monster between them – Dante, for abusing me, or my father for allowing it?

"Your father is home," Dante mutters. "Dry yourself."

Taking a deep breath, I lift my chin and clench my jaw as I step back inside my room.

My personal suite is lavish, containing everything I might need. It has a private living room, a bedroom, and an ensuite bathroom, but to me, it's nothing more than a gilded cage. No amount of luxury can hide the horrors these walls have seen.

I shoot Dante a dark glare of my own as I walk to my bedroom. I shut the door behind me and grab clean clothes from the closet, which I place on my bed. Reaching for my soaked shirt, I freeze when the door to my room opens with a bang against the wall.

Dante leans against the doorjamb, and crossing his arms over his chest, he sneers at me, "Faster, Principessa."

He now watches me when I bathe, dress, sleep – never giving me a moment alone. The threat of rape is always there. I know it's only a matter of time, and it makes dread imprint itself on my bones.

I'd rather die.

When that day comes, I swear I'll take my life.

I'd rather kill myself than let Dante have his sadistic way with me.

Hopelessness swirls in my chest, and I clench my jaw at the devastating feelings of despair, panic, disgust, and fear. They've become my constant companions.

I spend every moment I'm alone dreaming up ways to escape Dante, but even if I run to the ends of the earth, he'll find me.

I think he's addicted to the power he has over me. The fear he inflicts.

I pull my wet shirt off and quickly drag on a cashmere sweater while Dante taunts, "Soon, I'll fuck your tits and come all over your face."

I do my best to ignore the threat, but it's impossible. It makes fear coat my skin as it drags up the horrible memories of all the times Dante has crossed the line over the past four years. The now-familiar shame and repulsion once again rock me to my very core, and I have to fight hard to keep control of the devastating emotions.

With trembling hands, I switch out of my clammy jeans, moving fast to get the dry ones on. After slipping on a pair of heels, I walk to the bathroom and towel dry my hair before pinning it up in a bun.

When I step into the bedroom again, Dante darts forward, and grabbing hold of my arm, he yanks me through my private living room.

Repulsed by his touch, I rear back against his hold. "I can walk on my own!"

Dante stops to slap me across the cheek, and it has me yanking hard against his bruising grip on my arm. My defiance earns me a punch, this time harder, and it stuns me for a moment as I fall against the wall. Dante's fingers bite harder into my flesh, and I'm dragged down the hallway and stairs.

"Keep fighting, Principessa. It only makes me hard for your cunt," Dante threatens, and then I'm shoved into my father's study.

I come to a stumbling standstill in front of the large oak desk. I almost lift a hand to my aching cheek and bruised lip but catch myself in time. Not wanting to give Dante the satisfaction of knowing he hurt me, I fist my hands at my sides and level a scalding glare on my father's bowed head where he's glancing over a document.

My father lets out a sigh then lifts his eyes for a moment. He hardly takes notice of me before continuing to read the information.

How can a father care so little for his daughter? I'm his blood, yet he cares more for Dante and the business. I should be used to the sting of rejection, but it still hurts knowing I mean nothing more than the very chair he's sitting on.

"I'm going to send you to St. Monarch's once you turn twenty-one."

What?

My lips part on a silent gasp, and then my breathing speeds up as a glimmer of hope bursts through my grim existence. Father once told me St. Monarch's is the only neutral ground for crime families. Various services are offered there. Anything from training to sharpen your trade of choice to a resort that provides you with elite protection. There are also auction nights where anything illegal can be bought and sold.

I'll be surrounded by my father's enemies, but it doesn't scare me. Not when Dante is the enemy I fear the most.

"You're to learn whatever they can teach you so you can help take over the business when you marry Dante." Father's eyes snap up to mine, and he pins me with an unforgiving glare as his words shudder through me. "It should be an easy task. Don't disappoint me."

Marry Dante?

God. No. No. No.

My mouth dries with the impending death sentence because that's what it is. I will hang myself before vowing myself to Dante.

Knowing it would be stupid to argue, I bite my tongue to keep the words of protest from escaping.

"Lucian Cotroni is currently a guest at St. Monarch's. Beware of him. His father is the head of the Mafia. You say nothing to him. Do you hear me?" Father pins me with dark warning creasing his brows. "The Cotronis will not hesitate to kill in order to take our business. You avoid Lucian Cotroni at all costs. Understand?"

I quickly nod. Not that I know anything I could tell the Cotronis. Dante and my father never share anything business-related with me.

"I'm only sending you there to learn something of worth, and so you're out of the way. We have a new problem to deal with, and I need Dante by my side."

Which means he won't be with me.

I quickly nod again.

"Leave," Father barks, and then Dante grabs hold of my arm, yanking me out of the study.

I'm dragged back to my suite and shoved inside. Dante presses his body against my back, and a repulsed shiver races over my skin as his breath skims over my ear. "It's only a matter of time before you belong to me."

He shoves me hard, and the force has me stumbling into the back of my couch. I hear Dante leave, and then he locks the door, so I can't escape.

For a long moment, I stand still, processing what just happened.

I get to go to St. Monarch's. I'll be free of the villa. Even if it's just for a short while.

My hope begins to blossom, making the blood rush through my veins.

I don't know much of what happens at St. Monarch's, but I do know Dante won't be there.

God, I won't have Dante watching and following me. He won't be there to force himself on me or to beat me.

My lips begin to curve higher in a hopeful smile, and I press my hand to my excited heart.

I'm turning twenty-one next week. Only six days, and I'll be rid of Dante, even if just for a short while.

I'll finally taste freedom.

Chapter 3

LUCIAN

The Past - 20 Years Old.

Pristinely dressed in an Armani three-piece suit, I look at my reflection in the mirror. I have my father's features. A sharp bone structure with the usual Italian dark hair and eyes.

I take after my father in every way, which has made us closer than most fathers and sons. *Much closer.* I'm not just Luca Cotroni's heir but his confidant and only friend. With my father being the head of the Mafia, friends are not a luxury we can afford. It makes the bond of blood between us sacred and unbreakable.

"You ready?" Father asks as he walks into my suite.

A grin tugs at the corner of my mouth as I turn to face him. "I am."

His gaze sweeps over me, and then he gives me a proud smile. "Today, you will take your rightful place next to me." I watch as he pulls a gun from behind his back, and my eyes lock on the personalized Glock in his hand. "I had it made for you," my father says as he holds it out to me.

Lifting my hand, my fingers wrap around the handle that's engraved with our family name. *Cotroni.*

"Thank you," I murmur as I accept my first gun. It means things will change now. I'll no longer live the guarded life I've grown accustomed to. I'll now stand by my father's side during business deals. I'll attend meetings between all the families. I'll work with our allies, and I'll come face to face with our rivals.

The weight of the Cotroni name bears down on my shoulders. It's time to become the man my father's groomed me to be all my life.

His eyes lock with mine, and then he asks again, "Are you ready?"

I know what he's asking. Am I ready to make people fear me the same way they fear him? Am I ready to kill? Am I ready to rule the Mafia with a merciless hand?

"Yes," I answer, lifting my chin with surety and confidence.

My father places his hand on my shoulder, his eyes holding mine with a severe look. "You give no second chances. There's no place for mercy in our world. Show no weakness and fear. Never hesitate or second guess yourself.

Be sure. Be cruel. You have to make them fear you. That's where our power lies."

I nod, memorizing his words.

He pulls me into a hug, his arms wrapping around me like steel bands. "Above all, trust no one. It will only lead to your death."

As I pull back, I say, "But you trust me."

He lets out a chuckle. "You're part of me. Blood of my blood. *Famiglia*. I'm talking about everyone else."

Nodding, I glance down at the gun in my hand. "Thank you. It's beautiful."

He pats my shoulder then says, "Let's go. It's time for you to take your rightful place in the family."

Nerves spin my gut as I tuck the gun into the back of my pants. I adjust my jacket and leave the suite with my father. In silence, we walk down the hallway, and once we descent the stairs, my gaze goes over the men gathering below.

My eyes stop on Alexei Koslov, the best assassin the underworld has ever produced. Next to him stands his custodian, Demitri Vetrov. Together the two men are unkillable.

Thank God they are our allies.

Glancing at the other men, I notice Valentino *Tino* Lucas. Although he's from a rival family, we're civil. Tino might be tyrannical, but he knows better than to challenge us for the seat of power in the Mafia.

Nick Cabello represents the Cabello family. They've only begun dealing in arms the last decade, unlike our family, that's been at the head of the Mafia for four generations.

The thought makes me well aware of the legacy that will rest upon my shoulders. I'll have to make these men fear me or die trying. There's no other option.

I notice three families from the Bratva are present, but I begin to frown when I see a new face. An Asian man whose eyes are narrowed on my father.

My father stops on the fifth step, and I come to a standstill next to him. "Today, Lucian takes his place as my right-hand man. After he has attended St. Monarch's he will take over as the head of the Mafia."

I lift my chin with pride, then my father says, "We need to deal with unpleasant business before we can celebrate."

I glance at my father as he turns his attention to me. "What do we do with people who steal from us?"

"Kill them," I answer without hesitation because there's no place for mercy in our world.

Alexei shoves the Asian man closer and then forces him down on his knees.

"Mr. Chen thought he could get away with hiding profits from us," Father explains, and then he gestures from me to Mr. Chen. "Alexei was kind enough to hunt him down. Issue the punishment."

Pin prickles spread out over my scalp as my eyes snap back to my father's.

He wants me to kill?

There's no warmth in my father's gaze, which is dark with wrath.

Fuck, this is it. This is where I have to prove myself.

My eyes go back to Mr. Chen. I know better than to ask questions as I slowly reach for the gun at my back. I've seen my father kill many times before, so I know what to do. My fingers wrap around the handle, and I hold the Glock, so the barrel faces down.

I can't refuse or show any weakness because it will bring unforgivable shame to the Cotroni name.

This is it, Lucian.

I have to kill the thief and take my rightful place, making my father proud. I don't dare question my father's judgment.

I take the last five steps down and stop in front of Mr. Chen. My fingers flex around the engraved handle of my Glock as my heartbeat begins to speed up.

You can do it.

You have to.

No mercy.

I lift my arm and train the barrel on the man's head. For a moment, I glance up, and my eyes meet Alexei's. The most feared man after my father. Deadly. Merciless. He's not much older than me. Probably in his late twenties. Yet he's made a name for himself people cower before.

I have to do the same.

As I lower my eyes to Mr. Chen, I swallow hard, and my muscles tighten. A burning sensation spreads through my stomach at the thought of taking another man's life.

You have to.

Now.

I suck in a deep breath, and my finger curls around the trigger. Mr. Chen glares up at me, and then he spits on my shoes. That's all it takes for me to pull the trigger.

I watch as his head snaps back from the force, and then his body slumps to the side.

Breathe in.

I haven't spoken a word to the man.

Breathe out.

Yet I took his life.

The thought shudders through me, and it sinks deep into my bones, branding me a murderer. I expect to feel guilt, but instead, there's a rush of power.

"Good," Alexei says, but I can't tear my eyes away from the lifeless body.

I killed. For the first time, I took a life that didn't belong to me.

I feel my father's hand fall on my shoulder, and then he gives me a squeeze. "You've made me proud, my son."

I nod as I step away from the body and closer to my father. My breaths begin to speed up, and then Alexei chuckles. "Now we drink. He needs it."

The other men chuckle as my father steers me around the body, which the staff will take care of. We walk into the living room, and I take the tumbler of bourbon a server offers me.

I throw my head back, downing the amber liquid, and it draws another round of chuckles from the men.

My father pats my back, then says, "Next time, don't take so long to kill."

Next time.

This was my first kill, and it will be far from the last.

My gaze sweeps over the men celebrating my ascent to the top of the Mafia. Most of their smiles are forced, their eyes sizing me up.

It makes me lift my chin, and then I remember to tuck my gun away behind my back. I help myself to another drink, and then I watch. I memorize every dark glance, every lingering grimace.

I keep my head held high under the pressure. Half the men in this room are as old as my father. I know they won't be happy taking orders from me.

I'll just have to make them.

The thought has the corner of my mouth curving up in a daring smirk, and I pray to the almighty they see my father's blood pulsing beneath my skin.

Now it's kill or be killed. Rule or be ruled. Fear or be feared.

I, Lucian Cotroni, will never bend the knee. I will not cower. I will take my rightful place, and God help the man who tries to oppose me.

Chapter 4

ELENA

The Present – Elena; 21. Lucian; 24.

My heart is fluttering against my ribs as we're driven through the iron gates of St. Monarch's. The castle stands solid, wrapped in old money and extravagance. The gardens are flawless, and the grounds stretch so vast, I can't see the outer walls.

So beautiful.

Dante's palm connects with the back of my head, and I catch myself from slamming into the seat in front of me. "Listen to me!" he barks.

"I am," I bite the words out, giving him a defiant scowl.

God, it's only a matter of minutes, and then I'll be rid of this monster.

"You talk to no one. This is the training ground of the elite. No one here is a friend," he warns me for the hundredth time.

"I know," I mumble. Dante informed me of the different syndicate groups that rule the world of crime. The Mafia, the Bratva, the Cartels. Arms dealers like my father. Drug dealers. Assassins. The worst of the worst.

He also told me about the five people who are currently guests at St. Monarch's. Sergei Aulov, whose family is a part of the Bratva. Kim Yung, a smuggler, and there's also a custodian in training, MJ Fang. Isabella Terrero, also known as the Princess of Terror. I was told her mother is the head of the largest cartel. The last person is Lucian Cotroni, soon to be head of the Mafia.

They're all people like Dante and my father. Cruel and soulless.

I really don't intend to talk to any of them.

"If you're not learning the trade, then you stay in your suite," Dante grumbles.

"Mmh..." I have no intention of doing that. I won't attend any training sessions on how to trade arms. I'm going to spend every waking moment outside and learning how to fight, so I can defend myself against Dante.

I'm going to relish being free for once in my life.

The armored SUV comes to a stop, and not waiting for Dante, I open the door and climb out. I take a deep breath of the fresh Switzerland air. It's the first time I've traveled, and I can't get enough of the foreign scenery. St. Monarch's is situated near Geneva, and the view is idyllic, to say the least.

The chauffer removes my luggage from the vehicle, and unable to wait for a second longer to get away from Dante, I take the bags from the chauffeur and walk toward the entrance of the castle.

"Principessa!" Dante snarls behind me, his fingers clamping around my arm and yanking me to a stop. His body pushes into my personal space, and then his rancid breath hits my face. Before I know what's happening, he presses an unforgiving kiss to my lips. "Don't miss me too much."

Knowing I'm safe from being killed, I pull out of Dante's hold, and as I walk away from him, I say, "I won't. Not at all."

I hold my breath as I near the wide doors, on guard that Dante will grab hold of me again to punish me for what I just said. As I climb the stairs and reach the doors, I glance over my shoulder. I'm met with a deadly glare from Dante, where he's still standing by the SUV.

Elation washes over me from knowing I'm safe. For the first time in my life, Dante can't hurt me.

I hope he dies before I have to leave here.

Walking into St. Monarch's, I forget about Dante as my eyes take in everything. There's nothing outdated about the interior. Dark oak and golden furnishings lend a regal feel to the entrance hall. I glance up at the magnificent chandelier.

"Miss Lucas," a man dressed in a black combat uniform addresses me. He's holding a machine gun to his chest, the barrel facing down. "Welcome to St. Monarch's. I'll show you to your personal quarters."

"Thank you," I murmur as I follow after him.

"Madame Keller will welcome you officially at dinner," the man says. "You're free to move around the property as you see fit. There's only one rule; no killing."

I nod, then ask, "I heard there was an altercation a few months back?"

"Taken care off. The guards have been tripled for your protection. You have nothing to worry about," he assures me.

As we take the stairs up, the wooden steps creak beneath my feet, and the sound is at odds with the luxurious interior.

At least no one will be able to sneak up on me.

I'm led down a hallway. The walls and ceiling have been painted with battles of old.

The guard stops in front of a suite, and I watch as he unlocks the door that's engraved with square patterns. He pushes it open and steps aside.

I walk into my personal suite, and when the man hands me the key, I can't help but smile. "Thank you."

"You're welcome to explore St. Monarch's and the grounds. Dinner with Madame Keller will be in the dining hall at seven pm."

I nod, and when the man walks back down the hallway, the smile on my face grows.

I have the key to my suite. No one will be able to lock me inside for days on end.

Just as I'm about to close my door, the one opposite my suite opens, and my smile freezes. My gaze locks with a pair of intense dark brown eyes, and instantly a shiver rushes over my body.

Dante showed me a photo of Lucian Cotroni so I'd know who to stay away from, but... the picture was of a younger version of him, and honestly, it didn't do him justice at all.

This is not the boy version I saw in the photograph. This is a man. He's so attractive, I can't help but stare shamelessly at him. A tailored black suit covers his clearly muscled frame and broad shoulders. There's a dark dusting of hair on his chiseled jaw, square and strong. Flawless tanned skin covers his face, neck, and hands.

His hands. Veins line the back. As he adjusts a cuff, a ring on his right hand catches my attention. It looks like it's a family ring.

My gaze lifts back to his eyes. *Those eyes.* They're not cruel like Dante's, but mysterious and confident. And God, they're intense. It feels like he's staring right through me. Like none of my secrets are safe from him. Then an impassive expression hardens his face, and the moment shatters.

Lucian Cotroni – soon to be head of the Mafia. More dangerous than my father and Dante, as the Cotronis are the only family they submit to.

Fear slithers down my spine, and taking a step back, I shut the door between us.

I suck in a deep breath of air while thinking I'll definitely stay away from Lucian. Not because I was told to but from the power I could feel radiating from him. Life has taught me powerful people are cruel because there's no one to hold them accountable, no one who would dare cross them.

I turn to look at my suite, which is decorated with cream and gold furnishings. It lightens the interior. I have a private living room, a bedroom, and an ensuite bathroom. All modern and luxurious. Expansive bay windows lend natural light, and it makes the excitement return to my heart.

Taking hold of my luggage, I walk to the bedroom and begin to unpack. I want to get settled as soon as possible, so I can explore the castle and surrounding grounds.

For once, I can do whatever I want, and it makes my heart beat faster while I rush to unpack.

When all my belongings are neatly in their place, I kick off my heels and strip out of the tight-fitting jeans and top I'm wearing.

With Dante not here to leer at me while I get dressed, the constant weight that's been suffocating me lifts a little.

I choose a cream-colored dress and pull it over my head. The thin straps rest on my shoulders as the soft fabric falls to mid-thigh. I slip on a pair of sandals and then put my hair up in a messy bun.

So much better.

Feeling more relaxed than I've ever felt in my life, a smile spreads over my face as I walk to the door. Softly, I unlock it, and stepping out into the hallway, I glance around as I lock the suite behind me.

I don't have any pockets, and while I walk toward the stairs, I unclasp the necklace around my neck and slip the key onto it before fastening it back in place.

My eyes keep darting everywhere as I take the stairs to the lower floor. The only sound comes from the creaking wood beneath my feet. Curious to see what my new home looks like, I turn to my left and into the foyer. When I walk through an archway, I'm met with two hallways to choose from.

Deciding to explore the left one, I slowly make way through the art-covered walls as I glance into random rooms.

I find the studios where I'll hopefully learn how to fight. There is a variety of training equipment, and mirrors cover all the walls. There's no sign of the instructor, and I decide to stop by later so I can make an appointment for private training sessions.

I continue to explore, and when I reach another open door, I peek inside. Seeing weapons, I step into what seems to be the armory. A blonde-haired woman glances up from where she's standing by a broad counter containing handguns. Behind her, cabinets filled with more weapons line the wall.

"Miss Lucas. Welcome," she says, a professional tone to her voice. "I'm Miss Dervishi."

The instructors must've been told of my arrival.

I smile at the weapons trainer. "Thank you." Then I glance at the wide variety of firearms.

"Would you like to pick one? The shooting range is through that door." Miss Dervishi gestures at a doorway as I hear shots being fired. "There's also a more extensive shooting range outside."

"I'm just looking around," I explain as I walk closer to the doorway where the shots are coming from. "I'd like to start training tomorrow, though. Do I have to schedule a specific time?"

"Would you like private sessions?" she asks.

I nod as I glance back at her. "Preferably, please."

"I'm afraid I only have seven o'clock available. Would that suit you?"

"Seven is perfect. I'll be here."

I take a step into the shooting range and look at the stalls. There are ten, and only one seems to be in use.

Another round of shots begins, and I step a little closer until the target comes into view. Whoever's shooting is really good. The hole in the head of the target keeps growing as one bullet after the other hits the same spot.

Wow. I hope I can learn to shoot like that.

The shooting stops, and then a man steps out of a stall, the firearm he's using held firmly in his right hand.

Oh crap. Lucian Cotroni.

Our eyes meet, and it only takes a second for the impassive expression to return to Lucian's face, making him look dark and threatening.

For a second, the woman in me can't help but admire his strong features. He is handsome... maybe too handsome. Our eyes lock, and the deadly expression in Lucian's dark brown irises reminds me he's not just any man.

A different kind of danger emanates from him than what I'm used to feeling from Dante. Where Dante is depraved, this man seems in control of everything around him. He gives me the impression he doesn't act irrationally, and every move he makes is calculated.

I guess that's what it takes if you're going to be the head of the Mafia.

Lucian's strong fingers flex around the weapon's handle, and knowing how well he can handle a gun makes my fear intensify. My heartbeat picks up, and spinning around, I dart through the doorway and rush out of the armory.

Holy mother, that was intense.

I focus on calming my racing heartbeat as I hurry back down the hallway. With only six of us here, I get a feeling it's going to be hard to avoid the other guests.

I don't look into any more rooms as I pass by them, and when I finally reach double doors that are pushed open, I let out a breath of relief. Stepping outside, my lips part at the beautiful nature surrounding the castle.

Wide steps lead down to a path that's lined with trimmed trees and the occasional cast iron bench. Flower beds are scattered everywhere, bursting with colors.

My body moves forward as if it's being called by the path, and soon my feet find a comfortable pace as I follow it.

I take a deep breath of the fresh air and smile as the sun warms my skin. Lucian is soon forgotten as emotion wells in my chest from being able to walk outside.

God, I missed this. So much.

The sound of water catches my attention, and not long after, a beautiful fountain comes into view. It's situated in a courtyard that's framed by ivy. It looks like a secret garden.

There are two benches, the fountain obscuring the view between them. All the shade makes the air cooler, and I wrap my arms around myself as I step closer to the fountain.

The centerpiece is made of cherubs holding onto the dress of a woman. She stares longingly down at them as if they're her children. The sight makes a pang of sadness sweep through me.

It's heartbreaking that a statue is able to express more love than I've been given in my life.

Chapter 5

LUCIAN

The Present – Elena; 21. Lucian; 24.

Seated at my usual table for dinner, my eyes lock onto the raven-haired beauty as she walks into the dining room. She's wearing the same dress she had on earlier this afternoon, which is a surprise. Usually, guests make an extra effort when they're meeting with Madame Keller.

The woman is of average height, but that's where average ends when it comes to her. Her skin is snow-white, giving me the impression she's delicate and can easily be bruised. Her toned legs are shapely, an eye-catcher for sure.

My gaze follows the curve of her hips and breasts before locking onto her face again. For a third time today, something unknown stirs in my chest.

I'm used to women throwing themselves at my feet, but this woman has avoided me twice already. Earlier, in the armory, she practically ran from the sight of me. She now has my attention whether she wants it or not.

With my family being the head of the Mafia, we know everyone. Still, I've never seen this woman before, which makes her that much more intriguing.

I watch as she's greeted by Madame Keller, the architect of St. Monarch's. They talk for a moment, and then Madame Keller turns, and they head in my direction.

Well, the mystery of who this woman is will be solved soon enough.

As they near my table, I rise to my feet.

"Mr. Cotroni," Madame Keller says, her voice laced with respect for the title and power I hold. "We have a new guest." Madame Keller glances at the woman, then introduces her, "Elena Lucas. If I'm not mistaken, your families have business ties with each other."

"Lucas?" I ask, shocked to hear the name linked to the woman. My eyes narrow on her as I wonder why we weren't aware of her existence. Surprises are never a good thing in our world. Especially when it comes to Valentino Lucas. Things have been strained between our families for as long as I can remember.

Finally, Elena meets my gaze, and then fear tightens her features.

She definitely knows who I am.

Tilting my head slightly, I say, "I wasn't aware Tino had a daughter."

Elena doesn't offer me an explanation for the secrecy surrounding her. Instead, she lowers her eyes to the table as she softly says, "Mr. Cotroni, it's an honor making your acquaintance."

"Lucian," I offer.

"May we join you for dinner?" Madame Keller asks.

With my gaze still locked on the mysterious Elena Lucas, I reply, "Of course."

I take my seat again and watch as the two women sit down. Elena's spine is straight with tension, her eyes trained in front of her, obviously avoiding looking at me. It only makes me more guarded. My father taught me to be extra vigilant around anyone who can't make eye contact. It means they're definitely hiding something.

"Did Tino keep you a secret for a reason?" I ask, wanting to know the story behind her sudden appearance. My father also taught me to question everything and to trust no one.

"No," Elena murmurs, her voice soft and feminine.

A frown begins to form on my forehead, and my eyes snap to Madame Keller, who quickly explains, "Valentino kept Elena in isolation for her own protection."

"Where?" I ask as my gaze returns to Elena. "I've been to the villa and never saw you."

Why the fuck would Valentino Lucas hide his only heir from us?

"My father doesn't involve me in his business, which is why I was surprised he sent me here," Elena says, and then relief flutters over her features as a waiter interrupts us.

I wait for the ladies to place their orders before giving my own to the waiter. "Bourbon, neat. Filet, medium."

When the waiter leaves, Madame Keller's mouth tips up at the corners. Even though she's in her seventies, she still carries remnants of her beauty. "Elena is here to learn the trade. She's late in joining, so I hope you'll take her under your wing."

The corner of my mouth curves up as I let out a chuckle. "You know it's everyone for themselves in our world."

Madame Keller matches my chuckle with her own. "You have business ties. Her gain is your gain, is it not?"

"Right now it is." My gaze snaps back to Elena, who's still refusing to look at me. "Tomorrow, it might be a different story altogether," I mutter.

"I have no intention of attending the training sessions my father had scheduled for me," Elena finally speaks up. Her gaze darts to mine. "I won't take over from my father."

My eyebrow raises, and my eyes sharpen on her. "Why not? Is there another heir I'm not aware of?"

Elena shakes her head. "I'm an only child. I just have no interest in being a part of the Mafia."

With every word leaving her mouth, the mystery surrounding her deepens. I've never met anyone like her. Women born into the Mafia are raised as princesses. They're challenging and demanding. They hold their father's hearts in the palm of their hands, and because of that, they expect their future husbands to treat them like queens. They're outspoken and born socialites. From what I've seen so far, Elena is nothing like them. She's almost… skittish.

"Does your father know this?" I ask.

A server brings our drinks, and I take a sip of my bourbon as I wait for her answer.

Elena only shakes her head.

"Why are you here?" I ask.

Her eyes dart to mine, and before she can glance away, I capture them with my own. Her lips part, but when she doesn't answer me, I drop my voice low with warning, "Elena, why are you here?"

If it's to keep me occupied, so my attention won't be on the family business, Tino's made a big mistake. One he'll pay for with his life.

Fear dances in Elena's light brown irises, and then she lets out a slow breath. "I'm here for myself."

Nothing she says adds up, and it has me leaning a little forward. I take hold of the tumbler and twirl it slowly before my eyes snap back to hers. "Careful, Elena. I don't like secrets. If it's your family's intention to make a play for the head of the Mafia, then I suggest you rethink it."

Elena swallows hard, and then she rises to her feet. She gives Madame Keller an apologetic look. "Please excuse me."

Suspicion slithers down my spine as Elena walks away from the table but then she stops. I watch her shoulders rise as she takes a deep breath before she turns around and walks back to me. Suddenly her steps are sure as she lifts her chin. Her eyes lock with mine, and when she reaches the table, she says, "I have no idea what my father plans to do. I'm not here for you or anyone else. All I want is to be left alone. I just want to enjoy my time at St. Monarch's."

Rising to my feet, I close the distance between us. I stop mere inches from Elena, and instantly her eyes drop to my tie. She hardly reaches my shoulder, and it makes a different kind of power bubble to life in my veins.

I begin to lean down, and a soft scent drifts from Elena, making my mouth water. Attraction zaps between us, but then it's overshadowed by the fear coming off her in waves. It stirs the predator in me. She'd be so easy to capture, to dominate.

I allow my lips to touch her earlobe as I whisper, "Don't fuck with me. No one comes to St. Monarch's without an ulterior motive. If you think you can win me over with your beauty, you're wrong."

The air tenses between us as Elena lifts her chin higher. Even though she's scared shitless of me, she's still trying to stand her ground. I feel her breath fan over my jaw, and it's enough to make my body come alive.

Christ, this woman is dangerous. She's the kind men give their hearts and souls for.

Elena's words are clipped, "I'm. Not. Here. For. You." Another burst of sweet air is expelled from her lungs. "I have no interest in you or any other man. Especially one who's the head of the Mafia."

I pull back a little so I can capture her eyes. "Why are you here?" I ask one last time.

Elena's features tighten, and it looks like she's tearing a secret from her soul as she admits, "Freedom." Her shoulders sag a little as she takes a step away from me. When she turns and begins to walk toward the exit, she whispers, "I'm here for my freedom."

What the hell does that mean?

Is she trying to escape her father?

My gut tells me something is off about this situation, and it demands me to dig deeper until I find the answers.

My eyes snap to Madame Keller. "Tell me everything."

Madame Keller indicates for me to take my seat, and once I'm sitting again, she explains, "My little birdies tell me, Elena is to marry Dante Capone. He acts as her personal guard and Valentino's right-hand man."

Jesus, that alone explains a lot.

I hate the fucker.

My muscles tense as I grind the words out, "I know who he is."

Dante is old enough to be Elena's father. A violent man who takes joy in killing. Even someone as hard as me pities Elena if that's truly her fate.

"The birdies say she wasn't kept hidden for her safety," Madame Keller continues. Our eyes meet as she whispers, "She was held captive. Everyone who has met Dante Capone knows he's a depraved man. If you ask me, he doesn't have a soul." Madame Keller stops herself from saying more as she takes a sip of her wine.

Mother of Christ.

I've done my fair share of killing, but I certainly don't have a taste for holding someone captive. Especially a woman. Dante is sadistic, and the knowledge only makes new questions rear their ugly head.

What has Elena endured?

As Madame Keller sets the glass down, she murmurs, "I don't think Miss Lucas is here to spy on you."

Still, it doesn't make sense.

"Then why did her father send her here? If she was held captive, why would they let her go now?"

Madame Keller takes a deep breath as she reaches for her wine again. "There's underground chatter of a new threat. My source hasn't confirmed it, though."

"To the Mafia?" I ask as I pull my phone from my pocket so I can call my father.

"Yes," Madame Keller whispers darkly.

A server brings our meals, and while Madame Keller instructs him to take Elena's food to her suite, I get up and leave the dining room so I'll have privacy to make the call. I press dial on my father's number.

"Son," he answers almost immediately.

"I have news," I murmur softly, not wanting my voice to carry. "Tino has a daughter. Elena Lucas is at St. Monarch's. I don't know what their plan is. Madame Keller also informed me of a new threat, but I have no details yet."

"It was brought to my attention. I was just waiting for more information before calling you," Father tells me. "It's not Valentino. Someone stole Valentino's and our inbound shipments. It's an attack on the Mafia, not just one family."

"Christ," I mutter. "I should join you."

"No, stay at St. Monarch's. We can't be together until we know what we're dealing with."

I let out a breath, then ask, "And Elena?"

"Tino sent her there to keep her safe while we deal with the threat. Right now, they're our allies."

"So you knew about her?" I ask.

"She's nothing to worry about," My father explains.

I nod. "Keep me up to date if you learn anything more about the threat."

"I will. While you're there, see if the Bratva or Cartels have any information for us," Father instructs.

"Will do."

"Keep your head low and your guard up," he warns me.

"Don't worry about me," I try to reassure him.

"Impossible," he grumbles, and it draws a chuckle from me.

We end the call, and I return to the table. Meeting Madame Keller's gaze, I say, "Let me know the instant you learn anything new."

"For a price, of course," she replies, the corner of her mouth lifting.

"Of course," I mutter. Information is valuable in our world, and I don't expect her to give it away for free.

Lowering my eyes to my meal, my thoughts are inundated with the looming threat and Elena's surprise arrival.

One thing's for sure, life just got interesting.

Chapter 6

ELENA

After I enjoy my dinner, I draw myself a bubble bath. I soak in the balmy water for an hour without prying eyes roving over every inch of my exposed skin. It also helps my nerves settle from the altercation with Lucian Cotroni.

The man is as intense as a thousand suns, blinding and dangerous. I'm not going to lie, he is easily the most attractive man I've ever laid eyes on, but that means nothing to me. Lucian Cotroni will rule the very world I'm trying to escape from.

I actually contemplate leaving St. Monarch's, but not having any identification documents or money to buy fake ones, the idea vanishes quickly.

I'll just have to do my best to avoid Lucian.

I get dressed in a soft pair of jeans and a black cashmere sweater. Pulling on my sneakers, I'm hoping the dark clothes will make me blend in with the night when I'm outside.

Opening the door, I peek up and down the hallway before I sneak out. I quickly lock the door behind me and then rush down toward the stairs, hoping I won't run into anyone.

The guards only spare me a glance as I pass by them, and when I walk through the side doors, a smile begins to tug at my lips. Lightfooted, I take the stairs down to the path, and I glance up at the starry sky as I enjoy the silence of the night wrapping around me.

I'll just keep to myself. Hopefully, that will be enough to show Lucian Cotroni I'm not here for him, nor am I a threat.

When I reach the secret garden, my smile widens in wonder.

It's so beautiful.

Soft lights frame the fountain, making the water sparkle as it falls over the statue. I take a deep breath as my eyes savor the sight before me.

Staring at the woman whose longing gaze is locked on the cherubs, I wonder if my life would've been different if my mother hadn't left or died.

Again I ponder why she didn't take me with her if she is alive. There are so many unanswered questions surrounding her, it draws a sigh from me.

My thoughts turn to the impossible – escaping this life. I might not know much, but I know you don't just run away from the Mafia. There's only one way out. Death.

Awareness creeps up my spine, and my gaze quickly darts around the garden. It feels like someone is watching me, and my stomach tightens.

As I take a step back, Lucian's voice comes from the shadows to the left of me, "Stop." My body freezes, and then he makes himself visible as he steps out of the darkness by a nearby tree.

When he begins to walk toward me, I slowly inch around the right side of the fountain until we're both bathed in the lights.

Lucian stops, and thankfully he keeps his distance. He tilts his head, and his gaze drifts over my face.

I see the questions form in his eyes, and then he says, "You've piqued my interested."

I fist my hands at my sides to keep still while everything in me screams for me to run away from the danger this man represents.

My tongue darts out to wet my lips before I reply, "That was not my intention."

"You're unlike any woman I've met before," he states. He takes a step closer, and it makes my whole body tense up, which he notices. "You fear me?"

"I'd be stupid not to," I answer honestly. "You can kill me, and there's nothing anyone will do to stop you."

Like Dante, you can do what you want to me, and I just have to allow it because you're stronger than me.

Lucian takes a deep breath, and then he surprises me by saying, "I won't. Not unless you give me a reason." His gaze drifts away from me to the fountain. "You shouldn't be out here alone. It's not safe."

Before I can stop myself, the words spill from my lips, "That's a risk I'm willing to take."

Lucian's eyes snap back to me. "Every word that leaves your mouth intrigues me."

A frown forms on my face. "Again, that's not my intention."

I just want to be left alone.

The corner of Lucian's mouth lifts, and the sight makes my heart beat faster.

It's all an illusion, though. Lucian Cotroni is death and pain wrapped up in a strikingly attractive face and a body most women would probably drool over. He's more dangerous than Dante, with whom what you see is what you get. Lucian lures you in with a sexy smirk and his low voice – like a spider spinning a web.

Not wanting to be in his presence a second longer, I begin to walk toward the path leading back to the castle.

When Lucian suddenly takes hold of my wrist, my breath catches in my throat, and I instantly yank out of the light grip he has on me. The fleeting touch leaves heat branded on my skin.

My feet move fast to place my body out of his reach, and it has Lucian holding up his hands in a surrendering stance. I'd believe it if it weren't for the grim expression tightening his features.

"I have no intention of hurting you," he says, his voice low and cautious.

I don't believe you. Men like you only know how to destroy.

"I've learned something about you, but I don't know how much of it is the truth," he continues to talk. When I just stare at him, he asks, "Were you held captive?"

The question rips through the fantasy of freedom I've managed to weave around myself since I set foot on St. Monarch's grounds.

My heart begins to thunder in my chest as the memories of my 'captivity' creep through the cracks in my mind.

They're always there, lurking in the shadows, ready to claw at my soul… or what's left of it.

"I just want to be left alone," I squeeze the words out through a tight throat.

A dark frown settles on Lucian's face, and then he nods his head. "I'll send a guard to watch over you."

To my absolute surprise, I watch as he walks away without another word.

I let out a heavy sigh of relief, and lifting my hand, I place it over the panicked organ slamming against my ribs, while I watch Lucian's confident frame fade into the darkness.

He actually listened?

I didn't expect him to.

Seconds later, a guard walks toward me, and with a nod of his head, he stops near a tree.

Feeling a little safer, I glance back to the fountain.

Finally, I'm alone.

I do my best to shove down the horrific memories brought to the surface by Lucian's question. Taking a seat on a bench, I pull my legs up. I wrap my arms around my shins and rest my chin on my knees. Then I just listen to the water, and the sound feels cleansing.

Dante isn't here. It's just me, the night, and the beautiful garden.

My eyes lift to the statue's face.

Who do I pray to when God himself has forsaken me?

Her somber look is answer enough. *No one.*

What am I going to do? I can't return to the villa. I can't marry Dante. Just the thought of being bonded to Dante for life is enough to make my throat close up with panic and fear.

My body begins to tremble as hopelessness overwhelms me.

You have to learn to protect yourself, Elena. Learn how to shoot a gun. Learn how to fight.

The trembling subsides at the thoughts. St. Monarch's is the perfect place to learn the skills I'll need to kill Dante… before he kills me.

LUCIAN

Walking into the armory, I nod at Miss Dervishi. She's been at St. Monarch's for over a decade, giving training in weapons. She's helping Kim Yung, a smuggler, choose a gun.

Shots are fired in the shooting range and picking up a Glock, I check the clip. "Who else is here?"

"Miss Lucas," Miss Dervishi answers.

My gaze snaps to Miss Dervishi, surprised to hear Elena is here. Especially seeing as it's six in the morning.

Interesting.

The guards told me she goes to the fountain every day, so the armory is the last place I expected to run into Elena. Especially after not seeing her for the past three days, yet she's been constantly on my mind.

The other night, I learned a lot from my conversation with her. I have no doubt she was a prisoner in her father's villa. When I took hold of her hand, her reaction spoke volumes. I could feel the fear and panic vibrate off her.

There are still hundreds of unanswered questions, and the fact that I'm even thinking about them should make me worry. I've never had a personal interest in a woman, and not able to stop thinking about Elena should be warning enough for me.

Still, it's a warning I clearly intend to ignore.

With the Glock firmly in my grip, I walk to the shooting range. There are ten stalls to choose from, but I keep passing the empty ones until I reach the stall next to Elena. She doesn't notice me as she closes one eye while aiming at the target. Her tongue peeks out from between her lips, and then she pulls the trigger. Her whole body jerks, and she misses the target completely.

As cute as she looks at the moment, a frown forms on my forehead as I ask, "Have you ever handled a gun before today?"

I instantly regret speaking up when she lets out a squeak as she spins to me. The firearm falls from her hand, but then she scrambles to pick it up.

She must've been totally focused on the dismal job she was doing to have someone sneak up on her.

"I'll take that as a no," I mutter. "Why isn't Miss Dervishi in here showing you how to fire a gun?"

Elena places the weapon on the counter her stall provides before she answers, "I have a training session with her at seven. I just wanted to get some practice in."

"You'll end up killing yourself," I say, not happy about the fact Elena's allowed to handle a weapon when she knows nothing about it. I step closer while shoving my own Glock behind my back. When I reach for Elena's gun, a Heckler and Koch, I notice how she tenses. "Come stand in front of me," I order.

"I don't want your help."

My eyes snap to Elena's. "I won't offer a second time."

She lets out an annoyed huff but comes to stand in front of me. When I wrap my arms around her and my chest presses to her back, Elena takes a sharp breath, and she instantly starts to tremble. "Relax, I'm just going to show you how to shoot so you won't kill me while I'm here."

I take hold of her right hand and shove the gun against her palm. Then I bring up her left hand, forcing her fingers to wrap tightly around the handle. "Always have a firm grip on the weapon. Straighten your arms and lock your elbows, so the recoil won't make you jerk."

Elena nods, and leaning my head a little forward, my cheek presses against hers. "Keep both eyes open. Squinting won't help shit."

She nods again, her soft skin brushing against the bristles on my jaw as I line up the barrel with the target. Standing body to body with her is overwhelming, making every inch of me come alive with the undeniable attraction I feel toward her. Dropping my voice low, I murmur, "Pull the trigger."

Elena doesn't hesitate, and the next second, the shot rings through the shooting range. The bullet hits the target in the left shoulder, and the recoil makes Elena's smaller frame push back against my solid one.

"Not bad," I mutter.

Elena lets out a happy shriek, and turning her face to mine, there's a stunning smile around her lips.

Christ Almighty.

"Can you show me again?" she asks.

Her change of mood and bright smile catches me off guard, and all I can do is nod. She quickly positions her back against my chest, and then her grip on the handle tightens beneath my hands. The attraction deepens, and when I take a breath, my lungs are filled with her soft scent.

Fuck, I've never felt such a strong pull toward a woman before.

Struggling to keep my focus on the task at hand, I line up the barrel with the target, then I whisper close to her ear, "Pull the trigger."

Elena listens, and then the shot rings out around us, and the bullet hits the target in the right side of the chest.

"Oh my God!" Elena shrieks happily again. "That shot could kill someone, right?"

"It all depends. If you want to kill, you need to aim for the heart or head. Preferably the head," I say as I pull back from her because I'm a second away from getting hard, and

I don't think she'll appreciate my cock rubbing against her lower back.

Shots begin to sound up from the other side of the shooting range where Miss Dervishi is giving Kim Yung a lesson.

"Try again," I instruct Elena.

She nods and lines up the barrel with the target. When the tip of her tongue peeks through her lips as she focuses on taking the shot, the corner of my mouth curves up.

Standing close to her, I get to look at her while her attention is on shooting. There's a faint scar on her cheek, and I wonder how she got it.

Elena pulls the trigger, and her body jerks. My left hand darts out, and settling on her lower back, I help her keep her footing. The bullet misses the target making the smile vanish from her face.

"You make it look so easy," she mutters.

"Years of practice. You'll get a feel for it." I move to the stall next to Elena's, and pulling the Glock from behind me, I take aim and fire a couple of rounds.

When I pause, and I don't hear her firing any shots, I glance to my right and find her watching me through the bulletproof glass partitioning. "You need to practice."

Elena nods, and I only watch her take one shot that clips the shoulder of the target before turning my attention back to my own gun.

While I empty my clip, I think about how Elena has once again surprised me. She wants to learn how to protect herself, and it makes a protective feeling spread through my chest.

She might've been held captive, but she has fight in her.

After I've shot the last bullet in my clip, I glance at Elena's target. The corner of my mouth lifts when I see she's managed to hit it twice. Not kill shots, but it's a start.

I turn my head more, and then I'm met with a smile from her. "Thank you for helping me."

I nod as I turn away from her, leaving the shooting range. My eyes narrow as I try to make sense of the unexpected emotions the woman evokes in me.

I try to play it off as nothing more than compassion for finding out she was held captive... but deep down, I know it's not the only reason she's caught my attention.

Elena is like a wounded little bird trying to learn how to fly while she's surrounded by predators.

God help me, but it brings out a protective side of me I didn't even know I had.

The most confusing part is why I even care about a woman I only met four days ago.

Chapter 7

ELENA

I've just climbed in the bath when I hear the door to my suite slam open.

"Where the fuck are you?" Dante snaps, and I hurry to climb out of the tub, making the water splash. My heartbeat speeds up with panic as I grab a towel so I can cover my body.

Dante just stalks into the bathroom, and it has me saying, "I'm taking a bath. Do you mind?"

He's been crueler than ever since he caught me with Alfonso a month ago.

It feels like it only happened yesterday. I haven't been able to sleep, and my weight has dropped from the trauma, which seems to only worsen as the days pass.

Dante's lips pull up in a sneer. "I don't mind at all." Gesturing at the tub behind me, he says, "Bathe."

What?

No.

"Leave," I bite the word out as tremors begin to spread through my insides. I grip the towel tighter, and it catches Dante's eye.

He darts forward, and grabbing hold of my neck, he shoves me backward until my calfs hit the side of the tub, and I fall into it. Water splashes over the edge as Dante's vicious gaze rake over me.

"I said bathe yourself, Principessa!" He steps closer to the tub. "Or do you want me to bathe you?"

God, no.

Shame burns through me like hot coals, searing holes into my still traumatized psyche.

Not wanting Dante to touch me, I cling to the soaked towel with one hand while I draw my legs into the tub. With a trembling hand, I reach for my loofah.

"Drop the towel," Dante instructs.

My eyes snap to him, and horror floods me when he begins to unbuckle his belt.

Please, no. Not again.

My chin quivers, and I start to shake my head.

"We can always take this to your bedroom where I'll fuck you raw, Principessa. Drop the towel."

A heavy darkness falls over me as I force my fingers to let go of the wet towel. Ashamed and feeling horribly exposed, I bite back the hopeless sob building in my throat.

"Wash yourself," Dante orders again. *"Start with your tits."*

God.

Oh, God.

Help me out of this nightmare.

I'm shaking so much I almost drop the body wash as I squirt some onto the loofah. I used to love the smell of it. But now, it will forever remind me of this day.

The bathroom used to be a safe place for me, but that all changes as the sounds of Dante stroking his dick fill the air.

A tear sneaks out of my left eye, and I quickly splash water on my face, not wanting him to see it.

"Your tits are so fucking perky," he groans disgustingly.

I somehow manage to keep washing my body. I feel... dirty. I begin to scrub my skin harder as Dante's strokes pick up pace, and then he orgasms, and it hits the side of my face and shoulder in spurts.

I cringe away from him as a strangled sob escapes.

I should feel relieved when he zips himself up, but I don't.

"Soon, Principessa. Soon." With the ominous words hanging heavy in the air, he finally leaves.

A sob rips achingly from my chest as I begin to wash his orgasm off of me. Frantically, I let out the water, and I scramble out of the tub. I dry myself as I rush into my room, and grabbing clothes from the closet, I pull them on as quickly as I can.

Only when I'm dressed do I give in to my despair, hoping the tears will be able to wash me clean.

I shoot up into a sitting position, my breaths exploding over my dry lips as the remnants of the nightmare of the past shudder through me.

It's been happening more and more since I came to St. Monarch's, wreaking havoc with my psyche and emotions.

My skin crawls, and I feel sick to my stomach as I climb out of bed. Needing to get out of the confined space of my room, I strip out of my shorts and camisole. I tug on a pair of sweatpants and a long sleeve shirt, along with comfy sneakers. After pulling a brush through my hair, I leave my private suite in a hurry.

The hallways are quiet, and I keep my eyes down as I walk as quickly as I can to the side doors.

I've already been at St. Monarch's for almost two weeks, and the peace and quiet I find in the garden helps, but the nightmares keep ripping me out of the safety I feel here.

Once I'm outside, I don't slow down, and I begin to jog, just needing to get to the fountain.

Reaching the secret garden, I sink down to my knees by the marble edging. My eyes lock on the statue's face as I beg for mercy, "Please help me. Don't make me go back to Dante. Save me from him. I don't care how. Just save me from him. You can even take my life because I'd rather die than marry him. Please..." my voice grows strained as I force the last words out, "have mercy on me."

Desperation mixes with the all-consuming shame Dante has imprinted on my soul over the past four years.

It's just a statue, Elena. There's no God to listen to your prayer.

Feeling trapped in this never-ending nightmare, I lower my eyes, and then all the blood drains from my face when I see Lucian sitting on the bench to the left of me.

He's leaning forward, his forearms resting on his thighs and his hands clasped tightly together. Our eyes lock, and the grim expression on his face makes a chill sweep through me. Knowing he heard my prayer makes me wish the ground would swallow me whole.

After Lucian showed me how to shoot, I haven't spoken to him again. Whenever we run into each other, he only nods his head at me. It suits me just fine because I still consider him a threat. Just because he gave a shooting lesson doesn't mean I trust him.

I should get up and leave, but I'm unable to make myself move.

Lucian takes a deep breath before he says, "I can kill Capone, but that will start a war between our families." Slowly, he rises to his feet, and then he walks toward me.

Lucian stops next to me, and I have to tilt my head far back to meet his eyes. When he holds his hand out to me, I hesitate for a moment, not sure what to make of him.

"I can show you how to kill him," he says the one thing I've desperately wanted to hear.

Could he be the answer to my prayer?

Cautiously, I place my hand in Lucian's, and he pulls me up from the ground. When I'm standing in front of him, I ask, "Why would you help me?"

"When you kill Dante, and you take over from your father, I expect you to remember this moment. Your loyalty will belong to me."

It's a strategic move on his part. One I'm in no position to decline. I can use all the training I can get. I've seen him handle a gun, and I want to become just as good as him.

"When I take over from my father, my loyalty will belong to you," I agree, knowing that day will never come. I won't follow in my father's footsteps, but Lucian seems to have forgotten I told him that when we first met.

Once I've killed Dante, I plan on disappearing and starting a new life somewhere else… somewhere safe. But that's something Lucian doesn't need to know.

His fingers linger on mine before he lets go of my hand. I see the questions brewing in his eyes, but instead of asking them, he murmurs, "Go sleep, little bird. We start tomorrow morning."

Little bird? Instead of it sounding demeaning, it actually sounds as if Lucian might care. About me? How ludicrous. He knows nothing about me besides that I'm the daughter of Valentino Lucas.

I nod and begin to turn away from him, but then stop to ask, "What about your own training?"

The corner of Lucian's mouth lifts slightly, and it makes him even more attractive. "I'm almost done."

Needing to know how long I have, I ask, "When are you leaving?"

"If all goes well, I'll leave in a month." Lucian gestures for me to walk. "I'll escort you back to your suite."

It's when he does things like this that it confuses me. I've spent the past two weeks trying to figure out why he showed me how to handle a gun.

Why does he help me the one second only to practically ignore me for days on end? Not that I mind being ignored. I prefer it.

If Lucian thinks he can get to my father through me, he's going to be disappointed when he learns I mean nothing to my father.

We fall into step next to each other, and as the night swallows us, I become overly conscious of the man next to me. Power radiates in every step he takes. My hearing focuses on the rustle of his suit. The side of my body is hyper-aware of Lucian's muscled frame.

Who is Lucian really? The dangerous man I've been warned to avoid at all costs or...

"When you return home, you'll take over from your father, right?" I ask softly, filled with a weird need to get to know him.

"Yes."

So he will be the head of the Mafia in four weeks.

"Yet you're offering to help me," I state.

"The enemy of my enemy is my friend," he murmurs, and it has my eyes darting up to his face.

I'm sure he has many, but still, I ask, "Who's your enemy?"

"Didn't your father tell you?" Lucian's gaze drops to mine.

"He doesn't tell me anything."

"Our families are being targeted. Our fathers are trying to find out who the new threat is," he informs me.

"Oh." So that was the new problem my father was referring to before he sent me here.

Lucian and I step into the castle, and the narrow hallway has his arm brushing against mine. I glance up at him again as something begins to niggle at the back of my mind. A frown forms on my forehead, trying to figure out what it is.

There's no more conversation until we reach our suites. When I open mine, Lucian asks, "Didn't you lock your door?"

"I forgot," I admit. I was too upset from the nightmare to think straight.

Lucian moves past me, pushing my door open. I watch as he steps inside, and then my lips part as he checks all the rooms and possible hiding places.

A foreign sensation spreads through my chest as he comes to stand in front of me.

"Always lock your door. Just because we're on neutral ground doesn't mean we're safe."

I nod, and when Lucian passes by me, and crosses the hallway to get to his own door, I say, "Thank you." He glances back at me, and it has me continuing, "For helping me and checking my suite."

Lucian stares at me for a moment before he unlocks his door and steps into his own suite, then he murmurs, "Go inside, little bird. Be ready to train at six."

"Okay," Before I shut the door behind me, I add, "Good night, Lucian."

Our eyes lock for a moment, and a foreign sensation flutters in my stomach. I close the door quickly and make sure to lock it. Staring at the dark wood, hope and attraction stir in my chest.

Lucian Cotroni has the power to help me, but that doesn't mean I can trust him.

Careful, Elena. Don't fall for his charm just because he's shown you kindness. He's only helping you in exchange for your loyalty. It's all business for him.

My heartbeat begins to speed up when it sinks in he's going to show me how to kill Dante.

Yes, focus on that. It's the only thing that matters.

LUCIAN

While I strip out of my suit, my thoughts return to the hopeless expression I saw on Elena's face while she was praying.

I'm not going to lie, it was heartbreaking, to say the least, and that's not an emotion I'm comfortable with. Seeing Elena so vulnerable… made the protectiveness I felt toward her when she first came to St. Monarch's roar back to life.

I have to be careful, though. Thinking with my heart will only lead to my death. She's still Valentino Lucas' daughter, and it's the only reason I've kept my distance from her since I showed her how to shoot a gun.

It's been hard seeing her every day, and forcing myself to stay away from her has only made the attraction I feel toward her grow.

Naked, I walk to the bathroom and turn on the faucets in the shower. While I wash my body, I think about the offer I made Elena. If I help her, she will be bound to me by oath, and I'll have her support. She's desperate enough to promise me anything in return for protection.

Once I'm done showering and dressed in sweatpants, I check my phone. Not seeing any messages, I drop down on my bed and stretch out.

The sight of Elena kneeling by the fountain pops back into my mind. The raw desperation and fear, while Elena begged a statue to save her, reminds me of when we buried my mother. She died when I was eight, and I've never forgotten the sight of my father kneeling by her grave as he mourned her. She died of an aneurysm, and it was one hell of a shock to us. One moment she was with us and the next she was gone. My mother was the love of his life, and my father never recovered from the loss.

I don't know what kind of life Elena has lived, but something tells me it's one she'll never recover from. She could've been a fierce rival like the other women in the Mafia, but instead, her father turned her into a frightened little bird.

There's still fight in her, though. Not all is lost.

Careful, Lucian. You don't want to make her strong enough to take you down.

That would be the stupidest way to go out in the history of the Mafia.

———————

When I open my door at ten minutes to six, I'm surprised to find Elena waiting in front of her own.

There's no trace of the restless night she had on her face, and dressed in a pair of black leggings and a t-shirt with her hair tied in a ponytail, she looks ready for training.

"Morning," she says, a cautious expression in her eyes.

"Morning," I mutter as my eyes drift over her petite body. Once again, it strikes me how beautiful she is with a body made for nights of wild sex.

"I need coffee, or I'll kill someone," I mutter as I begin to walk, and when Elena doesn't follow, I order, "Come."

She falls into step next to me, and when we walk into the dining room, Madame Keller looks up from where she's enjoying her own coffee. A knowing smile spreads around her lips, and she greets us with a nod.

I take a seat at my usual table, and seconds later, a server brings my regular order. "Your espresso, Mr. Cotroni." He turns his attention to Elena. "What would you like, Miss Lucas?"

"A café latte, please."

While I enjoy my coffee, my eyes settle on Elena. She looks nervous again, as if last night didn't happen between us. Setting my cup down, I ask, "Did you manage to sleep?"

Her eyes dart away from mine as she answers, "Yes."

"You're a bad liar," I call her out, and it makes her look at me again.

We're interrupted when the server brings the café latte, and I change the subject. "We'll start with weapons training and then hand to hand combat."

"Grandmaster Yeoh trains me at four every afternoon," Elena mentions.

"I know." Just because we haven't talked doesn't mean I didn't watch her, and honestly, her fighting skills suck.

We finish our beverages in silence. When I get up, Sergei Aulov walks into the dining room. I've been meaning to talk to him. "Give me a moment," I say to Elena, and then I walk in the Russian's direction.

"I have some information," Sergei says when I reach him. I asked him to sniff around for me about the new threat.

"What?"

Sergei takes a seat at his table, then he gestures for me to join him. After I sit down, he says, "Word is the threat is closer than you think. It's someone in your circle."

"Can you trust this word?"

Sergei nods. "As much as it's possible to trust in our world."

Fuck.

The Mafia only consists of three families. The Cotronis, the Lucas', and the Cabellos. If Sergei's source is right, then it's either Lucas or Cabello.

Needing to speak with my father, I say, "Thanks, Sergei."

When I rise to my feet, he mutters, "Be careful, Lucian. We'd hate to lose an ally."

I nod, and pulling out my phone, I walk to where Elena is waiting by the doorway. "Go to the shooting range. I'll meet you there."

"Okay." I wait for Elena to walk away before I head toward the main doors of St. Monarch's. Stepping outside, I glance around before I take out my phone and dial my father's number.

"Son? What's wrong?" he asks because I don't usually call him so early.

"I spoke with Sergei Aulov. He says the threat is closer to home than what we think. It's either Cabello or Lucas."

"I know. Nick Cabello has gone silent. Either he's dead, or he's behind the attack. I've asked Alexei to track him down."

I glance back into St. Monarch's. "Are you sure it's not Tino?" I seriously don't want to help Elena, only for her to cut my throat.

"I'm sure," my father answers. "Don't worry too much, Lucian. Enjoy your last month there."

Easier said than done. "I'll always worry about you."

After we end the call, I take a deep breath before I walk back into the castle. On my way to the armory, my thoughts revolve around the looming threat and Elena.

I want to join my father, but he's adamant we're not in the same place right now. Which tells me we're in more danger than my father is admitting to me.

And then there's Elena. Honestly, the emotions she evokes in me are unwelcome, especially now when my head needs to be clear.

Walking into the armory, I choose the usual Glock I use and head into the shooting range.

Chapter 8

ELENA

After shooting a gun for hours, my finger aches, and the rest of my hand is numb. Lucian has been relentless and cold, with impassive expressions etched on his face throughout the training sessions the past couple of days.

I'm not sure if it's from him feeling burdened by helping me or whether something else is bothering him.

Walking toward the dining hall, I glance up at Lucian, and unable to bite the question back any longer, I ask, "Is something wrong?"

Lucian shakes his head, his thoughts seemingly miles away.

Just as we're about to enter the dining room, a guard calls out, "Miss Lucas, you have a visitor."

My head turns, and then the blood runs cold in my veins at the sight of Dante walking toward me. I instantly freeze, unable to form a thought while my heart starts beating out of control. Fear wraps its claws around me at the sight of the monster I thought I was safe from. I feel Lucian's presence next to me, and it makes my mouth go dry.

Oh God, why doesn't he go into the dining room? This is going to make everything so much worse for me.

When Dante gets close, Lucian suddenly steps in front of me, tilting his head at Dante.

"What are you doing here? Shouldn't you be working on finding out who the threat is?"

Dante's eyes flare with anger as they sweep from me to Lucian.

He warned me to stay away from Lucian, and now he's caught us together.

My thoughts instantly turn to the fateful day Alfonso was killed, and it multiplies my fear. My muscles tighten with the need to run, but my feet are frozen to the floor.

Unable to make a sound, I watch as Dante clenches his jaw. I can see it's taking more self-control than he has to answer Lucian with an abrupt tone. "We're doing everything we can. I'm here to talk to my fiancé." Dante's eyes narrow on Lucian, and it makes my heart hammer against my ribs. "Do I need your permission?"

Oh, Lord. Why did Dante have to come here?

Instead of answering, Lucian steps aside, and then he says the worst possible thing, "You know where to find me when you're done with your visitor, Elena."

This is going to be so bad. The only thing counting in my favor is that Dante's not allowed to kill me on St. Monarch's grounds.

My lips part, dread spinning a dizzying web around me. As Lucian starts to enter the dining hall, Dante grabs hold of my arm in an unforgiving grip, and I'm dragged through the foyer and up the stairs. When Dante shoves me down the hallway, and I realize we're headed toward my suite, I rear back against his hold. "We can talk in the foyer."

"Shut up," Dante snaps, and he yanks me so hard a sharp pain shoots through my shoulder. A gasp explodes over my lips, and then I'm shoved against my door. "Open it."

I shake my head, knowing if I do that, Dante will be able to do anything to me. He might not be able to kill me on St. Monarch's grounds, but there are much worse things than death.

"Bitch," he growls, and losing the little patience he had with me, he backhands me across the face. My cheek goes up in flames, and before I can recover, Dante spots the key

I keep on the chain around my neck and yanks it off, making the links bite into my skin before they break.

Within a second, Dante has the door open, and I'm shoved harshly inside.

Years of fear overwhelm me, and I'm unable to think straight. My breaths explode over my lips, and my heart is nothing more than a whisper, too scared to face the monster in front of me.

It's too late to hide, though. The monster is here, and there's nothing I can do because he's so much stronger than me.

The past two and a half weeks, I've let down my guard. I thought I was safe at St. Monarch's. It makes what's about to happen so much worse. The other times I was mentally prepared, but not today.

The thoughts are fleeting because Dante pounces on me, his right hand clamping around my throat. "You thought you'd be safe from me here? Wrong, Principessa." His knuckles slam into my jaw, and the blow has my ear ringing, and a dizzying wave of pain makes it hard to focus on anything.

Dante's grip on my throat tightens, cutting off my air supply. "I told you to stay away from Cotroni!"

His fingers keep digging into my skin, and it feels like he's trying to squeeze whatever air I have from my body. I begin to slap and claw at his hand while I strain to gasp for air.

"Have you let him touch you?" Dante asks, his gaze enraged with madness. "Have you let him fuck you?"

I try to shake my head as my vision grows dark around the edges.

"You're mine, Principessa. I've convinced your father to let us marry in two weeks." Through my fading vision, all I can see is the cruel gleam in Dante's eyes as his words rain down on me like acid. "I'll fuck you so hard at night you won't be able to walk by day."

My lashes begin to lower, as the meager strength I have leaves my body, and my legs give way beneath me.

He's going to kill me. The realization drowns me in horror, and then everything goes black as I slump to the floor.

LUCIAN

This is none of your fucking business.

Yet, I can't stop myself from going to Elena's suite. My mind tells me to ignore what I saw – Dante dragging Elena harshly away. My heart, however, refuses to turn a blind eye as I take the stairs two at a time.

Nearing Elena's suite, I hear Dante growl, "Have you let him touch you? Have you let him fuck you?"

For a moment, the corner of my mouth lifts, thinking Dante sees me as a threat. Rightly so. I'm half his age and more powerful than he can ever hope to be.

"You're mine, Principessa. I've convinced your father to let us marry in two weeks."

The news makes a frown form on my forehead.

"I'll fuck you so hard at night you won't be able to walk by day."

The door isn't closed all the way, and I slam my palm against the wood, making it swing open. What I see makes all rationality leave me – Elena's eyes flutter closed, and then she collapses to the floor.

Motherfucker.

Dante pulls his foot back to kick her, but I move forward, and grabbing hold of his shoulders, I yank him away from where he's towering over her.

I should do the whole world a favor and kill him.

Dante staggers back with a shocked expression widening his eyes when they focus on me.

Anger rushes through my veins, and it's more potent than anything I've felt before. I can't form words, so I instead resort to action. My fist connects with Dante's jaw, forcing his head back.

He shakes his head and then takes a threatening step toward me, but when I lift my chin, holding my arms wide to the sides, he pauses.

"I'll give you one hit, and then I'll fucking kill you," I bite the words out. "I dare you, Capone. Take a swing at me."

Dante clenches his jaw, but knowing he doesn't stand a chance against me, he backs down.

"Fucking, pussy," I spit at him. "You're nothing but a fucking runt." Knowing I don't have much self-control left, I order, "Leave."

Dante's gaze snaps to Elena, and it has me stepping in front of her, so he has to look at me.

The man has a death wish. I'll gladly introduce him to his maker.

"She's mine," he says as if it should matter to me.

Before thinking it through, I chuckle, "Was." I shake my head at him. "Does Tino know how you handle his daughter?"

It's Dante's turn to laugh.

What the fuck?

Definitely not the reaction I was expecting.

"Tino doesn't give a shit about her. Careful, Lucian. I'm the one who will take over from Tino."

The information makes the frown on my forehead deepen. "You can't take over if you're dead."

A confident sneer forms on Dante's face. "You don't have the authority to kill me. You're not the head of *la famiglia*."

"Yet," I mutter. My muscles tense as I close the distance between us until we're face to face. "You might have Valentino eating out of your hand, but don't forget I'm Luca Cotroni's son."

The reminder has Dante stepping back with a frustrated growl, and sparing me a glare, he reluctantly leaves Elena's suite.

When I turn around, I see Elena pushing herself up into a sitting position. Wildly her eyes glance around for Dante before they stop on me, and then her lips part as she sucks in a breath of air.

Anger burns through my chest as I move forward and hold my hand out to her. Elena places her trembling palm in mine, and I pull her to her feet.

Her tongue darts out to wet her lips, and it draws my eyes to the bruises forming on the right side of her jaw and around her neck.

"Did he leave?" she asks hoarsely. She keeps looking between the door and the floor. Anywhere but at me.

"Yes." My anger increases when pure relief washes over her face. Her chin begins to tremble, but she fights to rein in the emotions tightening her features.

I shouldn't care about this woman. She's nothing to me. Yet, I find myself gravitating to her, and for the first time, the thought enters my mind – I could marry her. That way, it will be a fuck you to Dante, and it will bring the two families together, showing us as a united front to our enemy.

Keep lying to yourself, Lucian. You fucking want her. The sooner you admit it to yourself, the sooner you can decide what the fuck you're going to do about it.

Elena begins to look very uncomfortable. Her eyes flit to mine before they lower back to the floor. "Thank you."

What a fucked up world we live in when a woman has to thank a man for saving her from an asshole?

I let out a sigh and walk to the suite's phone. Dialing room service, I order crushed ice for Elena's bruises. When I place the earpiece back, I turn to her and ask, "Are you hurt anywhere else but your face and neck?"

She lifts her hand self-consciously to her jaw then shakes her head.

I know it's a stupid question to ask, but I can't stop myself. "Are you okay?"

Of course, she's not okay. I can feel her distress radiating from her, and she's deathly pale, but still, she nods.

I only got a glimpse of how Dante treats Elena, and it's left me with a burning desire to kill the fucker.

How much has she already endured at his depraved hands?

I've always prided myself on being in control of everything. It's the way my father raised me. But since Elena walked into my life, I seem to have very little control over my actions. Once again, I find myself doing something totally out of character as I close the distance between us and wrap my arms around her trembling body.

She tenses for a moment, and then the trembling increases as she wraps her arms around my waist. Her hands grip hold of my jacket, her breath hitching. The sound rips through me, wreaking havoc with my own emotions.

I tighten my hold on her, and when I lower my mouth to her hair, I have to close my eyes from the overwhelming protectiveness and attraction this woman makes me feel.

Christ, it's unlike anything I've ever felt.

It's disarming.

I want her.

I want this wounded little bird with her big eyes and body made for sinful nights.

The dominance in me thirsts for her submissiveness. It calls to me, demanding me to make her mine.

Chapter 9

ELENA

It takes everything I have to not break down and cry. Nothing has ever felt as good as Lucian holding me. My thoughts are all over the place, but I manage to latch onto one. Lucian did what Alfonso couldn't – he made Dante leave.

For the first time in my life, someone stood up for me. This man whom I should fear has shown me compassion when I was drowning in despair. He protected me.

I tighten my hold on him, squeezing my eyes shut as I fight back the tears because I feel safe.

Safe.

I can't remember if I ever felt safe.

It makes me want to cling to Lucian forever, but knowing that's not a possibility, I loosen my grip around his waist. I bring my hands to his sides, but when Lucian doesn't pull back and instead tightens his hold on me, my eyes drift shut again. I take a deep breath of his aftershave and soak in the feel of his stronger body pressed against mine.

It's soothing instead of threatening.

Having someone show me something other than abuse begins to break down the walls I've tried to build up around myself. It exposes the parts of me I've worked so hard to keep hidden from Dante's cruelty.

The human being who was dying to feel a gentle touch.

The girl who only wanted to be loved.

The woman who wants to be free.

Knowing I won't be able to fight the tears for much longer, I try to pull away again, but still, Lucian won't let go.

And. It. Shatters. Me.

I splinter into a million pieces, each one showing a glimpse of the hell I've been subjected to.

I gasp against Lucian's chest, and my fingers dig into the expensive fabric of his jacket as the tears spill from my eyes.

He moves one of his hands to the back of my head, and he presses a kiss to my hair. Instead of it comforting me, it breaks my heart. It strips me bare because this man will rule the Mafia, which means he's brutal and dangerous.

There's no way a monster like Dante can be controlled by someone who's not a bigger monster.

And even knowing this, I don't want Lucian to let go of me. He's strong enough to fight all my demons. If only he wasn't a demon himself.

A knock at the door finally has Lucian's arms loosening their grip on me. His hands move to my shoulders, and I keep my head bowed, not wanting him to see my tears.

Lucian's breath fans over my forehead, and then his mouth presses against my skin. I squeeze my eyes shut, another overwhelming feeling of comfort rocketing through me. My stomach tightens and spins all at once, the sensation making me a million times more aware of the man in front of me.

The instant Lucian steps around me to open the door, I turn and flee to the bathroom. I shut the door behind me and take a moment to lean back against the wood, just needing to breathe.

I'm confused. Overwhelmed. Torn. A total mess.

It's because of Lucian and not Dante's surprise visit.

My heart wants to beg Lucian to keep holding me. My body is aware of his in a way I've never been aware of a man before. But my mind... my mind screams at me to run. To get away from the monsters in this world because it doesn't matter what they look like, what suits they wear, or how good their arms feel – at the core, they're all the same – evil and cruel.

Oh, Elena. Don't do this to yourself. You can't fall for Lucian just because he was nice to you. Yes, he's dangerously attractive, and yes, it felt amazing to be held by him, but he's still Lucian Cotroni. Everything he does has a motive. It's strategic. He thinks he can get to your father through you.

I keep telling myself this until I feel a little calmer. Walking to the sink, I open the faucet and splash water on my face, cooling my skin. I grab a towel from the rack and pat the drops away, being gentle over the right side of my face.

Then I lift my head and look at the mirror. There's an ugly bruise forming on my jaw, and Dante's fingers have left abrasive red imprints around my neck.

And for the first time, I feel overly self-conscious of the marks. I'm not at the villa where I'm locked in my room so no one can see them. Not that anyone there has ever cared.

What matters is that Lucian has seen them, and it makes shame burn hot in my cheeks.

God, I already care what he thinks of me.

I need to stop whatever's happening between us. I don't know what Lucian's intentions are, but I can control how I feel, and I refuse to fall for him.

When minutes have passed, and I know I can't hide in the bathroom forever, I loosen my hair from the ponytail and quickly pull a brush through it. I let the silky black strands cover the side of my face, falling like a curtain over the bruises. I take a deep breath before I walk to the door, and ducking my head low, I open it.

My heart instantly begins to beat faster, and I'm not sure if it's from the shame for the marks on my skin, or the undeniable attraction I feel toward Lucian, or both.

All I want to do is dart back to the bathroom, but instead, I slowly inch my way through the bedroom until I reach the doorway. Lifting my head slightly, I peek into the living room just as Lucian glances in my direction. We both freeze, him with a towel in his hand and me dying of embarrassment.

Lucian is the first to talk, his tone soft but still commanding. "Come here, little bird."

I swallow hard on the nervousness spinning in my stomach and walk toward him. When I'm within reaching distance, Lucian lifts his right hand to my face. His fingers brush over my skin as he pushes my hair behind my ear, and then he presses the towel to my jaw. It's ice-cold, instantly chilling my skin.

I lower my eyes to his chest, but then he steps closer to me while he lifts his left arm. His hand cups the back of my head, and it makes me feel surrounded by him.

"The ice will help with the swelling," he explains in a low tone that threatens to create an intimate bubble around us. "But you probably know this already." His words make my eyes snap up to his, which has him saying, "I'm guessing Dante's hit you before."

Does he want me to tell him? Would it even matter if he knew all the things Dante's done to me?

I search his strong features for the answers, but all I find is more confusion. Standing so close to him, with his aftershave filling the air, only makes my heart beat faster. It makes my stomach flutter and my skin tingle.

Do I want him to know?

My deepest fears. My darkest shame. My nightmares.

No, I don't want him to know. I don't want anyone to know.

The corner of Lucian's mouth lifts slightly. "You don't have to tell me," he says as if he can read my thoughts. "But..." He leans down until his breath warms my ear, "if you tell me, I'll probably kill Capone."

My eyes widen slightly, and for a moment, I'm tempted. God, I've never been tempted like this in my life. If I sacrifice my deepest, darkest secrets, Lucian will kill Dante.

As Lucian pulls back, his mouth brushes along the curve of my jaw. My breaths explode over my lips, and without thinking, I yank back, quickly putting a safe distance between us. The towel drops from his hand, and the icy slush spills onto the floor.

My eyes collide with Lucian's dark brown gaze, and the expression in them has my heart instantly thundering in my chest. He stares at me with predatory desire.

I've seen that look before. Many times as Dante defiled me.

The fear creeping through me is different, though. With Dante, the terror was always accompanied by disgust and devastating shame. It was traumatic.

With Lucian… it terrifies me for a different reason. There's no disgust. There's no shame. I'm only filled with an ungodly fear because it would be so easy to fall for him. It would be so easy to seek refuge in his arms. To have him fight my battles.

Only, it would cost my freedom, and it's the one thing I'm not willing to give up on. It's the only thing that's kept me going over the past four years.

Lucian looks like the possessive kind. Once he has me, I'll just become a prisoner again. The only thing that will change is the walls of my prison.

And God knows what new horrors they will bear witness to.

LUCIAN

Fuck, this is hard. I'm trying not to scare the shit out of Elena, but it's impossible to hide how I feel. The more skittish she becomes, and the thicker her fear grows, the more I fucking want her.

The darkest part of me wants to feel her tremble. I want to hear her beg for my mercy and not the goddamn statue out in the garden. I want her fearing only me so she'll fully submit.

It's fucking sick, but the desires are overpowering.

I suck in a deep breath of air, fighting the dominant side of me until my muscles loosen a little.

On my left shoulder sits the devil, whispering for me to take what I want. To make Elena mine. No matter the cost. No matter the blood, I'll have to spill. No matter the damage it will do to my family name.

On my right shoulder sits an angel, pleading with me to find compassion in my heart. To be gentle with this broken little bird. To not be just another man who forces himself on her.

Christ, right now, I want to flick the angel off my shoulder and listen to the devil.

I fist my hands at my sides as I fight for control over the intense emotions, and then I manage to take a step back.

Leave, Lucian. Before you do something, you'll regret.

My gaze rakes over Elena, where she's staring at me with wide, fear-filled eyes.

How did this happen? How has this petite woman manage to warm the coldest part of me?

Without a word, I turn away from her and stalk out of her suite. I pull her door closed behind me and take the couple of steps to my own. Unlocking it, I shove the heavy wood open, and walking into my living room, I slam it shut behind me.

Fuck.

Needing to find some clarity, I pull my phone out of my pocket and dial my father's number.

"Son?" he answers as always.

"Papà," I say, knowing it will get his attention. I only call him that when I need my father and not the head of the Mafia.

"What happened?" he instantly asks with concern lacing his words.

"I... I actually don't know," I admit. "It's Elena Lucas."

"What? Tell me," my father demands, his worry for me making his patience non-existent. After my mother died, I became my father's world. I know he lives and breathes for me. There's no one alive he loves more.

"She makes me feel," I force the words over my lips.

Christ, does she make me feel. Everything.

"Dio," he mutters 'God' in Italian. "Now's not the time, Lucian."

"I know," I bite out. "Trust me, I know."

"Don't act with your heart. Give me time. Once the threat has been dealt with, we can talk about Elena."

Time. It's something I don't have.

"She's marrying Dante in two weeks," I inform him.

"Merda," he grumbles. "This is really the last thing I need to worry about." He lets out an exasperated breath. "Are you thinking with your cock, or is it more?"

I wish it was only my cock. I'd be able to fuck her out of my system then.

"Lucian?" My father snaps when I take too long to answer.

Knowing I can't hide anything from him, I say, "I feel things for her I've never felt before. I have no idea what to make of it. I just... I want her, and it's clouding my judgment."

I'm weak.

God, she makes me weak.

That's not good at all.

"We have two weeks. Sort through your shit. If you still want her in seven days, I'll talk with Valentino."

I might want her now, but does that mean I want her for the rest of my life. Am I willing to marry her? Against her will?

I have no fucking idea. This is all new to me.

But I have seven days to figure out what the hell this is I'm feeling for her.

"Thank you," I mutter as I walk to the couch. I sit down and let out a heavy sigh. "Papà ... how did you feel when you met Mamma?"

He pauses for a moment, then he answers, "I was instantly obsessed. Your mamma bewitched me. She became the only thing I wanted. I would've killed for her. I would've taken her against her will if it was the only way I could have her."

I sit up straighter, a frown forming on my forehead. "But Mamma loved you... right?"

"Yes, I was lucky. She returned my feelings, and we got married a month later. Even though it was arranged by your nonni, we had no objections."

I knew my grandfathers were the ones who arranged the wedding to align the two families, but I didn't know my parents fell in love the moment they met. I never asked about their love because I didn't want to cause my father heartache.

I only know what I saw while my mother was alive. Their love was warm, and it filled our home to the brim.

Needing to know, I ask, "How do I know when it's love and not just lust?"

"You don't, son. To me, they are the same thing. You can't love what you don't want. The more I wanted your mamma, the more I loved her. With every passing day since she left, my love has only grown for her. She's the only one for me."

I rub my fingers over my forehead, not knowing what I actually feel for Elena.

Protective. Yes.

Attraction. Hell fucking yes.

Possessiveness. Yes.

But love?

"If in seven days, your feelings for the girl have grown, then you'll know. If they fade, you'll have your answer."

So far, they've only been growing.

I nod. "Okay." I swallow, then continue. "How are things there?"

"I'm starting to think I should've let you come home," my father chuckles.

"Yeah, next time, you'll listen to me," I tease him.

My father lets out a sigh. "Alexei says Cabello has gone into hiding. There's no sign he's been killed. We just have to find him now, and then the problem will be taken care of."

"That's good news," I mutter, wanting this shit to be over with as well.

"I have to go. Don't do something stupid. You hear me?"

"Yes, Papà."

We end the call, and I drop the phone on the coffee table. Leaning back, I settle into the couch and stare at the expansive windows.

Seven days.

It's not a lot of time, but it's better than nothing.

Chapter 10

ELENA

I've been doing my best to avoid Lucian for the past three days.

Even though I'm free to move around the castle and grounds, I've been hiding in my suite. I haven't even gone downstairs for my training sessions and meals, but instead, I order room service.

Which means I've had nothing but time to think. About everything.

Lucian.

My feelings.

Dante.

The impending wedding and death sentence.

Eleven days. That's all I have.

It's nothing. Just eleven days, and I'll either have to find a way to kill Dante, or I'll cross over to the afterlife.

Staring out of the window, my heart longs to feel the warmth of the sun on my skin.

Every night I wait until midnight before I sneak out of my suite to visit the secret garden. So far, I've been lucky, and I haven't run into anyone but the guards.

I'm not free. Not even at St. Monarch's.

It's better than being locked up in the Villa with Dante.

But I'm still not free.

A knock at my door draws me out of my thoughts, and I turn away from the window to receive the order I've placed for lunch. Not having much of an appetite, I got myself a platter of cheese, cold meats, and olives.

I unlock the door and open it, but instead of finding a server, I'm met with Lucian, a severe expression darkening his features.

I begin to shut the door, but his hand shoots out, slamming hard against the wood.

"What –?" Before I can say another word, Lucian grabs hold of my arm and pulls me out of the room. He reaches past me and closes the door. "What are you doing?" I demand to know, my heart starting to beat faster.

Lucian's hand clamps around mine, and then I'm tugged down the hallway. "I'm fucking done with you hiding," he mutters. I try to pull free from his grip on me, but it only has him tightening his fingers around mine as he threatens, "I swear to God I will throw you over my shoulder if you make a scene."

I follow him down the stairs, having to almost jog to keep up with his wider strides.

"Where are you taking me?" I ask while I search for a guard.

"Outside." It's the only explanation I'm offered.

"I'll scream for help," I warn Lucian, not sure if it will even help. Will they dare go against his wishes?

"Go ahead," Lucian says, his voice filled with confidence. "They'll only interfere once I've killed you."

"Once?" The word bursts from me as fear slithers through me. "So you can do anything to me, and they won't stop you?" My breaths begin to speed up. "God." I yank back against Lucian's hold. "Let go!" I stop walking, trying to twist my hand out of his.

"Christ Almighty!" he snaps, and then he turns to me. Lucian grabs hold of my sides, and the next moment I'm thrown over his shoulder as if I weigh nothing. I let out a startled shriek which he ignores as he begins to walk again, stepping through the side doors.

I start to slam my fists against his back. "Put me down! You can't do this."

A slap to my bottom makes my eyes widen, and a gasp explodes from me. Stunned, I hang over Lucian's shoulder as he carries me away from the castle. When we reach the secret garden, I'm tugged down the front of his body until my feet meet the ground. I stumble, but then Lucian catches my shoulders.

With my breaths exploding over my lips and my hair hanging in my face, I glare at Lucian. "What the hell do you think you're doing?"

"It was clear this was the only way to get your attention," he says, his features even darker than when I opened the door.

"My attention? For what?" I take a step backward, but my calves bump against the marble edging around the fountain.

"This," he snaps, and then he moves forward, and the meager space I've managed to put between us vanishes with one stride from him. His right hand shoots up, clasping the back of my head, and before I can even realize what's happening, Lucian's mouth crashes down on mine.

I freeze, stunned out of my mind.

He enters my mouth without any effort, and then velvet brushes over my tongue.

My shock turns to confusion turns to feeling overwhelmed in a matter of a second.

A roar ripples from Lucian, and I somehow manage to lift my hands to his solid chest. I want to push against him, to sever the kiss, but my hands won't listen.

Lucian's left hand finds my cheek, and then he forces my head to tilt to where he wants me as he deepens the kiss. It becomes hungry as he seems to lose control, and soon I'm struggling to breathe past the assault on my mouth.

A whimper escapes me, and I'm not sure why I made the sound.

I don't want this.

Yet, I do nothing to fight him off.

It's just another thing taken from me.

But still, I can't deny the fluttering in my abdomen and the quickening of my heartbeat. And it's not because I fear him. It's because it's the best kiss I've ever had.

Lucian's lips knead mine, his tongue stroking hard, his teeth tugging, demanding, claiming.

God, it's… forceful… intoxicating… earthshattering.

Where I could never mentally escape from Dante's assaults, I find my mind easily clouding over. It feels as if I'm being absorbed by Lucian. His power engulfs me. His manliness drugs me. His mouth demands that I focus only on how he's making me feel.

Where I only felt disgusted with Dante, it's the total opposite with Lucian. Not even Alfonso made me feel so... hypnotized.

Every single fiber of my being is focused on Lucian. My blood rushes through my veins, and before I know it, I'm kissing him back. I give in, not even trying to put up a fight.

I taste the mint on his tongue. I feel his warm breaths on my skin. His arms wrap around me so tightly it feels like he'll never let go.

God. God. God.

What is this?

My body melts against his, and my hands move up to his neck, my fingers trying to memorize the feel of his skin. My breasts push against his firm chest as my tongue savors his.

Another whimper escapes me, but it sounds different to my ears. There's no panic in it. Only need.

As quickly as Lucian invaded my mouth, he lets go of me, and within another second, I'm filled with the loss of his kiss and body as he puts a safe distance between us.

My eyes flutter open, and my hands drop limply to my sides.

I'm met with smoldering eyes, his chest rising and falling from the deep breaths he's sucking in. He lifts a hand to his jaw, and then his thumb swipes over his bottom lip.

And then reality sets back in, and my heart plummets to the ground from where it was soaring the heavens.

I thought I've felt fear before. I was wrong. I begin to tremble uncontrollably, and the warmth flees my body, filling me with ice.

Not because Lucian can physically hurt me, but because he can do the one thing Dante never could – Lucian can kill my soul. He can rob me of my dreams. He can make me a prisoner, and I fear I won't want to escape him.

LUCIAN

Mother of God.

I've been slowly losing my mind the past three days. My thoughts were consumed with Elena. My eyes constantly searched for her. But Elena hid from me, never leaving her suite.

Knowing I was running out of time, I knew there was only one way for me to be sure. So I yanked her out of her room, and like a fucking caveman, I carried her to the garden she loves so much.

And then I fucking kissed her.

I thought it would help me be done with her. I thought it would be the same as kissing any other inexperienced girl – unexciting and tasteless – and I'd finally get over my obsession with her.

But I was wrong. *Christ was I wrong.*

My hopes were smothered, and my concerns were met face to face with the most powerful emotions I've ever felt. Unrelenting need. Potent desire. Above all, my possessiveness increased tenfold.

I want Elena. More than anything I've ever wanted. She tasted like heaven. She felt perfect in my arms. When she whimpered, it made me instantly hard. It took more self-control than I thought I possessed to break the kiss because I was a second away from fucking her right here next to the fountain.

I can still taste her sweetness on my tongue, and it makes me lick my lips, searching for any hint of her left on them.

I drink in the sight of her rosy cheeks, the excitement from the kiss we shared staining her skin. Her breasts swell under her v-neck t-shirt with every breath she takes.

She looks like the goddess of sex until the blood drains from her face. Panic tightens her features, and then her eyes fill with fear. Her trembling hands catch my eye, and her gasps begin to come faster until I worry whether she's about to hyperventilate.

Honestly, I'm a little surprised by Elena's reaction. She kissed me back. She fucking melted in my arms. But still, she looks at me with horror. As if I fucking attacked her.

I take a step toward her, but her hands fly up in warning. "Don't!" Even her voice is strained with panic. She sucks in a frantic breath. "Don't ever touch me again."

Elena darts away, and I almost go after her, but the horror I saw on her face keeps me rooted to the spot.

Not now, Lucian. Give her time.

I let out a sigh and walk to one of the benches. I unbutton my jacket and sit down, my gaze settling on the fountain.

What the fuck do I do now? I got my answer, and in the process, I traumatized Elena.

I should've been more patient.

Fuck that. I waited three days for her to come out of her suite. That alone took more patience than I had.

Narrowing my eyes, I turn them toward the castle.

Maybe it's not me? It could be that the kiss brought up bad memories for her. If that's the case, it means Dante did more than just hit her.

God won't be able to help him if that's the case. I'll fucking rip his head off.

My phone begins to ring, and pulling it out of my pocket, I frown when I see Alexei Koslov's name flashing on the screen.

Thinking he can't get a hold of my father, I answer, "Lucian."

"It's Alexei," he says, his voice filled with the darkness I've grown accustomed to hearing.

"I know," I mutter. "Why are you calling?"

"It's your father. He's been killed." The words are abrupt, straight to the fucking point, but still, they don't sink in.

"What?" I begin to get up but sit down again when there's no strength in my legs.

"Your father's been assassinated." There's a moment's pause, then the Russian says, "I'll find out who it was. First, we need to get you to safety."

Papà... No. No. No.

Stupidly I ask, "Are you sure?"

"I'm looking at his body right now. Bullet to the head. You're a fucking sitting duck at St. Monarch's. Carson is coming to get you. Go to Madame Keller's office and wait there for him. Demitri and I are leaving Italy now. We'll meet you at a safe house."

"Alexei," I breathe, still not able to process what he's telling me.

"Lucian!" he snaps. "Go now. We're on our way."

Somehow I manage to get up, and I listen to Alexei tell Demitri, his personal guard, "Let's go."

I walk toward the side door, then Alexei shouts, "I don't hear you fucking running, Lucian."

And then it sinks in. My body darts forward, and just as I take the steps two at a time, the mosaic widow to my left shatters.

Fuck.

I move faster and slip inside just in time as another bullet shatters the glass door.

"They're here!" I snap into the phone. "They're fucking here."

I keep running down the hallway, and instead of going for the safety Madame Keller's office will offer, I turn right into the foyer and dart up the stairs.

I run down the hallway and then slam a fist against Elena's door. When she doesn't open, I begin to pound against the wood. "Open, Elena. You're in danger!"

Seconds later, she opens. I grab hold of her hand and begin to run again, yanking her behind me.

"Lucian!"

Ignoring Elena, I speak into the phone. "How far away is Carson?"

Carson is Alexei's younger brother, so I know I can trust him. The Koslov's won't turn on me. They have honor which means they'll die protecting me. They're the most important allies my father ever made, and right now, my life depends on them.

"Twenty minutes," Alexei answers.

I drag Elena down the stairs, and as we turn left in the foyer, gunfire erupts out by the front gate. Guards rush past us as I turn down the hallway that leads to Madame Keller's office.

One of the guards stops when he sees us and shouts, "Faster, Mr. Cotroni."

We're escorted the rest of the way and ushered into the office that's more secure than any other place on this goddamn planet.

Madame Keller takes hold of my free arm, her face filled with compassion. "I'm so sorry for your loss, Mr. Cotroni."

My father is dead.

The thought rocks me to my core, and I let Madame Keller pull me to a sofa as her guards usher the other guests inside. The door is closed and then locked.

I sit down, still gripping Elena's hand tightly. Slowly I turn my eyes to her pale face, and I can only manage to breathe as the realization robs me of all rationality.

My father is dead.

"Lucian?" Elena asks as she scoots closer to me. Her fingers stir in my hold, not to free her hand but to get a better grip on me. "What's happening?"

"They're here," I manage to say, my voice void of any emotion. "Fuck, they're here."

"Who's here?" She glances around the room and then at Madame Keller.

"Mr. Cotroni's father was just assassinated. I assume they're here for Lucian," Madame Keller explains.

Elena's eyes widen as her head snaps back to me. "Oh, God. I'm so sorry."

"They killed my father." The words drift over my lips, lost with disbelief. A relentless ache tears through my chest.

My mind begins to race, looking for answers to questions I haven't even thought of yet. My heart hammers against my ribs, trying to get away from the ruthless sorrow filling every inch of me.

"They fucking killed my father," I rasp.

I glance around the room at the other guests, some my allies and others my enemies, which makes me rein in the grief. A switch flips inside me, and it shoves the raw sorrow down to the darkest part of me. In its place, rage burns through me like wildfire. Letting go of Elena's hand, I get up and bring the phone back to my ear. "You still there?"

"Blyad'," and then Alexei roars, "you better be in Madame Keller's office! I swear I'll fucking beat the shit out of you once I get my hands on you."

"I'm in her office. I'm safe." Or rather, as safe as I'll ever be.

Alexei lets out a breath of relief. "Carson's close. Just sit tight."

I walk to the furthest side of the office and mutter, "Is it Cabello?" I need to know who I'll be hunting. "Is he behind this?"

"I'm not sure. All signs lead to him, but I think he's working for someone."

"Who?" I demand.

"A fucking ghost. The person has covered all their tracks."

Fuck!

Chapter 11

ELENA

Minutes become an hour, and all we can do is wait in Madame Keller's office, which looks more like an armory. Cabinets, filled with every kind of weapon, line the walls.

At first, Lucian paced the length of the office like a caged lion. After a while, he stopped in front of the one cabinet, and he's been staring at the guns ever since.

My tongue darts out, nervously licking my lips, and then I get up. Slowly, I walk closer to Lucian, not knowing what I'll say or do once I reach him.

Stopping next to Lucian, he doesn't move. His eyes remain trained on the weapons.

"I'm sorry for your loss, Lucian," I whisper, not knowing what he's going through.

Slowly, Lucian nods, and then he glances at me. For a moment, all I see is grief, and it makes me want to hug him, but then his eyes narrow. "Have you heard from your father?"

"No," I answer honestly.

Lucian's gaze snaps from me to where Madame Keller is sitting with a glass of wine in her hand, looking way more relaxed than I feel. "Any word on whether just my father was assassinated?" Lucian asks her.

Madame Keller holds up a finger, and I watch as she makes a call. She murmurs into the phone, and I can't hear what she's saying.

"You think my father might be dead too?" I ask, strangely not upset by the thought. *God, as long as Dante's dead as well.*

The thought lifts some of the darkness that's fallen around us.

Lucian shakes his head, and then he walks to Madame Keller as she sets the wine glass down and rises to her feet. I follow after him.

"Valentino is secure in his villa. There was no attack on him," Madame Keller informs us.

Which means Dante's alive. Damn. At least one good thing could've come from today.

"Interesting," Lucian mutters. I watch as he dials a number on his phone, and moments later, his voice is filled with anger as he says, "Do you think you're safe at your villa, Tino?"

My eyebrows lift when I realize he called my father. It has me shamelessly listening in on the conversation.

"Where the fuck were you when my father was killed?" Lucian asks. Seconds later, he snaps, "You better find out who's behind the attack. Until then, I might just think you're behind the assassination."

Oh. God.

If Lucian thinks my father had his father killed, what does it mean for me? I instantly step away from him, and it has his eyes snapping to me. Slowly, he shakes his head, then he says, "I have Elena. I'll keep her with me until you figure out who's trying to kill us all."

It doesn't sound like I'll be safe with him, not with the warning darkening every word.

Lucian ends the call then he tilts his head, his eyes locking with mine. "You're leaving with me as soon as Carson gets here."

"What?" I gasp. "Leave? Where?"

A two-way radio crackles, and then a voice says, "It's safe. The grounds have been secured."

"Thank God for small mercies," Madame Keller mutters, and then she gestures to the guards by the door. They open it, and not wasting time, I walk away from Lucian.

I don't know where I plan on going. If I stay here, I'll end up being taken by Lucian. If I leave... I might just get killed right outside the gates of St. Monarch's.

A man comes walking down the hallway, dressed in a dark blue suit. He looks scary as hell, and I step to the side so he can pass by me.

God, is there anywhere safe on this planet?

"Stop her, Carson," Lucian calls out from behind me, and the man instantly grabs hold of my arm. "She's going with us," Lucian explains, and then I watch like an idiot as the two men hug.

Too much has happened today, and it's hard to try to make sense of any of it.

Carson shoves me toward Lucian, muttering, "Yours."

I try to pull free as they pass me over like I'm a piece of property, but Lucian quickly grabs hold of me by the elbow.

"Ah, Mr. Koslov," Madame Keller croons behind us. "It's always a pleasure seeing you."

Carson leaves us to greet Madame Keller, and then Lucian begins to drag me down the hallway while he tells Carson, "We'll be ready to go in ten minutes."

"I'm not going anywhere with you," I warn him.

"Oh, little bird," he murmurs, his voice deadly, "you don't have a fucking choice."

I'm dragged back to my suite and shoved into my bedroom. "Pack your shit. We don't have any time to waste."

"I'm not leaving with you," I snap back at Lucian.

"Elena…" Lucian's voice is low with warning. "Don't fucking test me today."

He'll probably throw me over his shoulder again.

"Lucian?" Carson calls from the hallway.

"In Elena's suite. Come watch her while I get my belongings," Lucian says without taking his eyes off me.

"Don't do this," I resort to pleading. "I'm nothing to my father. It won't matter to him if you kill me."

"I have no intention of killing you, so calm the fuck down and pack your clothes," he bites out, the tension on his face clearly telling me he has zero patience left.

Carson comes into my bedroom, then glances between Lucian and me. "Why is she coming with?"

"She's Valentino's daughter." It's the only explanation Lucian offers him before he leaves us.

Carson's one eyebrow lifts, and it makes him look scarier. "I didn't know Valentino had a child."

"I'm not a child," I mutter as I walk to my closet. Not wanting to be dragged out of St. Monarch's with only the clothes on my back, I begin to pack.

Carson doesn't say anything else, but I feel his eyes watching my every more. "Can you not stare at me," I ask when it becomes too much.

"Why? Do you have something to hide?" he asks.

I let out a huff and pack faster. Even though I hurry, Lucian's done before me, and he comes back into my suite. "Did you bring vests?"

"Yes, I'll go get them quickly."

After Carson leaves, I shove the last of my clothes into the bag and zip it closed.

God, what will become of me?

"You're wasting your time taking me," I try one more time. "My father really doesn't care about what happens to me."

Lucian just stares at me with a clenched jaw. His phone begins to ring, and it takes his attention off me.

"Yuri," he answers, and after listening, he says, "I appreciate it. I'll be in touch about the shipment as soon as I get home. Don't worry, business will go ahead as planned."

He ends the call, and a moment later, Carson comes back with bulletproof vests.

I watch as Lucian takes off his jacket. He straps the vest on and then shrugs his jacket back on. Taking the other one from Carson, Lucian comes to me. I've never worn one and let him help me, not knowing what use the vest is if someone's going to shoot me in the head.

"Let's go," Carson says.

I take hold of my luggage, and with my teeth worrying my bottom lip, I walk out of my suite.

LUCIAN

With Elena walking between Carson and me, I warn her, "Don't try to run. If I have to carry you out of here, I'm going to be fucking angry, and that's the last thing you want right now."

"This is absurd. I'm worthless."

Her words grind against my last nerve, and I clench my jaw.

Carson stops by the guard at the door and takes the weapons he had to surrender when he entered St. Monarch's. He hands me a Heckler and Koch and a Beretta. I check both the clips before I tuck the Beretta behind my back. Holding the Heckler and Koch in my right hand, I glance at Elena. "You do exactly as I say."

The dismayed expression on her face changes into worry as she turns her eyes to the exit.

"Wait here," Carson instructs. He walks to the exit and scans the grounds, then gestures at us. "Let's make this quick."

"Move," I order Elena, and thankfully she doesn't decide now's a good time to put up a fight.

We leave the castle and hurry down the steps to where Carson's armored SUV is waiting. We load the luggage in the back, and then I open the back door and wait for Elena to get in. "Move over," I snap tensely, and then I get in next to her.

Carson slides in behind the steering wheel, and as he starts the engine, he says. "It's a fifteen-minute drive. There's more ammo and guns in a hidden compartment beneath your seat.

I duck forward and press against the velvet by my legs, which instantly springs open. "Got it."

He pulls away from the castle and drives toward the exit. As we near the guardhouse, the gates begin to open, and I check the clip of my gun again.

Elena sits quietly next to me as Carson steers us off the grounds. I instantly scan the area around us, consisting of a short stretch of road with trees lined on either side. We get to the main street, which leads through the town, and it makes the tension ease from my shoulders a little.

After we've made it safely away from St. Monarch's, Carson makes a call. "I have them." A moment later, he says, "Lucian and a woman, Elena Lucas." He listens then holds the phone over his shoulder for me to take.

Putting the device to my ear, I say, "Yes."

"Elena Lucas?" Alexei asks. "Why?"

"Security," I answer so Elena won't catch onto what we're talking about.

"Makes sense. Demitri and I are on the way. We'll meet you at the safe house."

Knowing I owe Alexei my life, I say, "Thank you."

"Of course." He lets out a chuckle. "By the way, the fee went up."

His words draw a chuckle from me, but it feels foreign on my lips. "I expected as much." The grim cloak of sorrow tightens around me, then I ask, "My father's...?" I can't force the word 'body' over my lips.

"In safekeeping."

"Thank you."

Papà... Dio, Papà...

I close my eyes as intense grief rips through me.

"We'll find out who's behind this and kill them," Alexei assures me.

"I won't rest until they're dead," I growl.

"Neither will I," Alexei murmurs darkly. "I considered your father a friend."

It means a hell of a lot to hear Alexei say that. He's the best there is, and knowing I have him on my side offers me some comfort.

We end the call, and I toss the device onto the passenger seat, then say, "Thanks for coming, Carson."

"Don't thank me yet. We have a tail," he mutters.

"Only one car?" I ask as I glance over my shoulder at the sedan carrying four men.

"Yes."

"Stop the car," I order.

Carson slams on the breaks, and it brings us to a screeching halt. I throw the door open, and as I get out, I remove the Baretta from behind my back. Lifting my arms, I open fire on the fuckers who dared to come after me.

People on the sidewalks scatter for cover while cars swerve to get away from the hell breaking loose.

"You come after me?" I shout as I let one bullet after the other fly. "You fucking kill my father and dare come after me?"

The fuckers should've invested in armor-proof windows because I take out the driver and passenger in front without breaking a sweat.

The other two in the back seat open their doors and take cover behind the metal, returning fire.

A bullet clips my jacket on my left arm, then Carson opens fire, using a submachine gun, and it riddles the sedan with bullets, killing the last two men.

"Fottuta feccia," I mutter, *you fucking scum,* as I walk closer and search the body on the passenger side. Carson helps, and finding the dead men's wallets and phones, we jog back to the SUV.

Once Carson steers us away from the crime scene, I begin to search through their wallets and phones for any information that can help us find out who's behind this.

"We should expect more. The scouts were only reporting where we are," Carson advises.

"I'm ready," I mutter as I open the first phone and check the call history. I press dial on the last number, and then a man answers, "Give me an update."

"You should've sent more than four men," I bite the words out.

There's a moment's silence, then the fucker asks, "Who am I talking to?"

"Take a wild fucking guess, asshole."

The line goes dead, and it has me cursing, "Fucking piece of shit." I meet Carson's eyes in the rearview mirror. "He had a Greek accent. What fucking Greek is moving in on my territory?"

"A soon to be dead one," Carson mutters. "We'll let him bring the war to us and then end it."

I glance at Elena, who's been surprisingly quiet, and then I see why. She's pressed herself against the door, her arms wrapped tightly around her waist and her hair hanging like a curtain between us.

Noticing how badly she's trembling, I reach over and brush her hair away from her face. She instantly flinches, the short bursts of air leaving her parted lips speeding up even more.

It's the look of terror in her eyes that makes me realize she's having a panic attack right next to me, and I didn't even know.

Fuck.

I slide closer to her, and taking hold of her chin, I turn her face to me. "Deeper breaths, little bird," I murmur, so I don't spook her more. She begins to gasp, and it has me lifting my other hand to her cheek. "Shh... you're safe," I say the only thing I can think she wants to hear right now.

It seems to help, though. Elena snaps out of the haze she was caught in and yanks her face free from my hands.

"Don't... touch... me," the words shudder from her.

I move back to my side of the seat, watching Elena squeeze her body against the door again.

She doesn't look like she's about to stop breathing anymore, and shaking my head, I turn my gaze to the scenery passing us by. Buildings, street lamps, people going about their business.

I close my eyes, my thoughts returning to my loss.

It's more than a loss, though. I've lost the only person who knew me inside out.

I lost my best friend.

My mentor.

I loved my father more than life itself, and his death has left a gaping hole in my heart that will never heal.

Chapter 12

ELENA

The shots ring in my ears.

Alfonso falls beside me, his eyes wide as blood trickles from his head.

My stomach churns at the memory that's so clear in my mind as if it just happened.

Lucian and Carson just killed those men. Right in the middle of the road.

Oh, God.

I wrap my arms tighter around my waist, trying to put as much space between Lucian and me.

Oh my God.

He killed them.

He just killed them.

I swallow hard on the bile, threatening to push up my throat.

I see Alfonso and Gino's bodies.

The blood.

The acidic smell of my vomit filling the air.

The taste of Dante.

I gag and quickly cover my mouth with my hand.

"Fuck, she's going to throw up," I hear Lucian say, but his voice sounds miles away.

I feel his hand on my back, and that's all it takes. I bend over, and unable to stop it, I vomit on the floor.

All my demons have been set free, and they close in on me until it feels like I'm going to lose my mind.

"Principessa," I hear Dante whisper dauntingly from the darkness. "I know you're awake."

I have to force myself to keep still, hoping I can convince him I'm asleep. I hear him move, and I squeeze my eyes tightly shut.

"We're here," I hear Carson's muted voice.

"I could fuck you right now," Dante says, no longer whispering, "and you'll just have to take every inch of my dick."

The trembling in my body grows as fear pulses where my heart should be.

"I've got her," Lucian says, and I'm only half aware of his arms slipping under me.

Suddenly Dante pounces, his hand closing around my throat, and it rips a terrified scream from me. He pushes

151

me onto my back, and his rank breath wafts over my face.
"Which hole should I fuck?" A cruel chuckle darkens the
night. "I'll let you choose, Principessa."

I hear voices. All male. I feel Lucian move, his arms strong beneath me, his shoulder solid against my cheek. His aftershave wars with the acidic smell of bile.

I'm laid down on a bed, and then I feel Lucian's cool palm on my heated cheek. I manage to open my eyes, and for a moment, I connect with his worried gaze, but then I'm yanked away by the demons.

"Choose," Dante growls, drops of spittle hitting my
face.

"Don't. Please," I beg, but it only makes him tighten
his grip on my neck, making it hard to breathe. My heart
hammers at a panicked pace.

I hear as he begins to unbuckle his belt, and it makes
waves of terror crash over me.

This is it. This is the moment I've feared most.

Dante leans closer to me, and then he licks the tears
from my cheek. "Choose, or I'll choose for you," he
threatens.

I'm so terrified he'll rape me, my lips part, and it feels
as if a piece of my soul is torn out along with the words.
"M-m-mouth."

He lets out another chuckle, and then he lets go of my neck as he moves back. *"You better make this good."* He frees his cock from his pants, then snaps, *"Now, Principessa. Before I change my mind."*

Quickly, I sit up, and my body shudders as I scoot to the side of the bed. A sob escapes me, and it has Dante saying, *"Puke and I'll fuck you raw. This time you swallow every last drop of my cum."*

Father... why have you forsaken me?

Another sob builds, but I swallow it down.

Dante grabs hold of my head, and even though it's the lesser of the two evils, it kills me to open my mouth.

He thrusts brutally into my mouth, letting out a sadistic chuckle. "Fuck, yes."

No.

It will always be no.

I squeeze my eyes tightly shut and pray it will be quick, but then Dante says, "Open your eyes and look up at me while I fuck your mouth."

God, he won't even allow me to escape the sight of him.

Knowing I have no choice, I do as he says, and the sight of him leering down at me makes bile push up my throat.

I swallow hard while he thrusts relentlessly into my mouth, shafting my lips.

And it becomes unbearably real.

It's revolting.

Inhumane.

Soul-crushing.

A vital piece of me dies as Dante finds his release, coating the back of my tongue and throat. I swallow hard on the last of my dignity... and then I'm left with what feels like an empty shell.

The last of the light dims, and darkness pours into me until it's all I am.

I shoot up from the bed, and not recognizing my surroundings, I at least spot the bathroom. Darting off the bed, I rush into it. I make it to the toilet just in time, and then my body convulses as I empty my stomach of its contents.

My mind swirls with traumatic flashes from my past.

My heart shrinks.

My soul withers a little more, and I wonder when it will just fade away.

"Elena," I hear Lucian say, and when he places his hand on my back, I flinch.

He killed those men. Without a second thought.

It's only a matter of time before he'll either kill me or make my life an unbearable hell.

I try to reach for the lever wanting to flush the toilet, but I can't get to it, and Lucian does it for me.

"Come," he murmurs, and then he places his hands under my arms and pulls me to my feet. He helps me to a counter, and I bend over the sink. Opening the faucet, I rinse out my mouth with the cool water.

I feel feverish from the panic attack and memories haunting me and splash some water over my face.

Lucian hands me a towel, and as I pat my face dry, I step away from him. Now that I know what he's capable of, every part of me is on high alert.

"Where am I?" I think to ask.

"A safe house."

"How long… was I…" I can't finish the sentence.

"Not long."

Lucian cautiously takes a step closer to me, and I quickly shake my head. "Please don't."

Instead of ignoring my plea like Dante would've, Lucian holds his hands up in a surrendering gesture. "You're safe."

I'll never be safe.

I shake my head. "Unless I give you a reason to kill me. Right? That's what you said."

Lucian lets out a heavy breath. "What do you expect of me, Elena?"

From the head of the Mafia?

Depraved cruelty. Death. Destruction.

"Nothing," I whisper.

LUCIAN

I'm tired.

I'm struggling to keep the grief from overwhelming me, and Elena scared the fucking shit out of me with the panic attack she had. Today has pushed me to my limits, and right now, I have nothing left in me.

Walking past her, I mutter, "There's food if you're hungry. If not, you can sleep. The bedroom's yours."

As I reach the doorway, she pleads, "Let me go."

I stop and suck in a deep breath. I'm trying to save her life, but still, she sees me as the devil.

Slowly, I turn to face her. Our eyes lock, and I say, "If I let you go, you'll be dead before midnight. Is that what you want?" When she just stares at me, I ask, "Do you want to go back to Dante?"

This time I get a reaction, a flash of panic tightening her features, and it has me continuing, "You see me as a monster because I killed men who would've taken our lives the first chance they got. It was either them or us. Do you understand that?"

Elena nods and wets her lips before she says, "I don't want any part of this world."

Shaking my head, I take a step towards her. "You were born into it, little bird. There's no other way out but death."

Her features tighten with a desperate expression. "I never wanted this life."

I let out a sigh. "It's the only one you have. The sooner you make peace with it, the better."

Lowering her eyes from mine, she looks down at the towel she's wringing in her hands. "What do you plan to do with me?"

I don't know.

When I don't answer her, she glances up at me again, her eyes filled with the same horror as when I kissed her earlier.

God, was that today? So much has happened, I've lost track of time.

Wanting to give her some peace of mind, I say, "I'm not going to let you go. I won't hurt you, and even though I said differently when we met, I won't kill you." I close the distance between us, and lifting my hands, I frame her face. "The safest place for you is by my side." I lean down and press a kiss to her forehead. "Get some sleep."

This time when I turn away from her, I walk out of the bathroom, needing some time for myself. I drop down on the couch and let out a sigh as I shrug out of my jacket. I unfasten the bulletproof vest and drop it on the coffee table, and then I lean back and close my eyes.

"Alexei and Demitri landed. They'll be here in twenty minutes," Carson murmurs from where he's sitting on the couch opposite me.

"Thanks."

Lifting a hand, I rub my fingers over my forehead, where a headache is starting to brew.

My father adjusts the lapels of my jacket even though they were fine. His eyes meet mine, and I take my chance to ask, "Let me stay, Papà. I don't want to leave you alone."

A caring smile softens his features. "It's just for two years, my son. Enjoy it while you can because once you join me, there won't be rest for your soul again. Not until you meet our maker."

I've been working with my father for the past two years, ever since I took my place next to him.

I've killed. Fourteen men and one woman.

The woman was the hardest even though she deserved it. Viola was our housekeeper. We caught her selling information about us to whoever was willing to pay the highest fee.

I let out a sigh, then lean in to hug my father. It's going to kill me to leave him alone in this big house.

My father's arms wrap securely around me. "Ti voglio bene."

"Ti voglio bene, Papà," I tell him I love him too.

The pain is searing, branding the sorrow onto my soul.

I'm caught in my grief until a knock at the door to the quarters we're staying in pulls me out of it.

The safe house belongs to a contact of Alexei. When we arrived, I had no time to look around because I was too worried about Elena.

Carson gets up to answer the door, and when he opens it, Alexei and Demitri come in.

I rise to my feet as Alexei hugs his younger brother, murmuring, "You did good."

Then Alexei looks at me, and his expression turns grim enough to make the fucking devil tremble in fear. He stalks over to me, and his arms wrap around me. The hug is hard and fast as he murmurs, "It was quick. He didn't suffer."

I nod as I pull back, his words making the rage in my chest intensify. "Just find out who's behind this."

"I will," he promises.

Our eyes lock for a moment, and when I see the loss in his merciless gaze, it offers me comfort to know I'm not the only one grieving my father.

"Thank you," I say.

"Stop thanking me, you're going to pay me," he chuckles, trying to lighten the mood.

It works. The corner of my mouth lifts.

Demitri comes to give me a brotherly hug which I accept. He's not the most talkative person, so I'm not surprised when he doesn't say anything.

As Demitri steps back, his head snaps to the bedroom. He's already halfway to the room before I think to say, "It's Elena Lucas. She's in there."

Demitri doesn't stop but glances into the room, and seemingly satisfied that Alexei's life isn't in danger, he turns back to us. The man has been trained to protect Alexei at all costs. It's admirable, to say the least.

"The private jet is ready. We need to go now," Alexei informs me.

"Home?" I ask to be sure.

Alexei nods. "If you go into hiding, it will show them they've won. You need to take over now."

I nod, agreeing with him. I also have to arrange for my father's burial.

The thought is sharp and suffocating. Trying to get away from the sorrow, I put on my jacket as I walk to the bedroom. When I enter, I find Elena sitting on the edge of the bed. She instantly gets up, her eyes darting between me and the doorway.

"Time to go," I say as I hold my hand out to her.

Elena hesitates, but then she comes to me. Her palm is ice cold when it meets mine, and it makes my fingers wrap tightly around hers. I pull her closer until our bodies are almost touching, and lifting my other hand, I brush my fingers over her cheek.

Fuck. She's freezing.

Letting go of her hand, I wrap my arms around her, trying to offer her some of my warmth, but instead, I find the comfort I've needed since I found out I lost my father.

Closing my eyes, I bury my face in her hair, and I take a deep breath, but then Elena tenses in my hold.

"Just for a minute," I whisper. "I need this."

She doesn't fight me and instead wraps her arms around my waist. It's exactly what I needed.

God, she even has the power to chase my grief away.

My hold on her tightens, and I savor the peace I find in her arms until Alexei's voice carries from the living room, "We need to leave."

Reluctantly, I step away from Elena, and taking her hand, I pull her out of the room. I link our fingers, and we follow the Russian men downstairs to where we left our luggage.

Not wanting to dig through Elena's clothes, I open my bag and pull a sweater from it. Elena's eyes dart to my face when I help her put it on. I adjust the fabric over the vest, and it makes her look small and fragile as fuck.

My gaze connects with hers, and I know with dead certainty I'm not going to let her go. Never. Just like my father was prepared to do with my mother, I'll take Elena even if it's against her will.

You were right, Papà.

"Weapons check," Alexei orders, yanking my attention away from Elena.

I walk to the table where they're standing and pull the Baretta and Heckler and Koch from behind my back.

We have enough weapons between the four of us, but I'm not so sure about ammo. Alexei talks to his contact to bring us what we'll need to make it to the private jet should we be ambushed.

We load fresh clips into all the guns and shove extra ones into our pockets.

Tucking the Baretta away behind my back, I again keep the Heckler and Koch in my right hand. Taking hold of my luggage, I glance at Elena. "Time to go."

She seems much calmer than when we left St. Monarch's and doesn't argue as she comes to me.

Demitri takes the lead with Alexei right behind him, and Carson brings up the rear as we're taken through a maze of hallways until we reach the back of the safe house.

"The car's bulletproof," Alexei's contact advises us, and he's the first to step outside into the night that's fallen while we were waiting. The man makes sure it's safe for us to exit, then gestures for us to come.

This is it.

I take a deep breath knowing the moment we step out of this safe house, my life as the head of the Mafia begins.

I'll never hide again.

I'll face my enemies head-on.

I'll kill anyone who opposes me.

I'll follow in my father's footsteps and bring honor to the Cotroni name just as he has.

And one day, I'll die just as he has, but before then, I will leave a legacy of my own.

Chapter 13

ELENA

Sitting between Lucian and Carson, I choose the evil I know a little better, and scoot closer to Lucian, so the left side of my body doesn't touch Carson's.

I keep telling myself Lucian's done nothing to hurt me. He doesn't shove me around like Dante does. He hasn't raised a hand against me... yet.

Instead, Lucian's hugged and kissed me, and even though it's been against my will, it's nothing compared to the depravity Dante has inflicted on me.

Lucian's the most dangerous man I know, and I still fear him, but I can't deny he's given me more comfort and affection than I've ever received in my life.

It's still confusing as hell.

I also can't ignore the fact that Lucian killed those men. What stops him from killing me when my father upsets him?

Carson's phone begins to ring, and when he moves to pull it out, his elbow connects with my side.

"Sorry," he mutters, and then he takes the call, speaking in Russian.

His language sounds angry as if he's threatening whoever's on the other side of the line's entire family with death.

I try to not make it too apparent as I press closer to Lucian, but still, he notices. Lucian lifts his left arm, and wrapping it around my shoulders, he pulls me against his side. I have to turn into him, so it's not uncomfortable. Not knowing what to do with my hands, I keep them clutched together on my lap.

God, my thoughts and emotions are a complete mess. How's it even possible to fear a man but still feel safe with him? Have I lost my mind?

My eyes lower to Lucian's legs, and though he's been in the same suit all day, it's still clean with not a speck of dust on it. He also smells good and not like a man that's been running half the day.

Definitely not sweaty and rancid like Dante.

The thought makes me mentally flinch, and as if Lucian can sense it, he tightens his arm around me. Lifting his other hand to my cheek, he nudges my head until it's resting against his shoulder, then he whispers, "Close your eyes and rest."

I doubt I'll find any rest while I'm surrounded by Russian assassins and the head of the Mafia.

My eyes drift over Lucian's white button-up shirt, his jacket, and then I lift them to his neck. Slowly they inch up, taking in the neat scruff on his jaw until they settle on his mouth.

Instantly I think of the kiss and how it felt to have his lips caressing mine. Strong and sure. Addictive and hot.

The thoughts make warmth spread through my body and up my neck.

If we were two ordinary people who met by chance, I have no doubt I'd fall in love with him in a heartbeat.

But we're not.

I'm Elena Lucas. A bargaining piece.

He's Lucian Cotronti. Head of the Mafia.

Still, I've never been kissed like that before. There was so much heat, it makes what I shared with Alfonso seem detached and childish. Keeping in mind, I was only seventeen.

Alfonso was my first… and, well, the only boy close to my age on the property. It's not like I had a wide selection.

'You still don't have a selection of men to choose from,' I remind myself.

You're marrying Dante in eleven days.

Unless Lucian can stop it.

My eyes dart up to his, and I realize he's been watching me stare at him all this time.

"What are you thinking?" he asks softly as if he doesn't want the other men to hear.

Figuring I have nothing to lose, I ask, "Can you stop the wedding between Dante and me?"

Lucian's eyes drift over my face before they lock with mine again. "Do you want me to?"

Without hesitating, I nod. "Yes. More than anything."

God, please!

My heart begins to beat faster as I wait for Lucian's answer to the most important question I've ever asked.

Finally, he nods. "There's no way you're marrying Dante. Stop worrying about it."

Just like that?

My breath explodes over my lips as pure relief floods me. "Thank you…" Unable to find more words, I repeat, "Thank you."

Lucian's dark brown gaze takes mine prisoner. The intense expression on his face makes my heartbeat pick up and my stomach spin as if it's being tossed around by a strong wind.

Alexei shatters the moment when he says, "We're five minutes out. Get ready."

Lucian pulls his arm away from me, and I slump back against the seat. When he takes the guns out to check them, my eyes lock on his sure hands and the weapons.

Hands that won't hesitate to take a life.

I wonder if he even feels bad about the men he killed. How many other lives has he taken? How many more will he still take?

What makes him any different from Dante besides the fact that he's more powerful?

Okay, I'll admit there's a lot that sets the two of them apart. For one, Lucian doesn't look like a monster, not like Dante. Lucian also hasn't abused me in any way.

Still, I've only known him for three weeks. A lot can change. Even with Dante, it took time before he started abusing me.

Yeah, it's probably a matter of time before Lucian will show his true cruelty.

When we enter an airfield, the atmosphere grows tense in the car. Demitri stops the vehicle and then orders, "Move fast."

Lucian shoves the door open, and then he gets out. I scoot to the side and climb out behind him. While Carson, Alexei, and Demitri keep an eye out, Lucian and I grab our luggage, and then I have to jog to keep up with the men as we make our way to the stairs.

As I climb the first step, Alexei takes my luggage from me, muttering, "Faster, little one."

I rush up the steps and into the cabin and keep moving toward the back of the lavish plane, where I take a seat in the corner.

A couple of seconds later, I watch as our luggage is placed in the overhead compartments, and then Lucian comes to sit next to me.

The Russians sit down on the opposite side of the plane, and I let out a relieved breath.

Moments later, we're moving, and I quickly strap myself in. As the plane gains speed, the only comfort I have is that I'll be back in Italy soon.

I glance through the window at the dark night outside, feeling a pang of sadness that I didn't get to explore Switzerland's beauty.

***

LUCIAN

After the moment we shared in the car where Elena asked me for help, she's been quiet.

I'm taking it as a sign that she's warming up to me. She wouldn't ask me for help if it was otherwise.

She's staring out of the window, and it gives me a moment to take a good look at her.

Her skin is smooth, and except for the old scar, the fading bruise on her jaw, and the marks on her neck, there are no other blemishes. She has a small button nose and big eyes, the light brown of her irises, not a color I've seen before. Elena is breathtakingly beautiful, there's no denying that, but it's not the reason I want her.

She's so damn feminine it calls to every part of the man in me.

She's not the strongest, and yes, she probably comes with a fuck-ton of baggage, but it will take more than that to scare me off. Actually, it doesn't bother me at all.

Maybe it's because I've lost my mind with grief, or because I just can't deny myself this one thing, but I make up my mind to arrange a marriage between Elena and myself.

Valentino will have no choice if he wants to keep the peace, and Elena will be too glad to be rid of Dante, so she shouldn't mind.

And me?

My eyes drink in the stunning woman beside me.

I'll have Elena. To fuck until lust turns to love.

Turning my gaze away from Elena before I start getting hard, I'm met with a smirk from Alexei.

The corner of my mouth lifts, no doubt he's already guessed what I'm planning.

Needing to know what I'll be walking into, I ask, "You saw my father?"

Alexei nods.

"Where was he shot?" I ask, the loss deepening my voice.

"He was meeting me at a café. It was probably a long-distance shot. They took him out before I got there."

God, at least he didn't know. It's all we can ask for when our time comes.

I find comfort knowing my father didn't suffer on his knees before he died. That would've killed me.

"Where is he now?"

Suddenly Elena places her hand on mine, and not wanting to lose her touch, I keep from looking at her as I turn my hand over and link our fingers.

"The morgue."

Christ, the two words rip through me, and I tighten my hold on Elena's hand.

"As soon as we've had the funeral, we'll get to work," I say, knowing I have to start thinking like the head of the Mafia and not the son of the greatest man who ever lived.

But first, I need to lay him to rest.

Now I only have an aunt left. My mother's sister, Aunt Ursula, is my last living relative.

I turn my head to Elena, and she glances at me.

And I'll have you. To have and to hold until death do us part.

As if Elena can hear my thoughts, she pulls her hand free from mine while a frown forms on her forehead, then she asks, "Why are you looking at me like that?"

"Like what?" I ask.

"Like you're planning something I'm not going to like," she explains.

"It's nothing for you to worry about," I assure her, not wanting to tell her yet I'm going to arrange a marriage between us. First, I need to speak with Valentino.

"Now I'm definitely going to worry," she mumbles as she goes back to staring out the window.

An hour later, as we near the landing strip, Alexei says, "Your guards will meet us at the airfield. I had them wait there. I get a feeling we're going to need an army to get you safely home."

I nod, then ask, "Will Bruno be there?"

He's my father's personal guard and in charge of all the other guards we have. It was his job to keep my father safe.

"Yes."

Good.

We start our descent, and soon the plane comes to a stop. I unfasten the seat belt, and rising to my feet, I wait for Elena to get up before I take her hand and pull her to the door.

Demitri opens for us and exits the plane first, with Alexei behind him.

I keep a tight hold of Elena as we take the steps down to the tarmac, not worrying about our luggage which one of the guards will retrieve.

Spotting Bruno, I stalk toward him.

He begins to shake his head, his face torn with guilt.

Pulling the Heckler and Koch from behind my back, I lift it to his head, then growl, "You had one job. You had to keep him safe."

He nods, knowing what's coming.

"Follow my father to the afterlife and keep him safe until I join him." Without a second thought, I pull the trigger, and Bruno drops to the tarmac.

Elena gasps and pulls against my hold on her, but I yank her back to my side.

"Bring his body and the luggage," I instruct Franco, who's next in charge. "You've just been promoted."

Franco nods and orders two guards to take care of everything, and then he gestures for me to walk. Speaking into a microphone, he says, "We're on the move.

I tighten my grip on Elena as I begin to walk, practically dragging her behind me. "Keep up, or I'll fucking throw you over my shoulder," I snap at her.

She picks up her pace, and then I hear a strangled sob as we reach the armored Mercedes G Wagon. Franco opens the door for me, and I have to shove Elena inside. Once I slide in beside her and Franco shuts the door behind me, I turn to her.

She's fucking pale again, her eyes too wide.

"Do I need to start warning you every time I intend on shooting someone?" I ask, feeling a little irritated.

She scoots away from me, shaking her head.

Franco climbs in behind the steering wheel, then he says, "Mr. Koslov will take the lead."

"Okay." Matteo gets in the passenger side, and it has me saying, "You'll be second in charge from now on."

"Thank you, Sir," he replies humbly.

"Who do we have that's good?" I ask Franco.

"Leo."

Leo is one of the older guards. He's been with us for over ten years, so I feel he's a good pick.

"Inform him that he's to guard Miss Lucas," I instruct. "Form a team which he will take charge of. I want five men with her at all times when she goes out."

I can feel Elena's eyes snap to me, and turning my head, I meet her shocked gaze. "Do you have a problem with the arrangements?" She quickly shakes her head, and it has me muttering, "Good because it's not negotiable."

Leaving the airfield, we form a motor brigade. Soon I'll be home, and then I'll have to face the sight of my dead father.

Chapter 14

ELENA

Just as I think I've dealt with one threat to my life, I have a new one to worry about. I'm not so sure I'm going to last long with Lucian. At the rate he's killing people, I'll probably be dead by sunrise.

I mean, my God, it's not normal.

Is it?

Is this what Dante and my father do when they're gone from the villa? Is this everyday life for them, and I didn't know because I was held captive?

It was easy for Dante to kill Alfonso and Gino.

Maybe that's why it's so easy for them to hurt me.

My eyes dart to Lucian, and the grim expression etched on his face makes me hesitate, then his dark gaze snaps to mine, and he mutters, "What now?"

Pushing through, I ask, "Is it normal?"

Lucian frowns, and shaking his head, he asks, "Is what normal?"

"Shooting people."

He lets out a chuckle that sounds more like a threat. "In our world, it is." The frown returns to his face, and he tilts his head. "You've seen your father and Dante kill... haven't you?"

The memory shudders through me. "Once."

Surprise tightens his features instantly. "Only once?"

I nod. "I've told you before I never had anything to do with the business."

"So the kill was personal?" Lucian asks.

The demons stir, and it has me glancing away from him. "It was very personal."

It was the day my life became a nightmare.

"Who?"

I shake my head, not wanting to tell him about it. "Forget I said anything."

I can feel Lucian's eyes on me as I stare out the window, regretting I asked the question.

Luckily silence fills the vehicle until we drive through two massive gates. We're driven up a long driveway and come to a stop in front of a modern-looking mansion.

When I get out of the car, I blink at the black walls.

Who paints their house black?

The devil.

The front door swings open, and a middle-aged woman comes out. The moment she sees Lucian, she rushes to him. I watch as they hug, Lucian holding her tightly to him.

"Zia Ursula," I hear him breathe her name, relief in his voice. "I'm glad you're here."

"I came as soon as I heard. I'm so sorry," Lucian's aunt says. She frames his face and kisses both his cheeks.

When they pull apart, Lucian turns to me and holds out his hand. "Come."

My eyes dart between him and his aunt as I walk closer. When I take hold of his hand, his aunt frowns at us. "Who's this, Lucian?"

"Elena Lucas," he introduces me. "Valentino's daughter."

Her eyes instantly widen on me. "I didn't know he had a child?" Lifting a hand to her mouth, she whispers, "Dio, you're the spitting image of your mother."

"You knew my mother?" the question bursts from me. Hope stirs in me, thinking maybe I can finally learn something about my mother.

"I only saw her at functions. We weren't close, but she had a beauty you don't forget easily." Lucian's aunt pulls me into a hug. "You're part of the la famiglia. Call me Zia Ursula."

"Let's go inside," Lucian says. He tugs me into the mansion while Aunt Ursula greets the other men.

My eyes dart around the interior. The walls are black inside as well, with light wooden floors forming a sharp contrast.

There are lights everywhere, so it doesn't appear dark like I thought it would. Actually, it looks stylish.

Lucian's home fits him.

A guard follows us up the stairs with our luggage, and I try to take in everything before Lucian opens a door and I'm pulled into a room.

God, even the furniture and bedding are shades of grays and blacks.

"You really like black," I mumble, and it draws a chuckle from Lucian.

"I do." He gestures around the room. "Make yourself at home. The suite is yours for the time being."

"For how long?" I ask, wanting to know what to expect.

The corner of Lucian's mouth lifts in a predatory way, and it makes my stomach tighten.

"I'll answer that question tomorrow." He lifts a hand to the back of my head and presses a kiss to my forehead, then he walks to the door. "I'll check in on you later. Get settled."

The guard sets my luggage down, and then he leaves with Lucian. With a sinking feeling, I watch as the guard shuts the door.

Am I a prisoner again?

When I don't hear the clicking of a lock, I frown and walk closer. Turning the knob, I'm surprised when the door opens.

Lucian's eyes dart to me from where he's talking to the guard right outside the door. He must see something on my face because he says, "You're not a prisoner, Elena. You can move freely around the house."

I nod, then shut the door, feeling a little better.

Turning back to the suite, I take in my temporary home. It's not bad at all... as long as I don't get killed while I'm here.

Walking to my luggage, I find my toiletries and clean clothes, opting for white leggings and an oversized shirt. I walk to the ensuite bathroom, and then I smile.

There's a dark gray matte oval tub standing next to a black stone brick wall, big enough to fit two people.

I open the faucets and begin to undress, in desperate need to just relax. When I sink down into the balmy water, I let out a sigh and leaning back, I close my eyes.

God, I needed this.

My thoughts begin to turn around the day's events. So much has happened.

One thought stands out, though. Even though Lucian lost his father today and he was attacked, not once did he take it out on me.

LUCIAN

Sitting in the living room, I stare at the empty fireplace.

I've spoken with all the guards and got them up to date with everything, especially my plans for the next couple of days.

After I showered and changed into a pair of black sweatpants and a t-shirt, I knew I wouldn't sleep tonight and came down here.

Closing my eyes, I can feel my father's presence. I expect to hear his voice at any moment. To have him sit down next to me. To have him joke about how stupid the people are he has to work with… the people I now have to work with.

Without opening my eyes, I can see him walking out onto the veranda and staring at the garden he loves so much.

I hear movement, and my head snaps in the direction of the stairs. Elena walks toward the kitchen, and dressed in white, she looks like an angel.

I watch as she searches for a glass. When she finds one, a smile stretches over her face, and it makes my own mouth curve up. She opens the faucet and fills the glass, and then she glances up, and the water splashes all over her as she startles. "My God, I didn't see you there."

I get up and walk toward her as she grabs a couple of paper towels to dry the counter with.

Christ.

The water has soaked the front of Elena's shirt, and I don't think she notices. The fabric sticks to her breasts, leaving very little to the imagination.

I begin to harden and stop on the other side of the marble island to hide my cock from her view. Then I tilt my head and say, "You spilled some water on yourself."

Elena glances down, and the next instant, she drops to the floor behind the island.

"I didn't see much," I say. *Just your nipples which quite frankly looked perky as fuck.*

"I have eyes. I know what you saw," she snaps.

"If it's any consolation, you have nothing to be ashamed of," I try to make it better. Knowing Elena's not going to come out of hiding, I grab hold of my t-shirt behind my neck and pull it off. I throw it to where she is and say, "Wear mine."

"Thank you." I hear her move, and then she finally gets up, holding her wet shirt in her hand.

Damn, she looks good in my shirt.

I instantly begin to harden again, and I have to take deep breaths to calm down my cock.

When I'm done admiring her, and my eyes go to her face, it's only to see her staring at my chest. Her lips are parted, and her eyes are glazed over.

The corner of my mouth lifts into a smirk. "Glad to know you like what you see. Now we're even."

It snaps her out of it, her cheeks flushing a soft pink. "Sorry. I didn't mean to stare."

I walk around the island and picking up the glass she put down in the sink, I pour water into it and then hold it out to her. "You were thirsty?"

"Thanks." Our fingers brush when she takes the glass from me, and it sends an electric spark zapping up my arm.

Elena must've felt it, too, because her eyes snap up to mine. She tries to hide her reaction by drinking some water, and then she takes a step backward, putting some space between us.

She clears her throat then asks, "Can't sleep?"

I shake my head. "Want to keep me company?"

"Ah... okay."

I gesture to the living room and follow her to the couch. I wait for her to pick a spot to sit and take a seat next to her. Turning my body toward hers, I say, "Tell me about yourself."

She draws her bottom lip in between her teeth as she thinks of something to share.

God, I get the feeling I'm going to walk around with a permanent semi.

"I like to read," she finally gives me something.

"Yeah? What?"

"Fiction."

"What kind of fiction? Romance?" I tease her.

When her cheeks warm to soft pink, I know I guessed right, and it makes the corner of my mouth lift.

"Yes, romance," she admits, and then she takes another sip of the water. "Your turn."

"I don't have time to read."

My answer draws a soft chuckle from her, and it sounds musical. "Tell me something else," she demands.

I like this. It's the first time we actually get to talk. It's relaxing.

"I was really close with my father. He was my best friend," I admit a truth.

Elena's eyes soften with compassion. "What's your favorite memory of him?"

I think for a moment. "There are so many." Placing my arm on the back of the couch, I pinch a strand of her hair between my forefinger and thumb. "Every Sunday, he'd grill steaks for us. We'd sit out on the veranda and talk about the most random things."

A poignant expression settles on her features. "That sounds so nice."

"You're not close with your father?" I ask, even though she's told me before, she means nothing to him.

Elena shakes her head.

"Is there a reason?" I tilt my head, keeping my expression calm because I want her to open up to me.

Elena glances down at the glass in her hand, and a long moment passes before she replies, "He just never loved me."

"Your mother?"

Elena shakes her head. "I don't know anything about her."

Slowly, I nod, absorbing the information. Pushing my luck, I say, "Tell me what your life was like."

She swallows hard and then takes a deep breath. "It was nothing like yours."

I let go of the strand between my fingers and place my hand against the side of her neck. When her eyes lift to mine, I lean closer. "Tell me, little bird." To encourage her, I add, "Give me something I can use against Dante."

Instantly she lifts her chin, and fight sparks to life in her eyes. She takes another deep breath. "You know he beat me."

Lying through my teeth, I say, "I only know what I saw, and that's not enough to kill him."

Her eyes dart away from me, and her features tighten. "What will be enough?"

"Give me the worst thing he's done."

Let me carry it for you, little bird. Open up to me.

"You'll kill him for it?" she asks, still hesitating.

"Yes," I promise. *He's already a dead man walking, but she doesn't need to know that.*

The longer it takes Elena to tell me, the tenser the air grows.

Christ if he raped her… I don't have a taste for torture, but for Capone, I'll make an exception.

Chapter 15

LUCIAN

A torturous minute passes without Elena saying anything, and needing a drink, I get up. I walk to the side table and pour us each a tumbler of bourbon.

When I sit down again, I hold the glass out to her. "It's better than water. It will help."

Elena sets the water down on the coffee table and takes the tumbler from me. She sniffs at the drink before taking a sip, and then her face lights up with heat. "God, what is this?"

"Bourbon." I settle back into the couch, and savoring the whiskey, I wait to see if she's going to talk.

I watch as her mind drifts off. She takes another sip, and then her shoulders hunch as if she's trying to make herself smaller.

"Promise you'll kill him." Her tone has changed. It's hollow, all the warmth gone.

My muscles tighten, and the words flow easily from my lips. "I promise."

The same expression she had on her face when we met flutters across her features as if she's tearing a secret from her soul.

My heart begins to beat faster, and then her lips part. There's no emotion in her voice as she says, "Dante killed a friend of mine. The only friend I ever had."

It's not what I expected to hear from her, but I sit still and listen.

"I used to sneak out of the house to meet Alfonso in the stables. Dante caught us together." She pauses to take another sip, and it reminds me of my own drink.

As I bring the tumbler to my lips, Elena says, "Alfonso was held at gunpoint while Dante forced me… to go down on him." She takes a moment to breathe, a sickening look on her face. "He killed Alfonso anyway."

I lower the drink, not sure I heard right. I stare at Elena until the words sink in like burning coals.

The motherfucker.

My breathing begins to speed up as rage floods my veins, and unable to sit still, I get up. I down half my drink as I walk toward the windows before turning back to Elena.

She hasn't moved a muscle, but her glass is empty.

I down the rest of my bourbon, then walk back to her. Taking the tumbler from her hand, I go to refill the glasses.

With my back to Elena, I force the question over my lips, and it comes out sounding harsher than I meant. "Did Capone rape you?"

I pick up the tumblers, and only when I hold the drink out to her does she shake her head as she takes it from me. "No. I was so happy to go to St. Monarch's because I knew it was only a matter of time before he did."

Taking a seat again, I slump back against the couch. I begin to twirl the glass between my fingers. "Was that the only time?" I ask, even though I know the answer already.

Slowly, I turn my head, and then I watch as Elena shakes her head. "No, it wasn't."

Christ almighty.

It explains everything. I now understand why Elena is so skittish.

My little bird doesn't have broken wings. They've been ripped off.

"I was seventeen," she whispers, her voice sounding lost. "The past four years have been hell, and I just want to get away from it all."

God.

Breathe.

Fuck.

"That fucking motherfucker." I try to focus on my breaths, but instead, images begin to flash through my mind.

Elena on her knees in front of Dante.

A roar rips from my chest, and I get up again. "Fuck." I begin to pace up and down, trying to get rid of the sudden burst of energy brought on by the rage. "Fuck," I mutter again, unable to say anything else.

I knew it was bad. I fucking knew it.

Christ.

I come to a stop and close my eyes.

It's the same as rape.

Four fucking years.

My hands begin to shake, and I quickly down the drink, hoping it will calm me down. I set the empty tumbler down on the coffee table before I throw it.

All I want to do is kill Dante. Right fucking now.

My eyes fly to Elena, and unable to think of anything else to say, I breathe, "Fuck, I'm so sorry."

My stomach churns at the thought of what she's been subjected to.

That fucking depraved bastard.

Her gaze lifts to mine, and the pain I see in them slices right through me. "You'll kill him?"

Murder echoes in my voice as I promise, "I will."

Elena nods and sets her empty glass down on the coffee table. She surprises me by letting out a chuckle. "Good, because even after everything he's done to me, I'm not sure I can do it." She shakes her head, and there's no amusement as she lets out another empty chuckle. "It's either him or me."

"It will never be you."

She gets up, and then she meets my gaze. Questions flutter over her face. "It makes me just as bad as you, right? I was shocked when you killed those men, but here I am asking you to kill one more."

"We're not bad if we kill bad people. We're doing the world a favor by getting rid of the scum."

Elena nods, appearing to be deep in thought. "We're all bad in someone's eyes."

"Not you," I argue, convinced to my very core she's the purest of us all.

Elena shakes her head, and then she begins to walk toward the stairs. "To Alfonso, I'm the villain. I should have left him alone, then he'd still be alive."

I watch her go up the stairs, and then I stare blankly at the spot I last saw her. My thoughts are filled with everything I've learned.

Images of her horror flash through me, only increasing my anger until my body shudders, begging for release.

Turning around, I walk to the gym, and leaving the light off, I head straight for the punching bag. With a roar, I slam my fist into the bag, and as it begins to sway, I picture Dante's face.

I'm going to kill him.

I'm going to fucking kill him.

I keep punching the bag until my hands start to ache, and taking a step back, my breaths explode over my lips as I focus on the pain.

ELENA

I didn't sleep at all. I sat on the bed, surrounded by regrets and shame.

I've been alternating between wanting to bash my head against the wall for telling Lucian what Dante did to me and thinking I did the right thing.

I'll probably have to go home, and if Lucian can get rid of Dante, then at least I won't have the monster waiting for me. Whether I marry Dante or not, if he's alive, he'll rape me. I just know it.

For the hundredth time, I think about Lucian's reaction. He seemed genuinely upset. I could feel his anger vibrating off him.

It just adds to the confusion. I don't think I'll ever understand him. On one side, he's a ruthless killer, and on the other, he seems to care about me. It feels like I've been given a puzzle that's missing half the pieces.

A knock at my door has my head snapping up. I scramble off the bed and go to open it. I'm surprised to see Aunt Ursula.

"It's time for breakfast. Come join me on the veranda," she says, and then she walks away.

I step out of the room, and shutting the door behind me, I follow after Aunt Ursula.

Crap, I should've changed out of Lucian's shirt. I pull an awkward face as we walk through the house and then out two massive sliding doors that have been pushed open.

Stepping out onto the veranda, my lips part as I take in the backyard.

The lawn is perfectly manicured and in total contrast with the black mansion. I realize why Lucian also gravitated to the secret garden.

There's a huge fountain in the middle of the yard, easily the size of a swimming pool. Different levels of water shoot into the sky only to gracefully fall back to the pool.

Trees are scattered around the property, offering plenty of shade, and flower beds provide a rainbow of colors. In the distance, I can see the ocean.

"Beautiful, isn't it?" Aunt Ursula asks.

"Yes," I breathe, still awestruck.

"Morning," I hear Lucian say behind us, and when I spin around, he's taking a seat at the table where three plates are waiting.

He's dressed in an immaculate suit again, and for a moment, it feels as if last night was just a dream.

Maybe it was.

Then he glances at me, and the anger etched on his face assures me it was definitely not a dream.

"Let's eat," Aunt Ursula says.

I take a seat at the table and look down at the bowl of muesli, fruits, and yogurt. Picking up a spoon, I scoop some up and take the bite even though I'm not hungry.

We eat in silence, and then Aunt Ursula asks, "How did you sleep, cara?"

I lift my eyes to her and force a smile around my lips. "Good, thank you."

I feel Lucian's gaze on me and focus on my breakfast.

A moment later, he says, "I have a meeting this morning."

"Here?" Aunt Ursula asks.

"Yes. When I'm done, will you come with me to the morgue?"

I swallow hard on the bite I just took.

"Of course," she answers, sorrow shimmering in the two words.

The rest of the meal proceeds in uncomfortable silence, and when we're finally done, I excuse myself from the table.

When I start to walk away, Lucian says, "You need to attend the meeting. It's at nine."

I stop, and glancing over my shoulder, I nod. "I'll be ready." I hurry to my room, and not knowing what to wear,

I dig through all my clothes. It takes me twenty minutes to decide on black pants and a blouse.

It will match the house.

The thought makes my lips curve up as I change into the clothes. I take extra care with my makeup and style my hair in a loose French braid. Slipping on a pair of high heels, I walk to the full-length mirror in the bathroom.

I take in my appearance, and satisfied, I leave the room. I have no idea what to expect, and when I walk down the stairs, and the living room comes into view, my eyes widen at all the men gathered there for the meeting.

I recognize Alexei, Demitri, and Carson but none of the others. As my gaze sweeps over everyone, it stops when I spot Lucian. He turns, and the moment he sees me, the grim expression fades from his face, and then his lips part.

It's only for a moment, then he walks toward me. When he holds out his hand to me, I take the last couple of steps and rest my palm against his.

He leans into me, murmuring, "You look beautiful."

"Thanks," I whisper. "Who are all these men?"

"Allies."

Franco comes toward us and informs Lucian, "Mr. Lucas just arrived."

My head snaps up. "My father's here?"

"Yes," Lucian mutters, and then he pulls me away from the stairs. I stand next to Lucian, not knowing what to expect.

The moment my father walks into the living room with Dante right behind him, it feels like my chest is going to close up.

Lucian pulls a gun from behind his back, where it was hidden beneath his jacket, and trains the barrel on Dante.

My heart instantly begins to race, and I hold my breath.

"What the fuck do you think you're doing?" my father demands.

"Killing this piece of shit," Lucian growls low.

My father steps in front of Dante, leveling a dark glare on Lucian. "Then it will be war between us. Are you sure that's how you want to start your reign as head of the Mafia?"

The air slowly leaves my lungs as Lucian lowers the gun. Instead of killing Dante like he said he would, he barks, "Capone, get out of my house."

No.

I yank my hand from his and lift it to my racing heart.

No.

Dante immediately leaves. Then my father smiles. "Good choice."

Lucian stares at my father, then he says, "I spared his life for a reason."

"Name it."

"A marriage between Elena and me."

Oh. My. God.

Betrayal begins to swirl around me like a dark mass, and I manage to take a step away from Lucian.

"An alliance between our families?" my father asks.

"Yes. We need to show a united front if we're going to win this war," Lucian answers.

They're talking as if it's everyday business… instead of my future.

My eyes lift to Lucian's face, and my hand moves up to cover my mouth as another wave of betrayal crashes over me.

This was Lucian's plan all along?

My father holds his hand out to Lucian, and then they shake on it… on an arranged marriage. On my life.

My father lets out a fake chuckle. "When will the big day take place?"

Lucian matches my father's chuckle with his own. "Is a week too soon?"

When they turn to me, all I can do is shake my head.

This is not happening.

"Congratulations on your engagement," my father says, his gaze resting hard on me.

My distress grows when Lucian takes a box from his pocket, and then he removes a similar ring to the one on his right hand. It's just smaller, a black oval stone set in gold.

Taking hold of my left hand, he slips it onto my ring finger, and then he leans in and presses a kiss to my cheek. "Trust me. This is the only way."

Trust him?

TRUST HIM?

I trusted him last night. I believed him when he said he'd kill Dante.

Yanking my hand out of his, I glare at him as he pulls back. "I'll never trust you," I bite the words out, and then I walk toward the sliding doors, and I don't stop until I've passed the fountain and most of the trees. Instead of a wall, there's a cliff at the end of the property. The ocean spreads out into the distance.

God.

I just got engaged to Lucian Cotroni.

I close my eyes, and the wind picks up, playing with the loose strands of hair framing my face.

I've been passed from one monster to another.

Chapter 16

LUCIAN

I watch as Elena storms away from me, and when Leo follows after her, I turn my attention back to Tino.

It was my full intention to kill Dante, but I can't afford another war right now. I know Elena sees it as a betrayal, but I'm not breaking my promise. I will kill Capone, just not today.

Tino looks smug. The fucker just secured an alliance with me. The thought that he'll become my father-in-law makes my top lip curl with anger.

I gesture for Tino to join the other men, and as we walk toward the living room, I roll my shoulders to try and get rid of some of the tension.

Hopefully, Elena will see reason soon. It's either me or Dante.

Alexei is the first to congratulate me, giving me a brotherly hug, and then the other men shake my hand.

"Good luck," Yuri says with a chuckle. "I hear Italian women are feisty."

It only sinks in then that Tino agreed. Elena and I are engaged. Within a week, she'll be mine.

I smile at Yuri. "Thank you."

With the congratulations out of the way, I get right to business. "The shipments will continue to move as planned," I assure the men.

"When will the funeral be held?" Tino asks, and I don't miss the smirk he tries to hide.

Fucker.

My hands curl into fists as I have to restrain myself to not beat him to death.

"Tomorrow. It will be intimate."

"We can attend?" Marko Nicollaj asks. He's the head of the Bratva, and I don't dare refuse.

"Of course. I'd appreciate it."

"Security?" Alexei asks.

My eyes lock with him, and for the hundredth time, I'm thankful for him. "Can you handle it?"

Alexei nods. "Consider it taken care of."

Gratitude floods my chest, and I place my hand on his shoulder. "Thank you."

"This threat? Any new leads?" Tino asks.

I let go of Alexei. "I spoke with a man yesterday. He had a Greek accent."

Tino's head snaps back, a dark frown forming on his forehead. "Greek? You sure?"

"I know a fucking Greek accent when I hear one," I growl at Tino.

"Why would the Greeks want to move in on our territory?" he asks, clearly dumbfounded, and it lessens the suspicion I had about him being behind it all.

"I don't know, but I plan to find out. I've asked for a meeting with Stathoulis." Peter Stathoulis is the head of the Greek Mafia. Though we have a strained relationship, I don't think he's behind the attack. But I'm hoping he'll be able to shine some light on who is.

We need to get to the bottom of this. Besides my life, billions of dollars are at stake.

Gesturing for a server to offer the men drinks, I turn my attention to Yuri. "Let's take care of your order."

I glance at Alexei, and he nods, receiving the silent message. As Yuri and I walk to the front door, Alexei and Demitri follow after us. We step out of the house and walk to where the truck is waiting.

I sweep my hand in the air, and it has Franco opening the doors to the trailer, then I gesture for Yuri to go ahead with the inspection.

I stand with Alexei and Demitri and watch as Yuri checks a couple of aircon units filled with weapons.

Seemingly happy, he nods. "Good." I wait for him to talk with his righthand man, and once he joins us again, he says, "I'm glad to see your father managed to get the flash grenades. Thank you."

"Of course." I gesture for Yuri to walk.

As we head back to the house, Yuri takes care of the payment on his phone, then he chuckles. "You make me a poor man, Lucian."

I let out a burst of laughter. "I doubt that's possible."

The truck's engine starts, and glancing over my shoulder, I watch as two of Yuri's men steer the metal beast down my driveway.

Thank God for the training my father gave me before I went to St. Monarch's, or I'd be fucked right now.

The meeting lasts for another hour, and then the men depart. Tino hangs back, and once it's just us and Alexei and Demitri, he says, "I trust you'll plan the wedding?"

Fucking asshole. He won't even give his only daughter a wedding.

"I'll have my aunt take care of everything. You don't have to worry about a damn thing."

Tino doesn't miss the aggression in my tone, and it makes the corner of his mouth curve up. "Soon, you'll be my son-in-law," he taunts me.

I take a deep breath so I don't lose my patience, and then I meet Tino's arrogant gaze with my own. "Don't make the mistake of thinking it gives you power over me."

"I wouldn't dare," he sneers. Without asking anything about Elena, he walks to the front door. "Good doing business with you."

I watch him leave, then shake my head. "Some people make it hard not to kill them."

Alexei lets out a chuckle.

Needing to check on Elena, I say, "Make yourselves at home." Turning my attention to Franco, I ask, "Where is she?"

"Near the cliff," he advises me.

I walk out onto the veranda and glance over the property as I make my way to the edge of the backyard. When I reach Leo, I nod at him. "Fall back."

He moves away until he's out of hearing distance, and then my eyes lock on Elena. She's standing with her arms wrapped around her, just staring at the ocean.

"The meeting's over," I inform her.

She ignores me flat out, not taking her eyes off the horizon.

"You're angry?" I ask.

She lets out a flabbergasted huff, and then she turns her head to pin me with a glare. "You think?"

I tilt my head. "I thought you'd be relieved. You don't have to marry Dante."

Elena turns to fully face me, fisting her hands. It actually looks like she wants to do me bodily harm. I've never seen her angry, and honestly, it's refreshing.

"You lied to me," she bites the words out.

"I did no such thing."

She lets out an offended gasp. "You said you'd kill Dante! I opened up to you... for what?"

"First, I'm going to kill Dante, just not today. Second, you opened up to me because I care, and you have no one else who gives a shit about you."

Slowly she shakes her head as if she's struck with dumbfounded amazement by my words. "You know nothing about me. How the hell can you claim to care about me?"

I take a step closer to her. "I know more than you think."

"Like what? That I was held a captive by my own father? That Dante could do whatever he wanted to me?" She takes a shuddering breath. "That tells you nothing about me."

I take another step closer, and it brings us within inches of each other. "It tells me you're a little bird with broken wings, flailing while surrounded by predators."

Elena's features tighten, and then a breath rushes over her lips, her cheeks staining pink as her anger grows. "You think I'm weak?"

When I lift a hand to reach for her, she slaps it away, and then she spits fire at me. "I've survived Dante for twenty-one years. I never gave up! Every time he beat me or forced himself on me, I got back up."

Elena shakes her head at me, and then she begins to walk away.

"Do not walk away from me when we're talking," I snap at her.

She swings back at me. "Screw you, Lucian. You think you're better than Dante? Than my father?" She stalks back to me, her eyes sparkling with rage, and God, she's never looked more beautiful. "You're the same as them. All I've ever wanted was my freedom, and you took it away from me. Don't make the mistake of thinking I'll be your wife.

Ring or no ring. Vows or no vows. I'm nothing more than your prisoner." A breath shudders out of her. "If you think I have broken wings, it's because you're the one who broke them when you arranged a marriage between us."

Adjusting my cuff where it's scratching at my wrist, it gives me a moment to focus on not losing my shit.

Then I lift my eyes to Elena's, and I stare at her as I choose my words carefully.

Slowly, I begin to stalk closer to her, and when I'm within reaching distance, my right hand shoots up, and I grab hold of her behind her head. Yanking her against me, my voice is low and threatening. "Do you want to go back to Dante?"

Elena only holds my stare, her lips sealed as her anger silently wars against mine.

"You asked me to stop the wedding between you and Capone, and I did. You asked me to kill him, and I will." When I take a breath, it's filled with Elena's soft scent. "The world is filled with monsters, Elena. At least you get one who won't rape and beat you. Count your fucking blessings."

I watch as my words hit her, her infuriated breaths matching mine.

"I have shit to take care of, so you'll just have to fucking deal with the fact that we're engaged, and nothing on this godforsaken earth is going to change that."

Done talking, I take hold of her hand and begin to drag her back to the house.

ELENA

Sitting in the back of the G Wagon, between Lucian and his aunt, I clamp my hands tightly together.

My anger simmers in my chest as I stare blankly ahead of me.

We're on our way to the morgue. I have no idea why Lucian's bringing me along.

Probably to make sure you don't try to escape.

I roll my eyes at the thought because it's ridiculous. I still don't have any identification documents or money, so I'm stuck.

The fight with Lucian exhausted me, and after not getting any sleep last night, I feel drained.

I've never fought with anyone like that before. Dante would probably have killed me if I spoke to him like that.

Yet, Lucian remained calm. It was a deadly calm, but still, he didn't lash out at me.

'The world is filled with monsters, Elena. At least you get one who won't rape and beat you. Count your fucking blessings.'

His words keep replaying in my mind. I'm not so sure I can believe them, though.

I mean, we're going to get married. What will happen on our wedding night? Will our union be consummated in blood because I will not give my consent? I won't agree to have sex with a man I don't know. Least of all, one who's taken me captive.

God, all I wanted was my freedom.

For a stupid moment, I actually thought Lucian could give it to me.

Stupid, Elena. You trusted the first person who showed you a glimmer of compassion. But it was all business for Lucian.

We stop outside a building, and I take a deep breath as we climb out of the car. Lucian grips hold of my hand, and when I try to pull away, he gives me a dark look filled with warning.

Alexei and Demitri join us from where they parked next to our vehicle. I don't know where Carson is. It looks like he left after the meeting.

Surrounded by guards, we enter the building, and I'm instantly freezing.

A man comes to meet us. "Mr. Cotroni, we were expecting you. This way."

My eyes begin to widen when I realize I'm not going to wait somewhere until Lucian's done viewing the body of his father.

Before we enter a room, Aunt Ursula begins to softly sob. My heart instantly goes out to her. Lucian lets go of my hand and wraps an arm around his aunt. He presses a kiss to her temple, then murmurs, "Let's say goodbye. Okay?"

She nods against his chest, and the interaction between them touches me deeply.

Lucian holds his aunt as they enter the room, and then Alexei places his hand on my lower back, softly nudging me to follow them.

I step inside, and my eyes instantly fall on the white sheet.

Oh, God.

Lucian lets go of his aunt, and then he steps closer to the table until he's right next to it. He tilts his head and reaches for the sheet. I hold my breath as the white fabric is pulled back, and then emotion inundates me as Lucian takes a shuddering breath. "Papà," he whispers, his voice drenched in sorrow.

Even though Lucian's my enemy, and I didn't know his father, compassion fills me.

Lucian places his hand over his tie, and then he leans forward and presses a kiss to his father's forehead. "Ti voglio bene, Papà." He murmurs something else I can't make out and then straightens up.

I watch as Lucian closes his eyes, sorrow shadowing his face. He takes a couple of minutes, just staring at his father before he steps away so his aunt can say goodbye.

She falls over Mr. Cotroni's chest and lets out a heartbreaking wail. Tears spring to my eyes, and I quickly blink them away. When I glance away from the tragic scene, my eyes collide with Lucian's.

There's no anger. Just need.

He closes the distance between us and wraps his arms around me. He needs comfort from me, and I push our differences aside.

Lucian buries his face in my hair, his body engulfing mine. For a moment, I hesitate, but then I lift my arms and wrap them around his waist.

"Thank you," he whispers, his voice rough with grief.

I nod against his shoulder, and thinking it might help, I rub my hand over his broad back.

Standing in the morgue next to Lucian's father's body, we find a connection. Although our situations are different, we both know the bitter taste of loss.

Lucian is the first to pull back. He goes to his aunt, and taking hold of her shoulders, he pulls her away from the body. She weeps against Lucian's chest, and he holds her tightly as if his strength is all that's keeping her from sinking to the ground.

We leave the morgue, and I'm surprised when Alexei again places his hand on my lower back. It feels as if he's offering me comfort.

While Lucian is focused on his aunt, Alexei leans a little down, and then he murmurs softly, "Lucian's a good man. He's doing what's right. Don't make his life hell for saving you."

Frowning, my eyes dart up to Alexei's, and then I see the warning, and it sends a shiver down my spine. "Always remember I have Lucian's back."

In other words, if I try to kill Lucian, Alexei will be there to take revenge.

I move away from Alexei, and he drops his hand. Before I can walk faster, he says, "Love him, and you'll have my protection. You choose how your future will play out."

I walk faster and catch up with Lucian and his aunt. Glancing over my shoulder, I give Alexei one last look. He smiles at me, and somehow it looks scarier than his usual grim expression.

Snapping my head forward, I place my hand on Aunt Ursula's back, choosing to offer her comfort instead of worrying about Alexei.

Aunt Ursula's hand searches for mine, and then she clasps my fingers tightly. The engagement ring digs into my skin, but I try to ignore the bite.

We all climb back in the G-Wagon, and when I'm seated between Lucian and his aunt, I reach out for Aunt Ursula's hand. She instantly grabs hold of mine with both of hers and gives me a thankful look.

Lucian takes hold of my left hand, and as my head snaps to him, he places my palm on his thigh. My eyes dart to his face, but he's staring out the window.

When I turn my attention back to Aunt Ursula, she gives me a trembling smile. "We've lost, and we've gained. Dorothy's ring looks beautiful on your finger."

"Dorothy?" I ask softly.

"My sister, Lucian's mother. It was her engagement ring."

Surprise flickers through me. Lucian gave me his mother's ring? Having seen how close he is to his family, I know it must be of great sentimental value to him.

Just then, Lucian brushes his thumb over the ring on my finger, the touch a soft caress.

Slowly I glance at him, but he's still staring out of the window. My eyes drop to where his hand is covering mine. I take in the veins snaking under his tanned skin. I feel the warmth coming from his palm and his thigh.

When there's a fluttering in my stomach, I close my eyes. There's a stab of disappointment in my heart because I know it's only a matter of time before I won't want to escape anymore.

Chapter 17

LUCIAN

Walking into the church, I glance at the people filling the pews.

Intimate, my ass.

Everyone is here to either make sure my father is dead or to pay their last respects.

I lead Aunt Ursula to the front and help her sit down. Leaning over her, I press a kiss to her cheek and whisper, "I'm just going to greet a couple of people, Zia Ursula."

She nods at me and then holds her hand out to Elena. As I straighten up, I glance at Leo, and he nods at me. I leave the two women in his care, and with Franco and Matteo flanking me, I walk to Peter Stathoulis.

When we spoke, he said he'd attend the funeral to offer his respects, and we could talk then.

When I reach him, his thick eyebrows draw together, making him look like an eagle, his gaze sharp and not missing a thing. We shake hands, and leaning closer to me, he murmurs, "Your father was a worthy opponent."

I nod.

"You're looking for a woman who goes by the name of Umbria."

My eyes snap to Peter's. "Umbria?"

"The Goddess of shadows, secrets, and darkness who lives in the underworld," he recites the old Italian myth to me. "Whoever she is, she's here for revenge. Look at past enemies."

Christ. There are so many.

But a woman?

"Are you sure it's a woman?" I ask.

He nods. "As sure as one can be."

What the fuck?

My mind begins to race through all the enemies I know of, but I can't figure out who she can be.

"Thank you."

Peter nods and then tightens his grip on my hand. "Maybe we can put our differences aside. Consider the information a peace offering."

Our eyes lock, and knowing there was no bad blood between our families, I nod. "An ally is always welcome."

He lets go of my hand and then takes a seat next to his wife.

I greet a couple of politicians and detectives, and some other prominent families before I take my seat next to Elena.

Just like the day before, I take hold of her left hand and place it on my thigh.

While the priest performs the service, I rub my thumb over the engagement ring, and it offers me the comfort I need to get through today.

When we're done with Mass, I get up and walk to the open casket. My father looks like he's just sleeping, and it breaks my heart, knowing he will never wake again.

I lean over him and press a final kiss to his forehead. "Addio, Papà."

I wait for Aunt Ursula and Elena to say their final farewells, and then we step aside.

The guards know to keep the press away, so at least we're not inundated with reporters as we leave the church. It's quiet in the back of the car, and when we reach the cemetery, Aunt Ursula begins to softly weep.

I close my eyes for a moment, tightening my hold on Elena's hand.

She's put her anger aside to offer my aunt and me comfort through this challenging time, and it tells me just how big her heart is.

When we climb out of the car, Elena wraps her arm around Aunt Ursula, and the sight offers my heart some warmth.

I link my fingers with Elena's left hand, and then the three of us walk to the mausoleum where my father will be laid to rest.

Well aware, this is the perfect opportunity for an attack, I'm overly conscious of my surroundings even though I have an army of guards protecting us.

One slip up, and it can cost me dearly. I could lose Elena or my aunt.

My gaze connects with Alexei's, and when he nods, silently assuring me everything is okay, the worry begins to fade.

My father taught me we don't have friends, but looking at Alexei, I know with certainty I at least have one.

Thank God for small mercies.

The day proceeds at a somber pace, and by the time we get home, we all sink down on the couches in the living room.

Alexei and Demitri are staying as my guests until we've taken care of the threat.

Aunt Ursula only sits for a minute then she gets up again. "Come, Elena."

I watch as the women head for the stairs and then turn my gaze back to Alexei. "Stathoulis said the threat is a woman who goes by the name of Umbria."

"Umbria?" Alexei frowns, and leaning forward, he rests his forearms on his thighs. "Is that supposed to mean something?"

"It's the name of an old Italian mythical goddess," I explain to him. "Stathoulis thinks it's an old enemy."

"Any ideas?" he asks.

I shake my head. "You know how it works. The whole family gets taken out, so there's no one left to do something like this."

Alexei thinks for a moment, then he asks, "A scorned mistress?"

I let out a bark of laughter. "Fuck no."

"Umbria," Alexei murmurs her name again. "I'll dig around and see what I can come up with."

"Thanks." Getting up, I leave them to work on the problem and go upstairs to check on the women.

I find them in the sitting room, which has a spectacular view of the Mediterranian sea. Leaning my shoulder against the doorjamb, I watch as Aunt Ursula shows Elena pictures of wedding dresses.

"What do you think of this one?" Aunt Ursula asks, tilting her head to Elena.

A funeral and a wedding. It sounds like the start of a bad joke.

Elena stares at the picture then she nods her head. "It's beautiful." There's no excitement in her voice.

"The mermaid style will compliment your figure," Aunt Ursula says, then she stares at the dress. "So chic." She sets the picture aside, then spreads a whole bunch of new photos over the coffee table. "Now for flowers. What do you like?"

Elena looks at all of them then she shakes her head. "They're all pretty."

My lips curve up, and I slowly walk closer. When I reach the couch, both women glance at me.

"Planning the wedding?" I ask the obvious.

Aunt Ursula gives me a playful scowl. "One week! That's all I have, so don't you dare interfere."

I hold my hands up in a surrendering motion while letting out a chuckle. "Oh, trust me, I won't."

I sit down on the arm of the couch, and leaning into Elena, I look at all the photos that have samples of bouquets.

I gesture at the St. Joseph lilies. "Those were Mamma's favorites."

My comment makes a sentimental smile form on Aunt Ursula's face.

"We can go with those," Elena says.

"The St. Joseph's?" Aunt Ursula asks to be sure.

"Yes." Elena gets up. "Excuse me for a moment."

I rise to my feet, and straightening my jacket, I say, "Thank you for doing this, Zia Ursula."

"Of course," she smiles at me.

Walking out of the sitting room, I go to Elena's room and tap my knuckles on the door. When she doesn't answer, I knock again and wait a couple of seconds before pushing the door open to see if she's even inside.

Elena swings around from where she was standing in front of the window. "I just need a moment," she says, her voice tight.

I step inside and shut the door behind me. Walking to her side, I stare at the landscaped garden below.

"Thank you for the comfort you've given my aunt," I murmur. "And myself."

"I'm not heartless," she mutters.

"I know." I turn to face her, but she keeps staring out the window. Lifting my hand, I take hold of her jaw and turn her face to me. "Why are you against marrying me?"

Elena's eyes lock with mine, and I see a million thoughts in her golden-brown irises.

ELENA

"Because it will cost me my freedom," I answer honestly. "I fought too hard to just give it up."

Lucian's eyes drift over my face. "What makes you think you'll have to give up your freedom?"

"Everything. This whole world you're in charge of." I take a breath, and my lungs are filled with his aftershave, which I have to admit, I'm growing really fond of. "Or are you going to tell me things will be different? There might not be a lock on that door now, but what stops you from doing it later? One day you'll lose your patience with me, and it will start with one slap."

Lucian moves his hand to the side of my face, and cupping my cheek, the touch feels tender. He steps closer until our bodies are almost touching, and then he says, "I could never hit you. Not even if you drive me up the walls."

He leans down and presses a kiss to my forehead. His lips linger, and I have to close my eyes against how good it feels.

"I just want my freedom," I plead, hoping to appeal to his heart.

He pulls back and captures my eyes. "You're free to come and go as you please, Elena. You're free to do anything you want."

A frown begins to form on my forehead. "You'll just let me walk out of the house? Right now?"

His eyes narrow slightly. "Yes…" tilting his head, he continues, "but you better come back. Make no mistake, I expect to find you at home when I return from work."

My eyes dart between his, looking for the truth in his words. "So during the day, I can do what I want?" I ask to make sure.

"As long as you have the guards with you. I also prefer you take my aunt along, especially for shopping trips. She loves those."

I frown again, and my heart begins to beat a little faster as hope begins to return.

"What happens the day I make you angry?" I ask.

Lucian's fingers brush down my cheek to the faint bruise on my jaw. "You pissed me off yesterday, and I didn't hit you." He shrugs. "We'll fight. We'll make up." Shaking his head, he pins me with a look of warning. "But we'll never lift a hand against each other."

I need to know more. I need to know how I'll pay for disobeying him because there's always a price to pay.

"So no punishments?" I ask. "We just fight, and that's it?"

The corner of his mouth lifts into a dangerously sexy grin. He leans forward again, and then he whispers in my ear, "Oh, you'll pay. Just not the way you think."

"How?" I ask while I keep perfectly still.

Lucian drops his hands to my hips, and slowly his palms brush over my curves until they reach my bottom. I let out a burst of air from the sharp sensation it causes in my abdomen. He then moves up to my back, and it feels as if I'm being hypnotized – focusing only on him.

My lips part, and when he lets out a breath of air on my ear, my eyes drift shut, and my body quivers.

"Piss me off, and I'll drive you wild only to leave you aching for my cock," he murmurs, his voice low and seductive.

A wave of warmth spreads through my body as if he's set it alight, and my mind clouds over like when he was kissing me.

Lucian's lips skim along my jaw, and when his mouth touches mine, I exhale sharply. My lips tingle with need for his, but instead of kissing me, he pulls away. The smirk returns to his face. "Do you have any other questions?"

I quickly shake my head.

"Good." Lucian presses another kiss to my forehead. "Don't keep my aunt waiting. She's excited to plan the wedding." And then he walks out of my room. I take the three steps to my bed and slump down on it, my legs too numb to stand.

My. God.

What was that?

I actually wanted him to kiss me. I've never felt that before, not even with Alfonso, and it leaves me staring off into space with amazement.

It takes me a couple of minutes to gather my senses that have been scrambled by Lucian. Then I remember what he said – I can come and go as I please.

Is it the truth, though?

Only time will tell. In six days, we'll be married, and I know there's no way I can stop it from happening.

The thought reminds me of Aunt Ursula, and getting up, I rush out of the room. When I walk into the sitting room, I say, "I'm so sorry for keeping you waiting."

Instead of being angry, she smiles at me. "Not to worry, cara. I understand you and Lucian need time to talk as well. Come sit."

I take a seat next to her and then look at the new set of photos on display. She points to one where lanterns lend a soft glow to tables decorated with white linen. "If you have the wedding at sunset, this will look gorgeous in the backyard."

I glance at her. "Will the wedding be held here?"

She nods. "It would be a shame to not use the garden."

Agreeing with her, I nod. "I like the lanterns. It makes everything look mystical."

"Good," she says with a happy chuckle. "We'll decide on the food and cake tomorrow." Turning to me, her eyes scan over my hair. "Are you going to wear it up or down?"

I shrug. "I don't know."

"Lucian will like it down. I think you'll look beautiful with curls."

"It sounds easy enough," I say, a smile curving my lips.

Aunt Ursula tilts her head as she places her hand on mine. There's a soft expression in her eyes. "Lucian is all I have left. He's like a son to me."

I nod.

"Please be good to him."

I nod again.

She pulls me into a hug, then says, "I know an arranged marriage is not every girl's dream, but he'll be a good husband. Give him a chance."

I nod again. "I'll try."

"That's all I ask," she says as she pulls back. She brushes a couple of strands away from my cheek, and her fingers skim over the bruise. "The Cotroni men don't hit."

I swallow hard and lower my eyes to the pictures on the table.

"I'm here if you need to talk about anything. I'd like to think we can become good friends."

My gaze darts back to hers, and when I see the sincerity on her face, my hope grows a little more. "I'd like that too."

Chapter 18

LUCIAN

Standing by the dining room table, I stare at all the cakes.

I'm going to die of a sugar overdose if Aunt Ursula forces me to take one more bite.

I look at Elena and ask, "Have you decided which one you want?"

She glances at me, then back at the selection. "They're all pretty…"

"But?" I ask.

Aunt Ursula lets out a sigh. "They're not right for the two of you."

The pâtissier steps closer. "There's a new trend you might like. A naked cake with lace buttercream. It won't be too sweet."

"I like the sound of that," I mutter, drawing a chuckle from Aunt Ursula.

The pâtissier fiddles on a tablet, and then he shows the women a picture that instantly makes Elena smile. "It's perfect."

My lips curve up, and I walk closer. Placing my hands on Elena's hips, I look at the cake from over her shoulder, and even I have to admit it's beautiful. "Is that the one you want?" I ask.

She glances up at me. "Yes. I like how delicate it looks."

"It's settled then." I press a kiss to her neck. "I have work to take care of."

"Don't be late for dinner," Aunt Ursula calls after me as I leave the dining room.

"I won't." My lips curve up, thinking how pleasant things have actually been since Elena and I spoke yesterday. She seems to be warming up to the idea of marrying me, and it didn't escape my notice that she didn't tense up when I kissed her neck.

Walking out the front door, Franco and Matteo instantly flank me, and we head for the car. I get into the back seat, and once Franco starts the engine, I say, "The harbor. A shipment came in."

"Yes, Sir." Then he speaks into the microphone, "We're on the move."

I take my phone from my pocket and dial Alexei's number. He and Demitri are chasing a lead, and I want to touch base with them.

Alexei answers, and I hear a grunt, then he says, "Koslov."

"Please tell me you didn't answer the phone while fucking," I chuckle.

"Not the kind of fucking you're thinking of," he replies. "I'm getting some information from someone."

Poor bastard.

"I take it you got a lead?" I ask as Franco steers the G Wagon out of the driveway.

"Fucking mercenaries. That's who she has working for her."

My eyebrows raise. "And?"

"You interrupted me. Let me finish, and I'll let you know if he shared anything of value."

"Okay."

We end the call, and tucking the phone back in the breast pocket of my jacket, I relax against the seat. Lifting my hand, I rub over the scruff on my jaw while I once again try to figure out who's behind the attack.

Mercenaries. Freelance guns for hire who don't live by any code.

Fuck, it can be anyone.

When we pull up to the harbor, there's a police car. I let out a sigh. "Merda." My motor brigade comes to a stop, and I shove the door open. Getting out, I walk to the police car, and when I reach the driver's side, I let out a sigh of relief when I see it's one of the detectives on our payroll.

"What are you doing here?" I ask.

He climbs out and gestures with a thumb at my shipment of incendiary grenades. "A call came in about suspicious activity."

Our eyes lock as I ask, "And? Did you find anything?"

He shakes his head. "No."

"Good."

I watch as he climbs back into the car, and then he says, "Oh, by the way, congrats on the engagement."

He must've read it in the newspapers. The Cotroni name is becoming a trending topic, and I don't like it one bit.

I nod and watch as he starts the engine and drives off.

"Everything okay, boss?" Matteo asks.

"Yes. Let's check the shipment and get out of here before a cop who's not on our payroll comes sniffing."

We get to work, and after I've made sure everything is there, the men start packing it into the aircon units we always use.

The whole process takes an hour, and then we can finally get out of here.

"Matteo," I call after him before he can climb into the truck, "Make sure that shipment reaches its destination."

"Yes, boss."

I get into the G Wagon, and then Franco takes us home. As we turn into the driveway, my phone begins to ring. Seeing Alexei's name, I grin. "I take it you're done," I answer the call.

"I am," he chuckles. "Now I need a drink."

"And?"

"I only found out she's Italian. The usual shit. Dark hair, dark eyes. Goes by the name of Umbria."

"Fuck, that doesn't help," I mutter.

"I'll keep digging," Alexei says.

"Thanks."

Franco brings the car to a stop as we end the call, and getting out, I let out a sigh. It really feels like I'm chasing a ghost.

When I walk back into the house, I find Elena and Aunt Ursula in the kitchen.

"Whatever you're making smells nice," I say as I walk to the side table to pour myself a bourbon.

"I'm showing Elena how to make beef and mortadella meatballs in tomato sauce," Aunt Ursula answers.

Picking up my drink, I unbutton my jacket and take a seat on the couch. I savor the bourbon while I watch the women cook, and it instantly makes me relax.

Elena glances up every now and then, and around the fifth time our eyes connect, she begins to smile.

Slowly the corner of my mouth lifts, and for the next thirty minutes, I keep staring at her, drawing smiles from her.

By the time dinner is ready, I'm getting hot. Rising to my feet, I take off my jacket and drape it over the back of the couch. I unbutton my cuffs, and while I roll up my sleeves, I walk to the dining room.

I stop by the head of the table, and the sight of my father's empty chair is a punch to the gut.

Aunt Ursula pats my back. "Sit down. He would've wanted it like that."

I take a deep breath and let it out slowly as I pull the chair out.

When I take a seat, Elena places a plate in front of me. "Good luck. It's my first time cooking."

I let out a chuckle. "As long as you didn't add poison."

"Damn, I should've thought of that," she teases me back as she sits down to my right.

When we're all ready, I hold my hands out to Elena and my aunt, and then I say a quick prayer of thanks.

Picking up my utensils, I cut through a meatball, and when I take the bite, Elena watches me closely.

I chew slowly, savoring the richness, and then I begin to smile. "Relax. It's good."

A wide smile spreads over her face, and it has me staring at her while she begins eating.

"Of course, it's good," Aunt Ursula mutters. "I taught her."

Letting out a chuckle, I take hold of my aunt's hand and press a kiss to her fingers. "Thank you."

ELENA

It's my wedding day, and I'm not as nervous as I thought I'd be.

My hands are still shaking, and I can't stop sweating, but I thought when this day came, I'd be making a noose to hang myself with and not getting ready to walk down the aisle.

I take deep breaths as I stare at my reflection in the mirror.

The past week was nothing like I expected it would be. Every day I spent with Aunt Ursula, I got to know her a little better. Yesterday she asked me if I wanted her to move in with us, and I didn't hesitate to say yes. I feel much better knowing she's here. Just in case things start to go bad with Lucian.

Luckily there won't be a honeymoon because Lucian can't take off from work.

I take another deep breath when my thoughts turn to tonight.

God.

My stomach clenches with nerves thinking tonight we'll have to consummate the marriage. My heart begins to beat faster, and a cold sweat breaks out over my skin.

Lucian's been nothing but nice to me this past week, and if I'm honest with myself, I'll admit I've started to develop feelings for him.

But still… I'm not ready to have sex with him.

God, I'm not ready.

Aunt Ursula comes to stand behind me, and then the smile on her face fades. "What's wrong, cara?"

I shake my head. "I'm just nervous."

When I turn to face her, she takes hold of both my hands. "It's normal to feel nervous."

I nod, and then I almost lick my lips but remember the lipstick I'm wearing just in time.

"Is there something else you're worried about?" she asks, her tone gentle.

My eyes dart up to her face before I lower them again. "It's about tonight," I admit.

"Oh... Ohhhh." She pulls me to the bed, and once we're sitting down, she says, "That's normal too. I drank so much at my reception, and honestly, it helped."

"You were married?" I ask.

Aunt Ursula nods, and then she pulls a face. "Biggest mistake of my life. Luca warned me, and I didn't listen. He turned out to be an abusive bastard."

"So you got divorced?"

She shakes her head. "No, I'm a widow. Luca took care of it for me."

My lips part when I realize Lucian's father killed Aunt Ursula's husband. "Oh."

"Still," she shifts to face me better, "I'm sure Lucian will be gentle."

Oh, God.

My cheeks go up in flames, and it has her frowning. "Are you a virgin, cara?"

Ohhh, God. I'm going to die of embarrassment.

I shake my head.

"Well, then you know what to expect," Aunt Ursula sighs.

Yeah, I don't think so.

There's a knock at the door, and then Alexei peeks into the room. "Are you ready?"

"Yes, but we'll wait another five minutes," Aunt Ursula says. "Make my nephew sweat a little longer."

Alexei lets out a chuckle then he shuts the door.

We really make Lucian wait another five minutes as we straighten out my dress, and then Aunt Ursula kisses both my cheeks. "Don't forget to breathe, cara."

I suck in some air and then let it out slowly.

"Are you ready?" she asks me.

No.

I'm not sure.

Do I have a choice?

Instead of voicing my thoughts, I nod.

When we come down the stairs, and I see my father, my stomach drops.

Dante's here?

Just as I think the question, Dante comes out of the guest restroom, and his eyes lock on me.

"Come, you've made us wait long enough," my father barks.

"Hush, Tino," Aunt Ursula chastises him. "If you have a problem walking your daughter down the aisle, I'll do it."

Without a word, my father walks to me and holds out his arm. I place my hand in the crook of his arm and can't help but think it's the first time we're touching in years.

And probably the last.

"Come, Mr. Capone. Surely you don't intend on walking down the aisle with the bride," Aunt Ursula snaps at Dante. He gives me a leering look before he follows after Aunt Ursula.

I tighten my grip on the small bouquet of St. Joseph lilies in my left hand. As we step out onto the veranda, *Pachelbel's Canon in D* begins to play, and it all becomes too real.

I don't know most of the people attending the wedding. As I look into the distance, my eyes lock on Lucian, where he's standing in front of the fountain with the priest and Alexei by his side.

He looks so handsome in his tuxedo, he holds my attention until I'm halfway down the aisle. Then Dante catches my eye, and the cruel expression on his face makes me instantly cold. My gaze darts back to Lucian, and our eyes lock.

Please don't hurt me.

His gaze snaps to Dante, then back to me, and as if he can read my thoughts, a soft smile forms around his full lips.

I won't.

Reaching the front, my father gives my cheek an air kiss, and then he nods at Lucian before he leaves to go sit next to Dante.

Lucian's eyes drift over me and then murmurs, "You look breathtaking."

I try to smile, but it probably looks like a grimace.

The ceremony begins, and with every word the priest speaks, the shaking in my hands grows. By the time we're done with candle lighting, my breaths are rushing from my lips.

God, I'm getting married.

This is it.

There's no running away.

When it's time for the vows, I feel faint.

I glance at the guests, and again my eyes connect with Dante's. He looks like he's going to pull a gun on us at any moment.

It could've been Dante standing in front of you.

Lucian reaches for my face, and placing his finger beneath my chin, he nudges me to look at him. When our eyes lock, all the guests disappear, even Dante, and then it's only the two of us.

And our vows.

Lucian takes hold of my left hand and gives it an encouraging squeeze, then the priest says, "Lucian, repeat after me."

The priest recites the vows, but all I hear is Lucian's voice as he promises, "I, Lucian Cotroni, take thee, Elena Lucas, to be my wedded wife, to have and to hold from this day forward, for better, for worse, for richer, for poorer, in sickness and in health, to love and to cherish, till death do us part."

"Elena, repeat after me."

My lips part, and then I hear my own voice, and it sounds much stronger than I feel as I say my vows to Lucian.

Lucian's fingers tighten around mine when I say, "Till death do us part."

It will be the only way to escape now that we've said our vows and exchanged rings. I only half noticed the ring Lucian wore on his right hand is the one we used as a wedding ring for him.

"Lucian, do you take Elena Lucas as your wife?"

Lucian doesn't hesitate. "I do."

This is it.

God.

"Elena, do you take Lucian Cotroni as your husband?"

My mouth dries, and I swallow hard. *At least it's not Dante.* Seconds pass before I manage to say, "I do."

"I now pronounce you husband and wife. You may kiss the bride."

Husband.

Wife.

Marriage.

Lucian lifts a hand to my cheek, and then he leans into me. His lips brush tenderly against mine, and it makes emotions rocket through me. Overwhelmed, I begin to blink to try and keep the tears at bay.

I feel Lucian's breath on my lips as he pulls back, and then the priest says, "Mr. and Mrs. Cotroni."

"Elena Cotroni," Lucian murmurs, a satisfied grin spreading over his face. "My wife."

Chapter 19

LUCIAN

My wife.

God, she's beautiful.

I can't keep my eyes off Elena and only listen with half an ear as Judge Fico rambles on about the new yacht he bought.

She's a vision in the wedding dress where she's standing next to Aunt Ursula. They're talking to a group of wives from the most prominent families in Italy.

"Excuse me," I say, and then I walk to Elena. Touching her elbow, I get her attention, and then I ask the other women, "May I steal my wife for a dance?"

The women all swoon as I tug Elena away from them. I move my hand down to hers and linking our fingers, I lead her to the dance floor that's been set up on the other side of the fountain.

A song with a beat is playing, and not caring, I pull Elena into my arms. I ignore the beat and instead focus on the female vocals. My hands brush over her back, and I savor the feel of her smooth skin.

The dress she's wearing is sexy as fuck, the back exposed all the way to her lower back. The possessive side of me wants to shrug off my jacket and cover her so no other man can see, but I suppress the urge.

Elena places her hands on my shoulders, and her eyes only meet mine for a second before she glances at the fountain.

"Look at me," I murmur. When her gaze locks with mine, my lips curve up. "That's better."

The current song fades away, and then an alternate version of *Take Me To Church* begins to play.

I pull Elena tightly against me, and moving a hand behind her head, I press my forehead against hers. I feel her exhale on my lips, and my fingers curl into her silky hair.

Slowly, I tilt my head, and I let my mouth brush against the corner of her mouth. We're breathing the same air as I whisper, "Move your hands behind my neck."

Elena does as I ask, and feeling her fingers on my skin makes streaks of heat flash through my body.

Not caring that we're surrounded by family and business associates, I nip at her lips. Elena closes her eyes, and then I claim her mouth. I've been slowly dying from not taking what I wanted this past week.

I gave her time to settle in, to get used to the idea of us. *No more.*

My tongue sweeps into her mouth, and then I devour her. I memorize the sweet taste of her tongue.

I lift both my hands, and framing her face, I keep her in place as my hunger grows.

My tongue strokes hard over hers, branding her mine.

My teeth tug at her lips, claiming her.

My lips savor Elena's, knowing I'll never taste anything as good as her again.

Elena's fingers tangle with my hair at the nape of my neck, and then she begins to kiss me back.

Fireworks explode above us, and the guests begin to cheer, and I couldn't care less.

This moment.

Kissing my wife.

It's all that matters.

A moan drifts from Elena, and I drink it like a man dying of thirst.

Christ, I want more of those moans.

We've passed decent, and we're well on our way to filthy by the time I force myself to end the kiss. I nip one more time at her swollen lips, and then we breathlessly stare at each other.

This time there's no horror to chase the excitement from Elena's cheeks. She doesn't run from me, and all hell doesn't break loose. Instead, Elena stares at me with wonder as if I performed some miracle.

We just look at each other as the music continues to play. The guests continue to enjoy the reception. The fireworks fade into the night.

Everything in me wants to drag her to our bed so I can spend the rest of the night claiming her body, but knowing it's too soon for her, I take a step back. "Thank you for the dance."

"Uh-huh," she mumbles, still staring at me with the same look of wonder on her face.

"Keep looking at me like that, and I'm going to send everyone home and drag you to bed," I warn her.

It snaps her out of the trance, and frowning at me, she mutters, "Then don't kiss me like that."

I let out a chuckle. "Not a chance."

As I take hold of her hand, I don't miss the smile tugging at her lips. I lead her back to Aunt Ursula's side and leave her in the safety of my aunt's company while I attend to some of the guests.

As I take a glass of champagne from a server's platter, Alexei comes to stand next to me. His eyes scan over my face then he smiles. "You look happy, my friend."

"Considering all the shit we're dealing with, I am." I take a sip of the bubbly drink. "Are you enjoying yourself?"

He nods, then Demitri comes to murmur something to him. Alexei's eyes snap to mine, then he mutters, "We have to leave. You understand?"

"Of course." I hold out my hand to him. "Thank you for being my best man."

I get a smile from him before he and Demitri walk to the veranda. When I glance back to the guests, it's to see Tino walking toward me.

Fuck. I hated having him and Dante here today.

"Son," Tino taunts me.

"Don't fucking call me that," I growl at him, instantly pissed off.

Our eyes lock, and for a moment, we stare at each other. The air begins to crackle with tension.

"Any news?" he finally asks.

"No." Even if I had news, I wouldn't share it with him.

A sneer begins to tug at his lips, then he mutters, "Enjoy my daughter."

I clench my jaw and watch him with unadulterated hatred as he walks away from me.

Needing to calm down, I glance to where the women are, and only seeing Aunt Ursula, I set the glass down on the nearest table and walk to her.

"Where's Elena?" I ask when I reach my aunt.

She smiles brightly at me. "She's just changing dresses. Leo's with her."

I instantly relax, knowing Elena has a guard with her.

My aunt wraps her arm around my waist. "Are you enjoying your night?"

A smile forms around my mouth as I place my arm around her shoulders. I give her a sideways hug. "I am. Thank you for the beautiful reception."

"You're welcome, but next time you plan a function, give me more time."

I let out a chuckle. "I will." Seeing how happy my aunt is, I ask, "You're still moving in, right?"

She nods. "Your wife already gave her permission, so you can't change your mind now. We'll bring all my belongings over tomorrow."

My smile grows. "I'm glad to hear that. It warms my heart that you and Elena get along."

Something catches my attention, and I glance back at the house. My eyes scan over all the guests, the guards, Tino, and then my smile fades. There's no sign of Dante.

"Excuse me," I murmur to my aunt, and then I walk toward the sliding doors. My stomach tightens, and sensing something is very wrong, I break out into a run.

ELENA

"Congratulations, Mrs. Cotroni," Leo says as he follows me to my room.

I glance at him from over my shoulder. "Thank you." Opening the door to my room, I say, "I'll just be a minute."

Leo nods at me and takes his position next to the door as I shut it.

The wedding dress is beautiful, but I need to change into something that doesn't weigh more than me. Luckily, Aunt Ursula planned ahead, and I have a white cocktail dress waiting.

I've been trying to prepare myself for later tonight, unable to think of anything else but Lucian and I consummating our marriage.

Nerves spin in my stomach, but after the kiss that left me breathless, I have to admit the thought isn't as daunting anymore. Maybe, just maybe, it will be the same as when Lucian kisses me.

Taking hold of the silk straps over my shoulders, I pull them down, and then the weight of all the fabric drops to the floor.

Standing in only a backless lace bodysuit, I reach for the cocktail dress. Slipping it off the hanger, the door to my room bursts open. My head snaps in that direction, and then I go ice cold.

Leo's lying on the floor, a crimson stain forming on his white button-up shirt as Dante comes in. He slams the door shut and then levels me with a cruel glare. His right hand is gripping a gun with a silencer on, which is why I didn't hear the shot.

Shock stuns me as my lips part. It's only for a second that we stare at each other.

Horror pours in.

Dread creeps over my skin.

Desperation shudders through me.

I clasp the cocktail dress to my front, and faced with the devil, it brings back awful memories of when we were in a similar position.

I dart toward the bathroom. Not that there's anywhere to escape to, but it might buy me time.

Dante grabs hold of my hair in a brutal grip, and strands are painfully yanked out. I let out a scream as I fall back against him. His rank breath instantly coats the skin on my neck and ear, erasing the bliss that still lingered from Lucian's kiss.

Fight, Elena. God, you have to fight harder than ever.

I slam my elbow back against his ribs, but a layer of fat protects him. I begin to struggle, my breaths rushing over my lips and my heart slamming against my chest.

Needing both my hands, I let go of the cocktail dress. I somehow manage to head butt Dante against the nose, and his hand frees my hair. I dart forward, but then his body plows into mine, and I crash to the floor with his full weight on top of me.

"Get off!" I scream. It feels as if I'm being possessed by a devil of my own.

Dante easily flips me over onto my back, and then the gun slams against my left cheek. Lights explode behind my vision. Intense pain fills the entire left side of my face. I slip in and out of consciousness, my limbs heavy.

Dante claws at the bodysuit, and I feel it rip.

Darkness swirls around me, threatening to drag me to the depths of hell.

My soul shrinks as my worst fear looms over me.

I hear a roar of anger, and then Dante's weight disappears off me.

Blinking against the shock from the punch, my vision comes back, and strength returns to my body. I manage to pull myself up and leaning back against the bathtub, I watch as Lucian kicks the gun away. He crouches over Dante, slamming one fist after the other into his face.

I've never seen Lucian so angry, his features cut from rage and vengeance as he beats Dante into a bloody mess.

Even though it's one of the most savage things I've ever seen, I can't look away. Time slows down. I hold my breath. I don't even blink, not wanting to miss a second.

Dante's grunts grow weaker, and then Lucian wraps his hands around Dante's neck.

Instead of horror, calm trickles through me as I watch Dante gasp for air.

Just like I did.

Dante bleeds.

Like I've bled many times at his hands.

His face distorts with panic, his tongue curling in his mouth as he makes gurgling sounds.

Die.

Please. Just. Die.

Years of abuse flashes between Dante and me. The shame. The disgust. The pain.

And then Lucian severs the link, strangling the last air from Dante.

Dante makes one last gargled sound, and then he stills. His eyes are wide open. His face covered in blood. His mouth left gaping for the last gasp of air Lucian refused to give him.

He's dead.

My heart beats violently in my chest, and then a relieved sob bursts from me.

Lucian climbs to his feet, and I watch as he rinses the blood from his hands. "Remove this piece of shit from my house," he barks, and it's only then I see Franco and Matteo.

They don't look at me as they pick up Dante's body, and when they carry him away, only blood remains on the tiles where he died.

Using the tub, I pull myself up on trembling legs.

Lucian shrugs out of his jacket, and then he comes to wrap it around my shoulders. His arms slip under me, and I'm lifted to his chest.

There's zero hesitation as I wrap my arms around his neck. I bury my face against him while my relief washes the horror away.

Lucian carries me to another room. He takes a seat on the bed, and then he holds me so tightly it borders on painful.

I hear him take deep breaths. I feel his body shudder against mine with residual anger.

"Thank you," I whisper, my voice raw with emotion.

Lucian kept his promise.

He killed Dante for me.

A calm feeling washes over me, and I hold my husband tighter.

It's only then I realize I've found the freedom I've been fighting so hard for.

I'm finally free from Dante.

I'm free.

Chapter 20

LUCIAN

Bless me, Father, for I have sinned.

I sure as fuck won't be asking forgiveness for killing Dante.

I suck in a deep breath, and then I pull back so I can see what damage the motherfucker has done to Elena.

The moment I saw Leo on the floor, fear flooded me, unlike anything I've ever felt.

What I found when I rushed into the bedroom ripped the air from my lungs. All I saw was Elena's discarded wedding dress. And then I heard the angry grunts coming from the bathroom, and it baptized my soul in fire and brimstone.

Seeing Dante on top of my wife, tearing at the meager clothes that covered her body, robbed me of my sanity. I couldn't stop if I wanted to and I sure as fuck didn't want to.

I've never killed a man with my bare hands until today. My only regret is that he didn't suffer more.

My eyes scan over Elena's delicate features, and the bruise forming on her cheek rips a growl from my chest. Her skin has split, and the sight of the thin trail of blood makes my body shudder violently with newborn rage.

Our eyes lock. Instead of trauma and fear, she looks at me with so much calm it makes the rage fade.

Elena moves her hands to my jaw, and then she surprises me by slowly leaning in and pressing a kiss to my mouth. "Thank you for keeping your promise," she whispers against my lips.

"Are you okay?" I manage to ask, my voice rough with emotions.

She moves her hand to her cheek and touches the bruise with the pad of her finger, and then she nods. "I'm okay."

I wrap my arms around her again and hold her tightly to my chest. Elena hides her face in the crook of my neck.

I lift a hand to the back of her head and curl myself around her.

God, if I hadn't noticed something was off...

The shock begins to fade, and the adrenaline flows from my veins. I just hold her because I'm not ready to let go yet.

Just like before, it takes Elena a moment, and then she begins to cry. Delayed shock shudders through her. "Thank you," she squeezes out. "Thank you, Lucian."

I press a kiss to the side of her head and take a deep breath of her.

The door to our room opens, and Aunt Ursula comes rushing in. "Dio! What happened?"

"Dante attacked her," I bite the foul words out through clenched teeth.

Aunt Ursula comes to place her hands on Elena's shuddering shoulders, and then I lose my wife as she turns to my aunt.

"Dio. Dio," Aunt Ursula keeps repeating when she sees Elena's face. "Come, cara."

I stand up and watch as Aunt Ursula takes Elena to the bathroom, and then I close my eyes. I take a couple of deep breaths before I walk out of the room to face Tino.

I hear him threatening Franco at the bottom of the stairs, and pulling my Glock from behind my back, I take the stairs down. I lift my arm and order, "Move, Franco. I've got this."

With the barrel of my gun trained on Valentino Lucas' forehead, I say, "You brought that piece of shit into my home."

"You killed my right-hand man," Tino spits at me, his face tight with rage.

"He attacked my wife." My finger tightens around the trigger. "You've allowed that motherfucker to abuse Elena for years and expect me to do the same?"

"She's my daughter to offer to whomever I want."

Christ almighty, give me strength.

Unable to stop myself, I dart forward and slam the butt of the gun against Tino's face.

"Lucian," Aunt Ursula shouts behind me. "Stop!" I glare up at her as she rushes down the stairs. "You have guests."

My eyes dart around the living room that's filled with most of the guests. They're all watching to see what I'll do next.

"Whether we like it or not, Valentino Lucas is part of the *la famiglia*," my aunt reminds me.

He's done nothing to deserve death. Not in the eyes of our shared allies.

I take a step back, and my fingers flex around the Glock. Struggling to rein in my anger, I bite out, "Get the fuck out of my house."

My eyes snap to Franco, and he immediately grabs hold of Tino's arm to drag him out if he has to.

Tino rears back and spits at me, "You owe me for the loss of Dante."

I close the distance between us until we're face to face, my eyes boring into his. "I. Owe. You. Nothing."

"You killed my man," he hisses, refusing to back down.

Again my fingers flex around the weapon and holding my ground, my voice is deceivingly calm as I say, "I'm letting you walk out alive. There's your fucking payment."

We continue to stare, and I inject every bit of hatred I have for this man into my eyes and voice. "Leave while you can still walk out on your own two legs."

The air grows unbearably tense, my body on high alert.

Tino is the first to take a step back. He gives me a glare, promising nothing good, and then he stalks out with Franco right behind him.

I let out a breath.

The war is just starting.

"What's a wedding without a little drama," Aunt Ursula laughs awkwardly. "Where's the music?" She claps her hands. "Let's continue to celebrate." She ushers the guests back outside, and soon music fills the air again.

Franco comes back inside. "He's gone."

"Leo?" I think to ask.

"In surgery. I think he'll pull through."

"Good." I tuck away the Glock behind my back and head up the stairs. "Have one of the men watch Tino. I don't trust him."

"Yes, Sir."

Opening the door to our room, I find Elena sitting on the bed. She's wearing a soft pink dress, and her curls cover the left side of her face.

I crouch in front of her and catch her eyes. "You don't have to go back to the reception."

Shaking her head, she stands up, and it has me rising to my feet.

"I want to go back."

I lift a hand to her face and gently brush my palm over the silky strands hiding the bruise. "Are you sure?"

For the first time, Elena takes hold of my hand out of her own free will and links our fingers. "I'm sure. We still have to cut the cake, and I'd like to dance with my husband again."

She's so fucking calm it's starting to worry me.

ELENA

Seeing the concern on Lucian's face, I step closer to him. I place my free hand on his chest and smile up at him.

"I'm okay, Lucian. I feel nothing but relief."

The concern still doesn't fade from his eyes. Moving my hand up to his jaw, I stare deep into his eyes. "I'm okay."

He covers my hand with his own and presses a kiss to my palm.

"Take me back to our wedding reception," I say.

Lucian nods, but still, he doesn't move.

"What?" I ask.

"I need a moment to calm down," he admits.

I pull my hand free from his and wrapping my arms around his waist, I press my right cheek to his chest. He instantly envelops me in a hug and buries his face in my hair.

We just hold each other for a couple of minutes, and then Lucian moves and presses a kiss beneath my ear. "Do you trust me now?"

Do I?

Lucian saved me from Dante while we were at St. Monarch's.

He came for me while his own life was in danger to make sure I was safe.

He stopped the arranged marriage between Dante and me and married me instead.

I lift my eyes to his.

He'll tear the world apart if I'm hurt. He proved that to me tonight when he killed Dante.

Lucian will protect me.

Like he's done from the moment we met.

"I trust you," the words flow over my lips.

Lucian might be a bad man, the villain in someone's eyes, but to me, he's the hero. He's not a monster like I first thought but my guardian angel.

He's cruel and unforgiving toward his enemies, but to me, he's comfort and safety.

My breathing speeds up as a blissful feeling warms my heart. "I trust you, Lucian."

The corner of his mouth lifts into a hot smirk, and then he closes the distance between us. He lowers his head, and when his breath fans over my lips, they part for him.

The kiss is tender, and then his tongue brushes against my bottom lip, making heat flood my abdomen.

Kissing Lucian is like drowning, only you don't want to come up for air. I fill my lungs with his aftershave. I move my arms up, wrapping them around the back of his neck, and my fingers get lost in his hair.

His tongue finds mine, and together they taste, they explore, they memorize the feel of each other.

My stomach flutters, a kaleidoscope of butterflies taking flight as I fall hard and fast for this man who's now my husband.

I fall in love for the first time in my life because it's safe. It's finally safe to open my heart – to the man who many have tried, but failed, to kill.

It's as if Lucian is guarded by death itself, and he probably is with Alexei having his back.

Lucian ends the kiss, tenderly nipping at my lips, and when I open my eyes, all I see is affection reflecting from his gaze.

The nervousness returns, but this time it's different. There's no fear, only anticipation. It's inexperienced and shy, making my cheeks warm.

My heart skips a beat at how handsome he is. He's all man, cloaked in fierce strength, determination, and dominance.

Lucian brushes his fingers over my bruised cheek. "If you keep looking at me like that, we're not going to make it out of this room," he warns me.

A smile splits over my face, heat spreading up my neck. "We've left our guests alone long enough."

Wanting to savor falling in love with him for a bit longer before we have to consummate the marriage, I walk to the door.

Lucian captures my hips with his hands before I step out of the room, and pressing his chest to my back, he says, "I'll be patient until you're ready. I don't want you to worry about tonight, amore mio."

My love.

My lips curve higher at hearing the term of endearment that's much better than little bird.

"Thank you," I whisper. "I just need a little time to get used to us as a couple."

"I understand." He gives my hips a squeeze and then nudges me forward.

When we step out onto the veranda, Aunt Ursula rushes to me. "There's the lovely bride. Come, let's get you a glass of champagne."

She takes hold of my hand, and as I'm pulled away from Lucian, I glance over my shoulder at him. He smiles at us, and then he rolls up his sleeves as he walks to a group of men.

Aunt Ursula takes two flutes from a server's platter and hands me one. "Drink, cara. You need it."

I take a sip, and not wanting her to worry about me, I say, "I'm okay."

She reaches a hand to my hair and brushes it away so she can see the left side of my face. "Tsk…"

I smile as she arranges the curls to cover the bruise again. "It will fade," I try to reassure her.

We're joined by three other women, and as the conversation turns to the latest fashion, I glance at Lucian.

The moment my eyes land on him, warmth spreads through me. I admire his broad shoulders and his strong arms.

I take a sip of the champagne to cool my insides, but then our eyes meet, and the corner of his mouth lifts.

My heart beats a little faster, and my lips curve up into a shy smile.

That's your husband, Elena.

My smile widens, and happiness courses through me.

Chapter 21

ELENA

It's almost three in the morning when the last of the guests leave, and while Lucian locks up and turns off the lights, I head up to my room.

Opening the door, I step inside and glance at the bathroom. The floor's been cleaned, and there's no sign of the struggle that took place earlier.

I walk to my closet, and when I open it and see it's empty, I pause.

"Everything's been moved to our room," Lucian says behind me. When I turn to him, he holds his hand out to me. "Come, let's get some sleep."

I walk to him and place my hand in his. He leads me back to the room we were in earlier, and once we're inside, he shuts the door.

"Your clothes are on the left side of the closet," he informs me, and then he begins to unbutton his shirt as he walks to the bathroom. "You want to shower?" he calls out as he turns on the faucets.

Nerves spin in my stomach. "Ahh… no, you can go first."

Lucian comes out of the bathroom… shirtless. My eyes instantly drop to his chest and the eight pack that looks like it's been carved from stone.

Damn.

I tilt my head as my eyes drink in the sight of the muscles disappearing into his suit pants.

"You're making it really hard right now," Lucian says, his voice low.

My gaze darts to his face, then to the closet. "Sorry. It's just… you look really good."

He lets out a chuckle then goes to take a pair of sweatpants from the closet. "I feel good too," he teases me.

I press my lips together, trying to hide the smile I can't stop from forming.

With a chuckle, Lucian walks back to the bathroom.

I move the closet, and opening it, I remove a pair of shorts and a t-shirt for myself. Then I stare at my underwear.

Should I wear a bra to bed?

I take a pair of panties and decide against the bra, wanting to be comfortable while sleeping.

I sit down on the bed and glance around the room while waiting for Lucian to finish showering.

Then the thought hits.

Lucian's naked in there.

My lips curve up at the thought, and I even find myself leaning a little to the side, but not able to see anything, I straighten up again.

Minutes later, he comes out, dressed only in a pair of sweatpants. His hair is wet, and there are still some drops on his shoulders and chest. "The shower's yours."

I get up, and as I walk past Lucian, his fresh scent carries to me.

God, he smells good.

I find all my toiletries in the bathroom. I tie my hair in a ponytail and brush my teeth. There's no door to close between the bedroom and bathroom, and it makes me a little nervous as I strip out of my clothes.

I turn on the faucets and step into the spray. Closing my eyes, I relax under the warm water.

While I wash my body, I think about the day. Everything was beautiful, and the wedding cake was delicious. Dante dying was the highlight of my day, though.

I don't care if it makes me a bad person for being glad he's dead.

Now I can bury him along with all the traumatic memories he left me with.

I rinse the suds from my skin, and closing the faucets, I step out of the shower and quickly dry myself. I get dressed then glance at the archway between the rooms.

This is it. Our first night sleeping in the same bed.

I take a deep breath to steel myself and walk out of the bathroom. Lucian's nowhere to be found, and I begin to frown, but then he comes back into the room with a glass of water. His eyes drift over me, and after he places the glass on the bedside table, he says, "In case you get thirsty."

It's on the right side of the bed. "Thank you. You're taking the left side?" I ask to be sure.

He pulls the covers back. "Yes, so I'm closest to the door."

My heart melts.

I walk around the bed, and I feel a little awkward as I climb under the covers.

Lucian turns off the lights, and then I feel the mattress dip as he sits down.

With my eyes not used to the darkness yet, all my other senses sharpen. My body becomes aware of Lucian's as he lies down, and then his arm wraps around my lower back, and he pulls me right against him.

My skin tingles everywhere we touch. The air is filled with his scent. My hands are stuck between my chest and his rock-solid one.

"Wrap your arm around me," he murmurs.

I do as he says, and splaying my fingers over his back, my palm takes in the feel of him. My lips curve up, and turning my head, I rest my cheek against his warm skin. I close my eyes, thinking I'll fall asleep quickly, but being highly conscious of Lucian, I lay awake.

Lucian begins to rub his hand up and down the length of my back, then he whispers, "Relax, amore mio."

"I am." I hesitate for a moment but then admit, "It's hard to fall asleep."

"Why?"

I lift my head to glance up at Lucian, but I can only make out his profile. "It's the first time I'm sleeping with someone." My eyes widen, and I quickly correct myself, "I mean… in the same bed. Just sleeping."

He's quiet for a while, then he asks, "Are you a virgin?"

I squeeze my eyes shut, and my face reddens. "No."

"Alfonso?" he asks.

"Yes."

Lucian moves his hand up and wraps his fingers around the back of my neck. "Sleep, amore mio. You're safe with me."

I rest my cheek against his chest again, and listening to the strong rhythm of his heartbeat, I'm eventually lulled into a peaceful slumber.

LUCIAN

Two weeks have passed since our wedding day. It's been a challenge, to say the least.

Every night I hold Elena, it takes all my willpower to hold back. I have to see her dressed in those cotton shorts which frame her ass perfectly, and the t-shirt does nothing to hide her nipples when she's not wearing a bra.

Her laughter fills the house. Her soft scent is everywhere.

My wife is happy, and all I want to do is fuck her.

I gave Elena a credit card, and with my aunt's help, she's getting comfortable using it. Every time I'm notified of a payment on my phone, it draws a smile from me.

It's mostly food and necessities, though. Elena hasn't bought anything for herself yet.

Dressed in my usual three-piece suit, I take the steps down and head to the veranda where the women are enjoying coffee.

The moment Elena notices me, she jumps up and rushes to pour me a cup of coffee.

I change direction to the kitchen, and coming up behind Elena, I place my hands on her hips and press my chest to her back. I rest my chin on her shoulder. "Thank you, amore mio."

"You're welcome," she replies happily while stirring some cream into the cup.

"I need you to do something today," I say as I take a step back so she can turn around. I accept the cup from her and enjoy a sip of the beverage.

"Sure. What?"

My eyes capture hers. "Buy something for yourself." Making sure she understands me, I add, "Clothes, perfume, jewelry, anything you like."

"Okay," she whispers, looking a little uncomfortable.

I set the cup down on the counter and place my hands on her hips again. I tug her closer to me, and she has to tilt her head further back to look at me.

"Let me take care of you." I lean down and press a kiss to her lips. "It's important to me."

Elena lifts her arms and wraps them around my neck. "You are taking care of me."

I take a deep breath. "Actually, redo your entire closet. Get rid of the clothes Tino paid for. I don't want them in my house."

Elena nods. "Okay."

I press another kiss to her lips and linger, wanting to savor her for a moment before I have to head out. When I lift my head, my eyes caress every inch of her beautiful face.

It's been six weeks since she walked into my life, and I fell irrevocably in love with her. My obsession with her has only grown.

I've become more possessive, especially of my time with her. When I get home, Elena knows to have everything done because I want all her attention.

"Ti amo," I tell her I love her before I can stop myself.

Elena's eyes dart over my face, her lips parting.

I know I moved much faster than her, and she's not ready to return the words

"Don't say it back. I just wanted you to know." I press a last kiss to her lips, then let go of her. I go to my aunt and kiss her forehead. Walking to the front door, I call to Elena, "Use the card. I expect to see a lot of notifications on my phone."

Elena lets out a burst of laughter. "I'll drive you crazy and make you think of me every ten minutes."

I give her a smile, and then it grows even more when Leo comes in. "My friend." I hold my arms open and hug him. "Welcome back." Placing my hands on his shoulders, I ask, "How do you feel?"

"Ready to work, Sir," he says. "Thank you for taking care of my family while I was in the hospital."

I had them stay in one of my hotels with protection, so nothing happened to Leo's wife and two children while he wasn't there to protect them. I also gave him one hell of a bonus and some time off for the bullet he took for Elena.

"Of course."

"Leo," Elena says, and then she hugs her personal guard. "I'm so glad to see you."

Leo looks a little awkward as he hugs her with one arm.

Elena pulls back. "I'm sorry you got shot because of me."

"It's my job, Mrs. Cotroni."

I pat his arm. "I'll leave Elena in your capable hands. It's good to have you back."

I step out of the house. Franco and Matteo flank me as we head to the car.

We spend the morning checking and dispatching a big shipment of Heckler and Koch MP5K submachine guns. I let Matteo take care of the delivery, knowing he won't fuck it up.

Every time my phone beeps with a notification from the bank, it puts a smile on my face.

When it's almost time for lunch, I call Elena's number.

"Hi," she answers cheerfully.

"Hi. Missing me?"

"Every second," she answers.

"Where are you? I want to join you and Zia Ursula for lunch." Elena checks with my aunt, then gives me a name of a restaurant. "I'll meet you there in fifteen minutes."

"Time to eat, Fanco," I say as I head to the car. Getting in, I give him the destination then relax against the seat.

During the drive, my phone rings, and seeing Alexei's name, I answer, "You're alive."

"Of course," he chuckles.

"Where are you?"

"Spain." He sounds disgruntled. "No one is talking."

"Fuck," I mutter. We're not winning. Every lead we find is a dead end. "Come back. I don't want you wasting your time."

"I'll see you tomorrow," he assures me.

We end the call, and minutes later, Franco finds parking near the restaurant.

Walking into the establishment, my eyes scan over the tables. Seeing Elena and my aunt sitting near the window, I walk toward them.

Elena glances in my direction, and then a smile spreads over her face. She gets up as I near the table, and then glass shatters.

Screams erupt.

Franco grabs hold of me, and my body swings to the side as a bullet hits me.

Elena's scream is sharp in my ears as Franco takes my weight, lowering me to the floor.

"Elena. My aunt," I snap at him, pressing my hand to the side where it's stinging like a motherfucker.

Franco throws one of the tables on its side to use as cover, and then Elena drops next to me on her knees with my Aunt and Leo right behind her.

Elena's face is pale, and she takes one look at the blood seeping through my fingers, then she pushes her hand behind me and grabs my gun.

I watch as my wife's face tightens with anger and worry, and then she yells at Franco, "You better keep him alive. If my husband dies, you die."

She pulls Aunt Ursula further behind the table. "Put your hand on the wound. We need to stop the bleeding." Elena grabs a table cloth and rolls it up. "Use this."

Aunt Ursula does as she's ordered, and pulling my hand away from the bullet wound, she applies pressure.

"I'm –" I begin to say, but Elena hushes me.

"We'll get out of here," she assures me, her features softening for a moment as she looks at me. "Just keep still. Okay?"

Even though we're under attack, I have to admit I love seeing my wife take charge. It's a potent turn-on.

I admire her for a second longer, then I say, "I'm okay. It's not deep." I take the gun from her and turn my attention to Franco and Leo. "What do you see?"

"Nothing. It could've come from anywhere," Franco replies.

Fuck. We're sitting ducks.

Chapter 22

ELENA

I take over from Aunt Ursula, and lifting the cloth away from the wound, I check it.

"I'm okay, amore mio," Lucian says.

Seeing blood seeping from his side chills my bones.

Stay calm, Elena. Stay calm.

I press the cloth hard to his side, then lift my eyes to his.

God, let us get out of here alive.

Lifting my free hand, I place it against his jaw, and just in case things go horribly wrong, I lean into him and press a kiss to his mouth. "Ti amo."

Sitting between shards of glass with only a table as cover, I say the words 'I love you' for the first time in my life.

Lucian's eyes darken to midnight. He grabs hold of the back of my head, and he yanks me back to him, giving me a hard kiss. Then just as fast, he lets go of me and moves into a crouching position. He throws the bloody cloth to the side and barks an order at Franco. "Get men to search every fucking building from where the shot could've been taken. I don't plan on sitting here the whole fucking day."

Then he turns his intense gaze to Leo, Aunt Ursula, and me. "Crawl to the back of the restaurant. I want the women away from the window," he instructs Leo.

When I look at Aunt Ursula and see she's visibly shaken, I nudge her to move. "Come. You go first. I'm right behind you."

"Dio. Dio. Dio," Aunt Ursula chants as she crawls ahead of me while Leo secures our backs.

"We're going to be okay," I try to reassure her. We take cover behind a counter where two waiters are hiding, and I pull Aunt Ursula into my arms. "Lucian will get us out of here."

Holding Aunt Ursula tightly, I glance around the corner of the counter, my insides twisted with worry for Lucian.

"Move back, Mrs. Cotroni," Leo orders, and then he guards us as we wait.

Soon I hear sirens in the distance and send a prayer of thanks up.

Seconds later, there's police everywhere. The surrounding area is secured, but we keep sitting behind the counter until Lucian comes to us.

"It's safe to leave," he says, but still, his eyes keep scanning the front of the restaurant, on high alert.

I help Aunt Ursula up, and then she signs the cross, whispering a prayer of thanks.

Lucian ushers us out of the restaurant to where Franco has parked the car right in front of the entrance. Only once we're safely inside the armored vehicle do I manage to take a full breath.

My hands begin to tremble, and to keep my mind from wandering to the worst that could've happened, I focus my attention on checking Lucian's wound.

My heart shrinks at the sight, and I'm instantly drowned in worry. "We need to get you to a hospital," I say when I see how his button-up shirt has been stained with blood.

"I'm fine, amore mio," Lucian says, his voice deceptively calm. My eyes snap up to his, and I see the anger brewing in his dark brown irises.

I could've lost Lucian today.

If that bullet had hit higher.

If Franco didn't pull him back.

Lucian takes hold of my left hand, and his thumb brushes over the ring on my finger. "I'm here. I'm fine. Don't worry."

I slump back against the seat and close my eyes against the unbearable pain the mere thought of losing Lucian brings.

I've been wrapped up in a happy bubble, enjoying my life for the first time.

I forgot.

I forgot Lucian's the head of the Mafia.

I forgot there are people out there who want him dead.

Every day Aunt Ursula taught me how to cook. While we went shopping. While we relaxed in the garden, learning to get to know each other.

Every day I lived in blissful peace – Lucian put his life on the line.

And I forgot.

When he held me at night. When he kissed me. Even when he told me he loved me this morning.

I forgot it could be the last time I see him. The last time I feel his arms around me. The last time I have his strength keeping me safe.

Tears flood my eyes, but I swallow them down.

Never again.

I'll treasure every second I have with him from this day forward.

When we get home, we're all quiet, processing the shock of the attack. Leo goes to check every room while Lucian walks to the side table and pours himself a drink. I watch as he downs it, and then he fills the glass again.

"Let me look at the wound," I say. Taking hold of his arm, I tug him to the couch and push him down on it.

Lucian rests the tumbler on his knee, slowly twirling it with his right hand while I push his shirt up. Needing the fabric out of the way, I say, "Take off your jacket."

He sets the glass down on the table and shrugs out of the jacket. I unbutton the shirt and push it over his shoulders, helping him out of the ruined fabric.

Aunt Ursula brings a first aid kit and sets it down on the coffee table.

Opening the kit, I remove what I'll need, and while I clean the wound, Lucian doesn't make a sound. He just stares ahead of him, murder in his eyes.

Franco comes to stand by us. "Is the bullet still in? Do you need stitches?"

My head snaps up to him. "Do you know how?"

Franco nods and gestures for me to move aside. I take a seat on Lucian's right and grab hold of his hand.

I watch as Franco takes tweezers from the kit along with what he'll need for the stitches, then I say, "Wait. He needs something for the pain."

"I'm fine, just stitch me up," Lucian growls.

Aunt Ursula turns away and walks to the kitchen. Franco makes sure the bullet isn't stuck inside, and when he pushes a needle through Lucian's skin, the sight makes my stomach churn.

Lucian's grip tightens on my hand, then he grinds out, "Give me the drink."

I quickly reach for it and hand him the tumbler. He downs the amber liquid, then throws the glass. It shatters against the wall, and my breaths instantly speed up.

With a racing heart, I sit frozen as Lucian takes his phone from his pocket. He dials a number, and a moment later, he growls, "She just tried to fucking kill me." Lucian grimaces as Franco pushes the needle in again.

Oh, God.

It all becomes real. It sinks in hard. It robs me of my breath.

"We need to find her and end this," Lucian snaps.

Not wanting to upset Lucian any more than he already is, I get up and walk away, knowing Franco will take care of the wound.

I rush up the stairs and into our room, and then I place my hand over my heart that feels like it's been torn in two.

I love him.

I love Lucian Cotroni, and the thought that he can die rips through me. Maybe not today, but one day I could lose Lucian in the blink of an eye.

Tears spill down my cheeks, and for the first time, I cry not because I've been hurt but because I fear losing the man that's shown me what it is to be loved.

LUCIAN

When Franco's done stitching me up, our eyes meet. "Thanks."

He nods, then says, "I'm going to go see if I can find any footage of the shooter."

"Take men with you. Be careful." I can't afford to lose my best man. He proved himself to me today.

Rising to my feet, I walk to where my aunt is cleaning the mess I made. "Sorry," I apologize.

She shakes her head, and when she climbs to her feet, I take hold of her arm. "Zia Ursula." Her eyes lift to mine, and then they flood with tears. I pull her against my chest. "I'm fine."

"This life… it will take you from me too," she sobs.

"Not soon," I try to offer her comfort. "Shh…"

She pulls away, then says, "I'll prepare something to eat."

That's how my aunt deals, she starts making enough food for an army. Leaving her, I go look for Elena.

When I get to our bedroom, I nod at Leo, where he's taken position right outside the door. "Take a break."

"Yes, Sir."

Walking into our room, I come to a sudden halt. Elena's busy pulling leggings on, and for a second, I get a good look at her perfect ass, covered in only lace.

Christ.

My eyes sweep up her back, and when I shut the door, she glances over her shoulder as she reaches into the closet for an oversized shirt.

Up until now, she's avoided getting dressed in front of me, and instead of pulling the shirt on as quickly as she can, she drops the fabric and rushes to me.

She throws her arms around my neck, and I almost let out a growl from only feeling her lace bra between us, her breasts pressing against my chest.

I'm tempted to within an inch of my sanity to throw her on the bed and fuck the anger and stress away. Instead, I wrap my arms tightly around her and savor the feel of her bare skin.

She lifts her head, and when our eyes lock, everything fades.

The attempt on my life.

The enemies at my door.

All I see is the love shining from her eyes. The fear for my life. The feverish heartbreak of almost losing me.

Lifting my hands, I frame her face. "Amore mio," I whisper, happy she's learned to love me but angry as fuck she had to witness a hit on my life. I wanted to spare her from that part of our lives.

"I was so scared," she whispers. "I can't lose you."

My eyes caress hers. "You won't lose me."

When she pulls back, she lowers her hand to the bandage on my side, the sight of it seeming to cause her pain. Probably more than I'm feeling.

"I'm okay," I say once again.

She shakes her head. "Sei la miglior cosa che mi sia capitata," she whispers. "Sei il mio tutto."

You're the best thing that happened to me. You're my everything.

The words settle deep in my heart. They burrow into my soul.

Taking hold of her chin, I lift her face to mine, and then I fuse my mouth with hers.

I kiss her with all the pent-up hunger that's been building since I laid eyes on her. My tongue thrusts against Elena's, showing her what I plan on doing to her tonight.

I'm done waiting.

She loves me.

I love her.

I'm not waiting a day longer to claim all of her.

If I could have my way, I'd fuck her right now, but I can't leave my aunt alone while she's in such a state.

I break the kiss and let go of Elena before I change my mind. "I'm taking the rest of the day off. Let's go relax in the living room." Because if we stay up here, I'm going to lose the little control I have.

I walk to the closet and pull a pair of sweatpants and a t-shirt out. As Elena picks up her shirt, I unbuckle my belt and step out of my shoes. Her eyes dart to me, and then she pulls the fabric over her head as I push the pants down my legs.

My eyes stay glued to her, and as soon as her head pops through the neck of the shirt, she glances at me.

There's no awkwardness on her face when she sees me standing, clothed only in a pair of boxers. She looks comfortable, and it puts me at ease.

I step into the sweatpants and pull on my t-shirt. The second I'm done, Elena takes my hand and links our fingers. She pushes up on her tiptoes and presses a kiss to my jaw.

The moment feels intimate between us, as if we've finally moved to the next phase of our relationship.

I tug her closer to me, and lifting my right hand to her cheek, I lean down and capture her mouth. The kiss is tender and slow, filled with our newfound love.

When I begin to pull away, Elena follows, and then she deepens the kiss. I let go of her hand, and clasping the back of her head, I tilt her to give me better access to her mouth.

She lets out a moan, and I instantly harden, the kiss going from loving to filthy in a split second.

My control slips, and grabbing hold of her ass, I lift her against my body. Elena wraps her legs around me, and I push her against the closet door. There's a stab of pain in my side, but I ignore it the moment I feel Elena's heat warming my cock. My tongue lashes at hers, and I thrust hard, my cock wanting to tear through the clothes between us.

Time fades. My stress eases off my shoulders. My anger retreats.

There's only Elena. Us kissing, exploring, and devouring each other's mouths.

My hips keep moving, searching for any friction I can find, and the temptation of the heat between her legs drives me wild.

I slip my hand under her shirt, and then my fingers feast on her soft skin. I explore the curve of her waist, her ribs, and then the lace covering her breast.

Wanting to see her face, I break the kiss. Breathless and with swollen lips, our eyes lock. I move the lace out of my way, and my palm takes the weight of her breast. My thumb brushes over her nipple, hunger ripping a growl from me as her lips part on a gasp from my touch.

"Christ, Elena."

I've never wanted anything so badly. I need to be buried deep inside her heat. I have to claim her.

Chapter 23

ELENA

There are none of the nerves I felt on our wedding day. Not after today. Not after almost losing Lucian.

Hunger. Unadulterated lust. Love. It's all I see on Lucian's face.

There's no cruelty. No depravity. No hatred.

My mind is clouded with my desire for Lucian. His kisses have left me feeling lightheaded, breathless, and filled with need for more of him. His touch sets my skin alight, making tingles spread through my body. My abdomen aches at the feel of his erection rubbing against me.

God. God. God.

I've never experienced something so all-consuming.

"Lucian, your phone keeps ringing," Aunt Ursula calls from outside the room, and it shatters the intimate moment.

Still, Lucian doesn't let go of me. "I'll be out in a couple of minutes. Let it go to voicemail," he calls back.

The corner of his mouth lifts as he stares at me, his desire not diminishing at all from the interruption.

Again his thumb brushes over my nipple, making my abdomen tighten with a sweet ache.

The things he makes me feel – it's indescribable. I'm intoxicated and greedy for more.

Another brush of his thumb and my back arches, pressing my breast harder into his palm and stealing a moan from me.

"Fuck." Lucian steps back.

My feet drop to the floor, and I have to lean against the closet because there's no strength in my legs.

"You need to leave, or I'm going to fuck you right now," he says, his voice low and rough with the passion we just shared.

"Give me a second. My legs are numb," I reply, still breathless from his touch and kisses.

"Christ." He fists his hands, his eyes boring into mine.

It looks like he's going to lose control any second, and then my eyes lower to his erection, tenting the fabric of his sweatpants.

Holy mother.

"Go, Elena. Now," he grinds out through clenched teeth.

Rushing out of the room, I straighten my bra, shirt, and hair. At the top of the stairs, I pause to breathe through the desire I still feel.

My God, that was intense.

And it was only foreplay.

What's it going to be like making love to Lucian?

I place a hand on my flushed cheek, trying to cool my skin.

Then my lips curve up because instead of fearing the moment we have sex, the thought only fills me with anticipation.

I take the stairs down and walk to the kitchen. Aunt Ursula glances at me, her hands not stopping from kneading the dough. "Is Lucian okay?"

I nod. "Yes, he just needed a moment." I stop next to her. "What can I do?"

"You can beat the eggs. We need two."

I get them from the fridge and crack them open in a bowl. Movement from the stairs catches my eye, and I watch as Lucian walks to the living room. He looks calm and collected as if he didn't just set my body on fire.

My hands move automatically, unable to tear my eyes away from Lucian as he drops down on the couch, checking his messages.

I begin to beat the eggs, my attention not at all on what I'm doing.

I remember the first time I saw Lucian. The dark expression on his face as he adjusted his cuffs. When he demanded to know what I was doing at St. Monarch's. The shooting lesson.

My eyes rake over Lucian's attractive face, the scruff on his jaw, his broad shoulders, the veins snaking down his arms. His hands.

God, his hands felt so good on my body.

I draw my bottom lip between my teeth as our first kiss flashes through my mind. Him coming for me when he was attacked. When he climbed out of the car, and I witnessed him killing for the first time. The night I shared my darkest secret with him. The promise he made and kept.

Has it only been six weeks?

It feels longer.

Lucian glances at me as he presses dial on his phone, then he places the device against his ear. Our eyes lock, and there's instant desire sparking between us.

"Dio! You've overbeaten the eggs," Aunt Ursula exclaims. "They're going to make clumps."

"Oh, sorry," I say, looking down at the mess I've made. "I'll start over." I get two new eggs and discard the overbeaten ones.

"Don't worry, cara." Aunt Ursula takes the bowl from me. "Go sit with Lucian. I can see your mind is elsewhere."

My cheeks heat, but I take the out she's giving me from cooking and walk to the living room. When I sit down next to Lucian, he picks up my left hand and presses a kiss to the ring on my finger.

"Don't worry. Come back," I hear him say, still on the call.

I snuggle up to his side and lean my head against his shoulder, our fingers linking. Closing my eyes, I listen to Lucian making one call after the other until my eyes drift shut.

LUCIAN

When I'm done with all the calls, I realize Elena's asleep against my side.

I set the phone down on the arm of the chair and then carefully move her until her head rests on my lap. My fingers brush over the silky strands of her hair as I stare down at my beautiful wife.

The air fills with the delicious aroma of my aunt's cooking as my thoughts turn to the attack.

I almost died the same way as my father.

I keep telling Elena and my aunt I'm okay, but I'm not. I'm fucking angry and desperate for revenge.

Umbria.

I'm going to fucking find you.

Elena stirs, and then her eyes flutter open. She turns onto her back and blinks up at me.

"Nice nap?" I ask, my tone giving away none of my feelings.

She nods then sits up. "Are you done with the calls?" she asks.

I nod, frustrated there isn't more I can do to find Umbria.

Unable to sit still, I ask, "Want to go for a walk with me?"

"Sure."

Rising to my feet, I take hold of Elena's hand and walk to the sliding doors. I push it open, and as we step out onto the veranda, I lock my fingers with hers.

"Clear the area," I say to Franco. "I want privacy."

"Yes, sir," Franco replies, and then he orders the men to withdraw out of the backyard.

We stroll in silence toward the fountain, the sound of the falling water comforting.

A soft smile forms around Elena's lips, then she murmurs, "You were the answer to my prayer."

I know she's referring to the night I overheard her begging for mercy from a statue.

I give her hand a squeeze, and then she glances up at me. "So much has changed."

"Yes, but you still can't shoot for shit. We need to start with lessons again." Just in case. If I take another hit with Elena nearby, I need to know she can handle a gun.

"We can start whenever you have time," she says.

We keep walking until we reach the cliff. Elena lets out a sigh, her lips curved with a contented smile.

I pull her into my arms and looking down at her, I ask, "Are you happy, amore mio?"

Without hesitation, she nods. "Except for the incident. I hate the thought of you being in danger."

"It's the life we've been born into."

She pulls a disgruntled face. "It doesn't mean I have to like it."

"Of course not." I lean down and press a quick kiss to her lips. "But, I have to admit I loved seeing you take charge. You also won't hear me complain about the attention I got."

My words make her grin. "You don't need to get shot. I'll give you attention whenever you want."

"Yeah?" I lean down as she nods, and I press my mouth to hers. I tug at her lips, my tongue only touching hers for a moment before I pull back enough to capture her eyes. "What kind of attention are we talking about?" I murmur. I draw her bottom lip between my teeth then soothe it with my tongue.

"Any kind," Elena breathes against my mouth.

"Be specific," I demand while I move my hands to her ribs. My fingers curl into her, and I drink in the feel of how petite she feels under my touch.

Elena's eyelashes lower, a dreamy expression on her face that makes me hard as fuck.

"I'll kiss your bruises," she says, and pushing up on her toes, her lips skim over my jaw, moving to my ear. When her teeth tug at my earlobe, I let out a growl, brimming with desire.

My hands move up, and I capture her breasts in a biting hold, unable to be gentle. My thumbs rub her nipples into tight peaks.

"And?" I ask, my voice hoarse with want.

Elena tugs at my earlobe again, then her breath fans over my skin. "I'll massage the stress from your muscles."

My lips curve up as I lower my mouth to her neck. I suck on her skin. "I like the sound of that." My left hand slides down her curves, and when I palm her between the legs, I ask, "Like this?"

Lifting my head, I rub Elena softly while watching her face closely.

Her lips part, her cheeks flush, and then she nods. "Yes. Like that."

My eyes are locked on hers as I move my hand up, and pulling the waistband back, I push my hand under the fabric. As my fingers brush over Elena's soft curls, I place my other hand behind her head.

I spread her open, and a growl ripples from me as I touch her clit. Her hands fall to my chest, and she grabs hold of my shirt, fisting it tightly. Her eyes clouded with desire. Her lips parted and begging for my tongue

"I'm going to fuck you tonight." The words rumble from my chest as I increase the pressure on her clit, rubbing her hard. I tug at her lips with my teeth. "I'm going to bury myself deep inside you." She moans against my mouth, her grip on me tightening, her hips beginning to match my rhythm.

We're lost in our own bubble of desire, standing on the cliff, with only the Mediterranean Sea and nature as witnesses to the moment when I make my wife orgasm.

"Lucian," she gasps, her features tightening with need.

I tease Elena's opening, and it makes her lift on her tiptoes. She presses her face against my neck, her fingers gripping my shirt to the point I think she might tear it right from my body. "Dio." Her breaths become sharp, and then I push my finger inside her, savoring how fucking tight she feels.

My cock strains. I fucking ache. Torture has never been this sweet as Elena trembles in my hold. Her body stiffens, and then her gasps and moans create a symphony I'll never forget as she comes apart.

Her mouth finds mine, and I inhale her breaths and taste her moans. I greedily devour every single one as she rides out her orgasm.

Chapter 24

ELENA

I'm unable to think.

Unable to speak.

My body's been possessed by Lucian. My insides quiver as I'm overcome with pleasure, unlike anything I've ever experienced.

I gasp, moans the only sound I can make while he touches me like I've never been touched before.

I experience a level of intimacy with Lucian I haven't had before.

"Beautiful," he murmurs into my mouth. "So goddamn beautiful."

There's no shame. There's no guilt.

I feel beautiful in his arms. Treasured. Loved.

I come down from the heavens he took me to. Lucian pulls his hand away, and then he sucks my release from his finger, making residual tingles of pleasure ripple through me. Framing my face, his mouth adores mine, causing emotion to burst in my chest.

I find my worth in his love.

Lucian senses the emotions crashing over me, and he pulls back to lock his gaze with mine.

I see the woman I am in his eyes.

I now understand how two souls can become one because without me having to say anything, Lucian wipes the tears from my cheeks. "My love for you runs deeper than the bottomless pits of hell because that's how far I will go to find you if you're ever taken from me." He kisses me tenderly. "Do you understand what you mean to me? How precious you are, amore mio?"

I nod, bathing in his words, reveling in his love. "Angelo mio," I whisper because that's what Lucian is to me – my angel.

Our mouths meet again, and we kiss for what feels like hours. A breeze from the ocean plays around us. The crashing waves against the rocks below are the only sounds we hear.

Until Aunt Ursula calls, "Where are you? It's time to eat!"

Lucian releases me with a chuckle. "Coming," he shouts so she'll hear him, then he shakes his head at me. "You bewitch me, my wife."

"I think it's the other way around," I laugh as we walk back toward the house. He wraps his arm around my shoulder, drawing me to his side. "Careful of your wound," I say as I try to pull back.

"I'm fine," Lucian mutters, tugging me back to him.

"I don't want to hurt you," I argue.

"Stubborn woman," he playfully grumbles as we take the steps up to the veranda.

"You made me this way," I tease him.

"Mmh… seems I'm doing a good job."

"You are." We glance at each other as we walk into the living room, and then Lucian pulls me closer for one last kiss before he leaves me so he can go to the guest restroom.

I join Aunt Ursula in the kitchen and glance over the feast she's prepared. Pasta with mussels and cream. Bruschetta. Antipasti chopped salad, the salami making my mouth water.

"Wow, it looks delicious," I praise her.

"Today, we celebrate life," she says, seemingly back to her usual high-spirited demeanor.

I help her carry the food to the dining room, and when we're ready to eat, Lucian comes to take a seat at the head of the table. He holds our hands and says a prayer of thanks, and then I pick up his plate and load it with food.

When I set it down in front of him, he murmurs, "Thank you, Amore mio." Then he reaches for Aunt Ursula's hand and gives her hand a squeeze, teasing her, "I should upset you more so you can cook like this every day."

She gives him a disgruntled look. "Don't you dare. My heart won't last."

We enjoy the meal and watching Lucian savor every bite sets me at ease. At least he has a healthy appetite.

Then it strikes me how calm he looks, like every other day he comes home from work, and it makes me wonder if there have been any bad days he hasn't shared with us.

The thought doesn't sit well with me.

Not at all.

He glances at me and smiles as if he wasn't shot earlier. His eyes begin to narrow on me. "What?"

"You'll tell us if you have a bad day, right?" I ask, spearing a piece of salami.

He sets down his knife and reaches for my face, tucking a strand of hair behind my ear. "No. I won't bring my work home. It has nothing to do with you."

A frown instantly forms on my forehead. "Yet, you expect me to spend the money you bring home?"

"Yes. It's the way things are, amore mio."

My temper flares. "I refuse to wear clothes bathed in your blood."

"Well," he lifts an eyebrow at me, a look of warning tightening his features, "then you'll just have to walk around naked."

"Dio," Aunt Ursula mumbles under her breath.

Just then, Alexei walks into the dining room. Lucian gets up, mutters an excuse, and then he follows Alexei out of the room.

I slump back in my chair, shaking my head.

"It's the way things are done, cara," Aunt Ursula says.

"I'm going to die of worry," I say. "Every second, I'll worry whether he's okay."

"It's the price we pay for love." My eyes dart to Aunt Ursula's.

It's the price I'll pay for falling in love with the head of the Mafia.

I know it won't help to fight Lucian on this matter, but still, I'm not happy with it. I let out a sigh and pick up my fork again and begin to eat.

Lucian comes back into the dining room, dressed in a fresh suit. He places his hand on the back of my neck, and bending over me, he presses a quick kiss to my mouth.

"I'm going out. I'll be back later."

My lips part as he goes to kiss Aunt Ursula on the forehead.

"But you said you're taking the rest of the day off," I finally say.

His eyes lock on mine, his expression grim. "Something came up."

Not knowing if he's angry with me or something else, I ask, "Is everything okay?"

"Of course, amore mio."

I watch him walk out and jumping up, I call, "Wait."

Lucian stops, and as he turns around, I slam into him, wrapping my arms around his waist. "Please be careful."

His arms engulf me. "I will. Don't worry."

I lift my face to his. "Ti amo."

Instantly a smile forms, and it chases some of the tightness from his features. "Ti amo," he repeats and gives me another chaste kiss.

He pulls free from me, and I try to memorize the sight of his confident posture as he walks out of the house with Alexei.

Please bring him back to me.

LUCIAN

Sitting in the back of the G Wagon, I put on a bulletproof vest.

Alexei watches me, worry in his eyes, which I'm not used to seeing, then he asks, "You sure about this?"

"Yes," I mutter, even though I'm not sure at all. "Just make sure I don't end up dead."

I'm going to be bait, hoping to draw out whoever took a shot at me into the open. It's a shit idea, but it's all we have right now.

It's only Franco, Demitri, Alexei, and myself. Matteo and the rest of the guards are on standby near my club, so they're not seen with us.

"Approaching the club," Franco murmurs into his microphone.

I put my shirt back on over the vest, and after buttoning it up, I shrug on my jacket.

Hopefully, this won't all be for nothing. I really want to get my hands on the fucker who shot me.

I watch as Alexei checks his rifle, which he's going to hide under his coat.

Franco parks close to the entrance. As we all get out, my eyes scan the surrounding buildings. The setting sun reflects off the windows, making it hard to see anything.

With the hair raising on the back of my neck, I take a deep breath. Alexei falls in next to me, with Demitri taking the lead and Franco bringing up the rear as we walk toward the doors. The bouncer unhooks the golden rope and stands aside for us to pass.

"Mr. Controni," he greets me as we walk inside the empty club as it only opens at nine pm. Instead of going to the VIP section like I'd always do when I come to Vizioso, we head up to the roof.

The manager comes toward me, and I wave him away. "I'm just here for a drink."

"Enjoy, sir."

"You ready?" Alexei asks as we head up the stairs.

"It has to be done," I say, and then I walk out into the open. My skin instantly begins to prickle, knowing a bullet can hit me at any moment.

Fuck.

Keep your shit together, Lucian.

"Stand by," Alexei mutters to Franco. "You do everything I say. Don't hesitate."

"Yes, Sir," Franco answers.

I move around the pool toward the bar, and I have to fight the urge to glance at the buildings around the club.

"You're doing good," Alexei whispers next to me.

"Yeah, still breathing." My words draw a chuckle from him.

When we reach the bar that's still being stocked for tonight, I order a bourbon for myself and vodka for Alexei. I don't bother asking Demitri, knowing he doesn't drink on the job.

The bartender pours the drinks, and as I pick up the tumbler of bourbon, Demitri grabs hold of me and yanks me away from the counter. The tumbler shatters in my hand, right where my head was a second ago.

"Move, Franco. Hotel roof!" Alexei roars. He crouches, his rifle aimed in the direction the shot came from.

My heart pounds in my fucking ears as I draw my Glock from behind my back.

I watch as Alexei tracks the fucker through the scope on his rifle, and then he fires a shot. Getting up, he mutters, "I took out his knee so he won't get far."

Suddenly Demitri fires a shot, and a waiter drops to the floor, a gun scattering to the side. All the staff instantly holds up their hands as Demitri scans over them.

"There's more," he murmurs. "I can feel it."

I don't come here enough to know who's an employee and who's not.

Alexei checks the surrounding buildings through his scope while Demitri guards us, and seeing the two men work together, I understand why they're the best.

Thank God they're on my side.

"Matteo has him. Let's go," Alexei says. I get up from the crouching position. Alexei draws a Heckler and Koch from behind his back, holding the rifle in his left hand.

Demitri takes the lead, the three of us on high alert as we head to the stairs. My finger flexes on the trigger, every muscle in my body wound tight as we move down the steps.

"Come out, come out, wherever you are," Demitri whispers as we step into the ground floor section. "I can feel you."

I raise my arms, my gun ready as my eyes go from one employee to the next. A guy pops up from behind the bar, and as he jumps over the counter, I pull the trigger, along with Demitri.

He drops down between the barstools, a bullet to the head and one to the chest.

I quickly glance around, and when I see the manager staring at us with shock, I train my gun on him. "You fucking search every employee before they're allowed on the premises," I bark.

"Yes, Mr. Cotroni. I'm sorry," he whimpers.

"Clean up this shit, and you better be ready to open at nine, or it's coming out of your pay."

"Yes, Sir."

"Let's go," Alexei says.

When we walk out of the club, Franco's already waiting with the G Wagon's engine running. As soon as I climb into the back, I ask, "Where's the fucker?"

"Matteo and the men are taking him to the docks."

"Good."

"Fucking mercenaries," Alexei mutters. "He won't talk."

"At least I'll get the satisfaction of killing him."

When we reach the docks, I shove the door open, and with my Glock still firmly in my grip, I walk to the man Matteo has on his knees.

The man's eyes lock on me, dead and impassive. There's not even a sign of pain from the knee Alexei shot out.

He knows what's coming.

I train the barrel of my gun on his forehead. "You come after me?" I grit the words out through clenched teeth. "Big mistake."

He just keeps staring at me with zero emotion.

"Who do you work for?"

"Umbria."

Again with the goddess shit.

"They all keep saying the same thing. It's not even fun torturing them anymore," Alexei mutters.

I press the barrel against his head. "I will fucking find out who you are and hunt your family to the ends of the earth. Who the fuck do you work for?"

He shakes his head. "I was hired by a man."

"Greek?" I ask.

He nods. "I only know him as Zeus."

These code names aren't helping shit.

"Any distinct markings. Anything, and I'll make it quick."

"Nothing. We never met face to face."

Fuck.

My eyes lock on the mercenary's, and then I pull the trigger.

He slumps to the side, blood trickling from the bullet hole.

"Feel better?" Alexei asks.

"No, not at all," I mutter.

Alexei pats my back. "Go home. Hold your wife. Tomorrow's a new day."

I shake my head as I let out a deep breath. "We have to end this. It's been a month."

"She's growing impatient," Demitri suddenly says. "Three men at the club where you weren't even supposed to be, tells me she's desperate to end this just as much as you."

Alexei stares at Demitri, who seems to be deep in thought. "What are you thinking," he asks his custodian.

Demitri glances from Alexei to me. "Around-the-clock security on full alert. She's going to come out of hiding. Soon."

"Not soon enough," I mutter as I begin to walk back to the car. Glancing over my shoulder, I ask, "Staying at my place?"

"Yes."

We all get back into the G Wagon, and as Franco drives us home, my mind keeps replaying what Demitri said.

I just wish I fucking knew who she is. This Umbria shit is working on my nerves.

I shrug out of my jacket and unbutton the shirt so I can remove the vest, not wanting Elena to see it.

"Wear that vest whenever you go out," Alexei says.

"I will," I assure him.

He might be an assassin, but he's one of the most loyal people I'll ever have the privilege of knowing in our line of business.

When Franco steers the car up the driveway, I adjust my cuffs and straighten my clothes. I shove the looming threat to the back of my mind so Elena won't see the worry on my face.

God knows, she's worried enough today.

Tonight I just want to bury myself inside my wife and forget the world outside exists.

Chapter 25

ELENA

I'm a second away from chewing my nails. I've cleaned the kitchen and washed the clothes we managed to get before the incident at the restaurant.

Now I'm rearranging the closet. Anything to keep me busy.

The door opens, and my head snaps in its direction. When I see Lucian, I rush to him. "God, I was so worried," I say as I wrap my arms around his waist.

I close my eyes and send up a prayer of thanks for bringing him safely back to me.

Lucian hugs me back, then he places his finger under my chin and nudges my face up. "I don't want you to worry about me."

"I'll always worry," I whisper, my eyes searching his for any sign that he's not okay.

He lowers his head and presses a soft kiss to my mouth, then he says, "I'm just going to shower."

I pull away from him. "You didn't finish your meal earlier. Can I warm it up for you?"

The corner of his mouth lifts as he pulls his jacket off. "No, I plan on eating something else tonight."

"Oh? What? I can prepare it while you shower and have a drink."

A wolfish grin spreads over his lips. "Don't leave the room."

When he walks into the bathroom, my eyes widen with realization.

He meant me.

Oh, God.

I need to get ready.

I rush to the closet and begin to dig through the lingerie I got. I pull a white set out, seeing as it will be our first time making love.

Knowing Lucian showers quickly, I strip out of my clothes as quickly as I can. I pull on the white lace panties and matching lace nightgown that clips together beneath my breasts. My hands flutter over the lace, straightening it out.

Taking deep breaths, I listen for when the water turns off. Then I remember my hair is in a ponytail, and I quickly yank the tie out, fluffing the stands with my fingers.

The water turns off as I gather my discarded clothes and shove them into the closet for the time being.

I spin around and wonder if I should sit down on the bed. Lie in a sexy position? Maybe I should –

Lucian comes out of the bathroom, and I freeze. He has a towel wrapped around his waist. His eyes sweep over me, and then he stops dead in his tracks.

He stares at me until my cheeks start to warm.

"Christ, Elena," he breathes. "You're breathtaking."

"I wanted to wear something special for you," I say, happy to see the appreciation and desire swirling in his eyes.

"You can wear that every night," he mutters, still staring at me.

Lucian fists his hands at his sides, and when he doesn't come to me, I walk to him. My eyes search his, and not seeing anything but desire, I lift myself on my tiptoes and press a kiss to his neck, taking a deep breath of his scent.

I hear him exhale sharply, then I ask, "Why aren't you moving?"

"If I do, I'm going to throw you on the bed and fuck you. I'm trying to regain some control so I can take it slow for you."

My lips curve up, and I begin to walk backward until I feel the bed behind me. "I want you, Lucian. You don't have to hold back."

I'll take him any way I can have him.

I sit down on the bed and scoot to the middle, and it's all it takes for Lucian to rip the towel from his waist and stalk toward me.

My eyes instantly drop to his erection. There's no revulsion as I take in how perfect my husband is. Every inch of his body is hard muscle. He's much bigger than what I've seen, and even though I don't think he'll appreciate me calling his cock beautiful, it's the only word I can come up with.

Lucian takes hold of my thighs and yanks me to the edge of the bed, and it makes the lace move up, exposing me from the waist down.

"You have no idea how hard it was to wait," He says as he reaches for the nightgown, unclipping it.

My heart begins to beat faster, and my stomach flutters as Lucian nudges the right side of the lace away from my breast. Slowly he does the same with the left side as if he's unwrapping a gift.

His irises darken to midnight black as he stares at my breasts. "God, I'm a lucky bastard," he says, his voice rough and low.

No, I'm the lucky one to have a man look at me with so much love and desire.

His palms brush down my waist and hips, and then he takes hold of the lace panties and pulls them down my legs.

"On second thought, forget the lace. I prefer you naked," he says gruffly as he lowers himself to his knees. He pushes my legs open, and my face reddens from being exposed to him like this.

Lucian leans forward and presses kisses to my inner thighs, and then he moves up to my hips and abdomen. "Jesus," he breathes as he drags his nose over my strip of curls. Then my eyes shoot wide open, and my lips part on a gasp as his tongue swipes over my clit.

Holy...

He sucks hard, and it makes my body tighten and melt all at once.

Mother...

I'm still adjusting to the new sensations when Lucian lets out a deep growl. Then I have to grab hold of the covers, and my back arches from the intense pleasure his tongue and lips create between my legs.

I can only gasp, my jaw slack.

His tongue lashes at me until I'm overly sensitive. His lips knead my clit into oblivion, and when he pushes a finger inside me, I crash into an inferno of pleasure.

I make sounds I never thought possible. My body convulses as if I'm being electrocuted. Waves of pleasure crash over me, my skin alive, my breaths sharp and fast.

And it's all just from Lucian's skilled mouth and hands.

I'm still gasping for air, my fingers almost tearing into the covers from the tight grip I have on them when Lucian moves up my body. He presses kisses all over my abdomen and ribs until he reaches my breasts.

I finally regain some control back over my body, and letting go of the covers, I bring my hands to his hair as he sucks my nipple into his mouth.

My fingers weave through Lucian's damp strands, and when his teeth tug at my hard bud, I arch into him.

"Lucian," I moan, losing my mind from everything he's making me feel.

He pushes his arm beneath me and moves me up the bed, and then his body presses against mine. Skin to skin. Every inch.

His sculptured solid chest to my soft skin. His abs against my stomach. And his erection between my legs.

Lucian's eyes capture mine, and I'm overwhelmed by the love I see in them.

I can't believe there was a time I feared him. If I had a crystal ball to see this moment, I would've run to Lucian the first time we met.

I relish the feel of his body on top of mine as I move my hands to his shoulders, down his arms, and then back up until I reach his neck.

"I love you so much," I whisper. His expression softens at my words. "You're the first person I said those words to."

"I'll be the only person to hear them," he demands, and then his mouth fuses with mine.

LUCIAN

Jesus, it's hard to take it slow.

My body shudders from the effort it's taking to kiss Elena tenderly while she's naked beneath me, her legs spread for me, her pussy's heat setting my cock on fire.

I rub myself against her as my hands brush down her sides and back up, memorizing the feel of her curves.

Elena naked. I'll never see anything as beautiful again.

Then she lifts her hips, pressing her pussy against my cock, and she moans into my mouth.

And. I. Fucking. Lose. My. Mind.

Tender vanishes.

Gentle has no place here.

The kiss turns filthy, demanding more moans from my wife.

My lips and teeth work Elena's until they're swollen, plump for me to feast on.

Her eyes are clouded with lust, her breasts pushing against my chest with every breath of air she takes.

Fucking otherworldly.

I move my hand down, my knuckles brushing over her toned stomach and gripping hold of my aching cock, I rub myself over her opening and clit to lubricate the head.

The angel on my shoulder tells me to ask her if she's ready.

The devil says fuck that shit, I've waited long enough.

I push the head of my cock inside her, and then I meet resistance from her tight inner walls. It rips a growl from me, and I thrust hard, forcing my way into her because God help me, I need to be buried deep inside her right now.

Elena lets out a soft cry, her features tightening.

"Amore mio," I whisper, and I begin to press kisses to her face, trying to ease the discomfort I've caused her.

Her arms wrap tighter around my neck. "I'm okay."

My eyes close from how fucking amazing it feels to be buried deep inside her, and I take a moment to memorize how perfectly she wraps around my cock.

Our eyes lock, and then I pull out. I watch closely for her reaction as I thrust back inside her warmth.

Elena's lips part, and her pupils dilate.

I rub my pelvis against her clit, and when she makes a small sound of pleasure, I ask, "Enjoying the feel of my cock, amore mio?"

She nods, her lips curving up. "God, yes."

I pull out again and thrust in harder, and when she gasps and her eyes drift closed, I demand, "Eyes on me while I'm fucking you."

They open, looking like melted gold. Sinful and seductive.

I begin to move, and every time the head of my cock hits against her deepest depths, I go faster. Harder.

Elena's tight walls and heat strip me of my control, and I begin to worship her with my mouth and hands. I rub my whole body against hers as I sink deep, wanting my scent on every inch of her. I want to brand her skin with the feel of mine so she'll never forget this moment. She'll never forget I'm her husband and the only man who gets to sink balls deep in her hot pussy.

I claim her the only way I know how. Hard. Fast. Desperate to dominate all of her.

I lay my sins at her feet. My vows at her heart. My love at her soul. I give her all of me.

My weakness and strength.

The good and evil.

The lover.

The killer.

And Elena takes all of me as her mouth devours mine. Her hips begin to move, meeting my thrusts.

A symphony of love builds around us. Elena's moans. My harsh breaths. Our skin meeting. Her slick heat coating my cock.

"Christ," the word bursts from me as pleasure begins to spiral down my spine. I push my hand between us and pinch Elena's clit. "Come for me, amore mio."

I angle my cock to hit a different spot and finding my wife's G-spot, a grin spreads over my face when her lips form a silent cry of pleasure. Letting go of her clit, I grab hold of her thigh, pulling her leg up over my hip, and then I focus on assaulting her G-spot until Elena's thrashing beneath me.

"Lucian," she cries, and I crush my mouth to hers, wanting to taste her orgasm as it rips through her.

"Dio. Dio. Dio." Her chants fall on my lips. She arches, her breasts rubbing against my chest, her nails digging into my skin, and then her body tightens. "Lucian," she whimpers.

Her face fills with ecstasy, and then she comes hard on my cock, clamping around me, forcing me over the edge until I'm jerking inside her. My body shudders against hers, and a low growl is ripped from my chest.

With our eyes locked, we live only in this moment as we create mind-blowing pleasure together.

I lower my head and capture Elena's lips. Bringing my arms up, I frame her face with my hands, all of my body pressing against hers as I slow my rhythm until I'm lazily plunging inside her.

Residual pleasure rocks through her, making her spasm around my cock.

When I finally still inside her, I nip at her lips one more time before I lift my head, and then we stare at each other.

Emotion fills Elena's eyes until they sparkle.

"I love you so fucking much," I say.

She lets out a sputter and then presses her face to my neck.

I gather her in my arms, my body enveloping hers, and I hold her as she sheds her past and finds the freedom she so desperately needed in the safety of my love.

"I'm sorry," she says, her voice strained and small against my skin. "This is all I ever wanted. It's overwhelming to know I'm finally loved. "

I tighten my hold on her, pressing kisses to her hair, her ear, her neck. "Don't be sorry, amore mio. Let me take all of your demons. I want you to know only peace."

"You're my peace," she says as she lifts her face to mine. "Tutto mio." *My everything.*

My mouth finds hers, and we spend hours kissing, loving, devouring each other. We share our darkest secrets and our dreams. Our whispers fill the air as I take Elena in every possible position until I'm finally sated in the early hours of the morning.

Chapter 26

ELENA

Waking up, I stretch my tender body against Lucian, where I'm lying half over him.

His arm tightens around my shoulders, and he presses a kiss to my disheveled hair. The sheets are rumpled around us as the memories of last night come to me.

The way Lucian loved me… God, I didn't even know it was possible to experience such pleasure, to feel so much, to get lost in another person the way I got lost in him.

I cried, breaking in the safety of his arms, and he took all of my demons.

He wiped the cruelty and depravity from my life.

He released me from the shackles of my past.

Then he taught me how to love with all my heart. He showed me how to pleasure him in every way but one.

Lucian refused that I go down on him. Even when I told him I'm okay with it.

It was not negotiable.

Now that my mind is clear of desire and pleasure, I realize Lucian knows me better than I know myself. It would've tainted our night because I don't think it's something I'll be able to do without being reminded of the past.

Suddenly Lucian flips me onto my back, and he presses a kiss to my neck. "Stay in bed and get more sleep. I need to go to work."

Lifting my hand to his jaw, I brush my fingers over the bristles. "Be careful."

"I will." He gives me a chaste kiss then gets up. I turn onto my side, tucking my hands beneath my head as I watch my husband walk to the bathroom and as he gets dressed.

"I like it better when you're naked," I say, a teasing tone to my voice.

He chuckles and comes to give me another kiss, then he trails his nose down my neck and to my breasts. His lips tug at my nipple, making my desire increase, but then he gets up and walks to the door. "I'm going to be hard the whole fucking day," he mutters as he opens the door. "Ti amo."

"Ti amo," I say, a happy smile on my face.

When Lucian shuts the door behind him, I stretch out again and then roll over to his side of the bed. I bury my face in his pillow, taking a deep breath of his scent.

My husband.

Thinking how Lucian just walked into my life and took what he wanted makes me feel giddy, and I let out a soft chuckle.

God, I'm so in love with him. My stomach is constantly fluttering with butterflies. My heart melts.

And he chose me.

Out of all the women he could've picked, he chose me.

I'm so lucky.

So happy.

Taking another breath of his scent, I get up and walk to the bathroom. I open the faucets and pour some bubble bath into the tub.

While the water runs, I brush my teeth and hair, tying the strands back into a bun so they won't get wet.

With happiness hovering around my lips, I close the faucets and sink into the balmy water. While I soak my tender body, I remember how passionately Lucian made love to me. His hands on my skin. His mouth kissing every inch of me. How his body moved against mine while he filled me.

And his eyes.

God, his eyes.

They were dark as night, dominant and intense.

Ugh, why did he have to work today?

I finish my morning routine, and once I'm dressed in a brand new pair of jeans and a baby-yellow silk blouse, I slip on my high heels and go look for Aunt Ursula.

Finding her out on the veranda, I pour myself a cup of coffee and go sit by her.

"Did you sleep well?" I ask before taking a sip of my beverage.

"Yes, cara, and you?"

I didn't sleep much but answer, "Very well." Setting my cup down on the table, I stare out over the backyard.

"You look beautiful in the new outfit," she compliments me. "We should finish our shopping from yesterday."

My lips curve up. "Yes, I've taken all my old clothes out and placed them in bags. I thought we can drop them off at a shelter."

"That's a good idea. We'll leave as soon as you're done with your coffee." Aunt Ursula gets up to take her empty cup into the house, then I hear her say, "We're going shopping, Leo. Bring the car around to the front."

I finish my coffee and go rinse the cup out, then I go get my phone from where it was charging in the living room. I notice a message from Lucian and open it.

Lucian: Do you feel me between your legs?

A smile splits over my face.

Me: Yes, and everywhere else.

He types his reply instantly.

Lucian: Good, because I can still feel you wrapped around my cock.

God.

My body flushes with desire.

Me: I can't wait for tonight.

Lucian: You better be naked in bed when I get home.

Me: What about dinner?

Lucian: I'm only hungry for your pussy.

Oh. My. God.

I let out a giggle, my cheeks heating from his words. Wanting to tease him as well, I type out a reply I never thought I'd type in my life.

Me: I'm aching to have you fill me with your cock.

My eyes widen at the message, and before I can change my mind, I press send.

Lucian: Christ, now I'm walking around hard as fuck.

Me: Good, because my panties are soaked. We're even.

Lucian: You're killing me.

"Are you ready?" Aunt Ursula asks.

"Yes." I type out a last message.

Me: I'm going shopping with Aunt Ursula. I love you. Be safe.

Lucian: Love you most.

I tuck the phone in my handbag then walk out of the house with Aunt Ursula.

"Let's start at that little boutique we were going to go to next," Aunt Ursula says as we climb into the back of the other G Wagon.

Leo gets into the passenger side with Marcello behind the steering wheel. The rest of the guards fill the car behind us as Marcello steers us off the property.

"Okay," I smile at her. "These jeans are really comfy. I'd like to get another pair."

"And they sit well on you," she compliments me.

"You have a good eye. You picked them."

She lets out a chuckle. "Years of practice."

I'm changing out of a red cocktail dress into my own clothes when my phone begins to ring.

Slipping my foot into the one high heel, I dig the device out of my bag, and seeing my father's number, I frown.

What does he want?

I press answer. "Yes?"

"Elena," a woman's voice comes over the line. "It's Eva... your mother."

Stunned, I quickly place my hand against the wall to keep my balance as my legs go numb. Goosebumps spread over my skin.

What?

"Mamma?" I ask, not sure I heard right.

Is this real?

"If you really have to call me that," she says, her voice biting.

My heart begins to race, and my mind spins into chaos.

Oh my God.

She's alive?

My mother's alive!

A cold sweat spreads over my body as the shock hits full-on, ripping the air from my lungs.

"I thought you were dead," I manage to whisper, not even sure if this is real or a dream.

"I was." She takes a deep breath. "I have Lucian. Come to your father's villa, and I'll let you say your goodbyes before he dies."

Her words pour over me like acid, eating away the blissful happiness. It feels like my mind short circuits, not able to make sense of what I'm hearing. Unable to think of an appropriate reaction.

A strangled sound escapes me. "Don't. Please," I repeat the words I've said so many times before when I was faced with the horrors of life.

"You have fifteen minutes. Come alone, or you won't even get a goodbye."

The world spins around me as the call ends, and I stand frozen, my breaths rushing over my lips, not able to form a coherent thought.

Lucian.

No.

No.

No.

Keep calm, Elena. You need to save him.

Somehow I think to slip on the other shoe and gather my handbag.

Deep breaths.

God.

Focus, Elena. Lucian needs you. You can deal with the shock later. Right now, you need to focus on what has to be done.

Leo and Aunt Ursula can't know.

A sob ripples over my lips, but I swallow the shock and fear back. I take another deep breath, lifting my chin and forcing a smile around my lips.

Taking hold of the red cocktail dress, I close my eyes.

You can do this.

You have to.

For Lucian.

I open the door and stepping out, my voice is filled with false excitement. "Oh gosh, I love it. Can you pay while I run to the restroom? My bladder's going to burst."

I shove the dress in Aunt Ursula's hands, and she chuckles at me as I turn to the attendant that's been helping us. "Where's the restroom?"

"Just through that door, to the left," she smiles at me.

I glance at Leo, where he's standing near the store's entrance, as I run to the restroom. I shut the door behind me and lock it, then turn to the gold stained glass window.

Panicking, I can't find a way to open it, and picking up a trashcan, I smash it through the glass. Knowing someone probably heard the noise, I hurry through the opening, slicing my arm open. I cover the cut and run down the alley toward the street.

My heart hammers against my ribs, my breaths bursting desperately over my lips as I pray one prayer after the other for Lucian's safety.

God, my mother's alive.

She's here.

As the shock keeps hitting me in waves, I dart away from the store, praying Leo doesn't see me. The high heels make it hard to run, and I stop to quickly take them off.

"Mrs. Cotroni!" I hear Leo shout somewhere behind me.

Just then, I spot a taxi and rush toward it.

Jumping into the back, I give the driver my father's address. "Quick! Hurry!"

As he pulls away, I watch Leo run toward the car, his face torn with worry.

I'm sorry, Leo.

I lean back against the seat, and closing my eyes, I start to pray. I don't know what I'm going to do when I get to my father's villa.

How is this happening?

She's alive?

God, she has Lucian!

Can I even reason with her?

Why is she doing this?

"Faster," I say when it feels like the driver is taking his time. "It's urgent."

It feels like time crawls, and when the taxi finally pulls up to the villa, I pay the fee and climb out. I don't even think to put on my shoes as I rush to the gate. My heart beats in my throat as it opens, and then a man dressed in a black combat uniform steps in front of me.

He grabs hold of my arm, and without a word, he drags me up the driveway to the front door of the mansion I had hoped to never enter again.

I have no idea what to expect.

My mother's here, inside the house.

Lucian. God, Lucian.

My emotions toss inside me like wild waves.

Everywhere I look, bodies lay scattered, and I recognize none of the men standing guard.

So much blood.

So much death.

My phone begins to ring, and it has the man yanking my handbag away from me. With my heart thundering in my chest, I'm taken to my father's study and shoved inside the room.

My phone rings again, and the first thing I see is my father, tied to a chair, his face beaten and his shirt bloody.

Then I see an older version of me, and the sight of the mother who I thought was dead shocks me to my core.

She's really alive.

I can't help but feel hurt that she left me behind. I have so many questions filling me, but then I realize there's no sight of Lucian.

"Where's my husband?" I ask, not caring about what she does to my father or me.

Her lips curve up as her eyes glide over me, and then she points a gun at me. "I see you got your father's intelligence. I doubted whether you'd fall for the lie, but I had to try. Lucian Cotroni's not an easy man to kill, and using you as bait was the only hand left for me to play."

He's not here.

Lucian's safe.

Oh, thank God.

In a trance where fear wars with relief, I begin to shake my head, not understanding. "Why?" I manage to ask through the shock, still dulling my senses.

She gestures with the barrel of the gun at a chair, and then the guard shoves me toward it.

Refusing to take a seat, I meet her gaze again. "Why are you doing this?"

Again my phone rings, and then it really sinks in.

Lucian's not here.

It was a trap.

I realize how stupid I was. I just reacted out of fear without thinking of calling Lucian.

Elena... what have you done?

Slowly I turn my head to the guard holding my handbag.

Lucian's probably trying to get a hold of me.

"Why am I doing this?" she lets out a bark of laughter, then she slams the gun against my father's head. "Tell your daughter why I'm doing this."

"Fuck you," my father spits. "Kill me, you fucking bitch."

Hard until the end. My father still refuses to bow or show emotion.

A heavy hand lands on my shoulder, and I'm shoved down on the chair. I glare up at the guard, and as he raises his hand against me, my mother says, "No, Zeus. Don't hit her. Bring me the bag."

Confusion spills into my heart because she stopped one of her men from hurting me.

Does it mean she cares?

Maybe I can reason with her after all?

Maybe she won't kill me, and she'll spare Lucian because I love him?

I watch as he hands her my bag, and then she digs my phone out. "Lucian seems to really care about you. Let's hope it's enough to make him come here."

Chapter 27

LUCIAN

Alexei and Demitri are standing by the cars while Franco and I check the shipment of CA-415s and incendiary grenades that just came in.

As Franco opens another crate, my phone begins to ring. I pull it out of my pocket, and seeing Leo's name, worry instantly floods me.

"What's wrong?" I snap into the phone.

"Mrs. Cotroni ran away. She went to the restroom, broke the window, and took a taxi. I couldn't get to her in time," he says, sounding out of breath.

"Why the fuck would my wife run away?" I shout, instantly losing my temper.

"There was no sign she was upset. We were in the store. She went to try on a dress then gave it to your aunt to pay for while she went to the restroom. She showed no distress whatsoever," Leo explains, sounding puzzled by what happened.

"How long has it been?"

"Five minutes."

"Get my aunt safely home. I'll find Elena," I order. Ending the call, I walk to Alexei. "Elena's gone. Leo says she escaped from a restroom and ran away."

"What the fuck?" Alexei instantly straightens up. "Why would she run?"

"I have no fucking idea. She was happy." I bring Elena's number up on my phone and press dial. It just rings before going to voicemail.

I keep doing it until Demitri takes hold of my arm. My eyes snap to his, and then he shakes his head slowly. "She's not going to answer."

I don't like the look on his face, and it makes ice pour through my veins. "No." I shake my head, my legs losing all feeling. I lean back against the car to keep myself standing as the realization sinks in. "Dio." I breathe, placing my hands on my legs as my stomach lurches. "No."

"You think they got to Elena?" Alexei asks Demitri.

"Yes."

I keep shaking my head, unable to accept it.

"Makes sense," Alexei says, "Bait to get Lucian to come to them. That's what I would do if it was too hard to just kill the target. Using a loved one as bait makes the job cleaner."

My heart clenches into a tight fist, and needing air, I push away from the car and begin to stalk, sucking in deep breaths.

Elena.

Amore mio.

God, please, not this.

Not my Elena.

My phone begins to ring, and seeing Elena's name, relief rushes through my veins, making me feel lightheaded. "Amore mio," I answer, wiping the sweat from my forehead with my forearm.

"Not quite," a woman replies. "Listen carefully, Mr. Cotroni. You come alone. I see your guards, she dies. You try anything, she dies. You come alone."

My eyes drift closed as the worst feeling I've ever felt shudders through my body.

Unbearable pain.

Excruciating loss.

Unadulterated rage takes over every part of me. "Where?" I squeeze the word out through a tight throat.

"Valentino's villa. You have fifteen minutes."

Somehow my mind still seems to work as I demand, "I want proof of life."

The call ends, and a moment later, a message comes through. I open it and stare at the photo of my wife where she's sitting on a chair.

I drink in the sight of her, and then I see the blood running down her arm.

Motherfucker.

I recognize Tino's office.

Alexei places his hand on my shoulder, and in a daze, I turn my head to him.

"You need to stay focused," he says.

"I have to go alone," I mutter, unable to form a half-assed plan.

Elena.

Flashes of her begin to fill my mind.

Her smile.

Her eyes.

The musical sound of her laughter.

Her moans.

Her warmth.

"You're not fucking going alone," Alexei barks, and then he slaps my face. "Snap out of it. We need to go."

Shaking my head, I try to focus as we walk to the car, then only do I think to say, "Franco, bring all the men and load that crate of grenades. Leave the rest. We're going to Tino's place."

We pile into the car, and Alexei instantly begins to form a plan. "We attack full force."

"I won't risk Elena's life," I disagree.

Alexei gives me a look filled with warning. "Now more than ever, you have to trust me."

Christ.

If not him, then who?

I take a deep breath to try and calm down enough to focus. "I'm listening."

"If you go in alone, you're both dead. It's as simple as that. We attack with everything we have, and it will force Umbria to use Elena as a hostage. That way, you don't die, and we stand a chance of getting Elena out of there."

Alexei is right.

Fuck.

I nod. "Okay. We attack." I turn my attention to Franco. "Call all the guards from the house. Have them bring a rocket launcher. Leave only Leo with my aunt."

"Yes, Sir."

I feel agitated, fear dancing around the edges of the darkness closing in on me.

Then it hits again.

Umbria has my wife, the love of my fucking life.

My heart.

My soul.

God, if Elena dies. If anything happens to her. I will tear the fucking world apart.

My heart clenches, my muscles tightening, my hands thirsting for revenge.

I'll fucking create hell on earth to get her back.

I reach behind my back and pull my Glock out, and then I look down at the Cotroni name engraved on the sides.

'You give no second chances. There's no place for mercy in our world. Show no weakness and fear. Never hesitate or second guess yourself. Be sure. Be cruel. You have to make them fear you. That's where our power lies.'

My father's words echo through me.

Today I'll either join my father, or I'll show the whole goddamn planet to never fuck with me again. To never touch what's mine.

My eyes lift to Alexei's.

"If I'm going down, it will be fighting."

"I'll be right by your side, brother," he says, with no fear in his eyes.

I pull the extra ammo and guns we always keep in the G Wagon from the hidden compartment and begin to push clips into my pockets.

No fear.

No mercy.

I'm coming, amore mio.

ELENA

My mother slams the gun against my father's head again. "I've waited so long for this moment," she sneers. "The mighty Valentino Lucas has fallen."

My eyes dart around the room, searching for a weapon or a way to get out.

You have to do something, Elena. Before Lucian gets here.

My gaze falls on the letter opener on my father's desk, and as soon as I move, a shot rings through the air. A bullet slams into the wall behind me, tearing a shriek out of me as I bounce back with fright.

"Don't move," my mother yells. "I just need you alive, not in one piece," she threatens.

Shaking like a leaf, I sit frozen.

She glances between my father and me, her features tight with her thirst for revenge. "I'm surprised she's still alive. I didn't think you'd let her live."

My father remains quiet, his eyes not showing any emotions.

"You see," she goes on as she leans back against the oak desk, "Valentino wanted a son. He had no use for a daughter. It took me seventeen hours to give birth to you, and then he beat me to within an inch of my life because I pushed a girl out."

Her words hurt, each one ripping at my heart. For a moment, I begin to feel compassion for her.

"I was left for dead on the side of a road," my mother gestures to the guard next to me, "where Zeus found me. He took care of me and then taught me everything I needed to know, so I could take my revenge."

God.

Horrified, my eyes fall on my father.

I can't believe I come from such cruelty.

Conscious that Lucian can be here at any moment, I ask, "Why did you kill Mr. Cotroni? Why are you going after Lucian?"

My mother lets out a bitter chuckle. "I was engaged to Luca. I was in love and happy, and then he met Dorothy, and I was handed down to Valentino. Discarded like trash."

She pushes away from the desk, her hate-filled eyes landing hard on my father. "If Luca had kept his promise to me, I wouldn't have been repeatedly raped by this monster." She hits my father again until blood flows freely from his nose and mouth.

"Lucian is innocent," I argue, just wanting to save his life. I don't care what she does to my father.

Another bitter chuckle escapes her. "What little innocence there is in this world is destroyed by men like the Cotronis and your father."

"Why did you wait twenty-one years?" I cry. "You just left me with them, knowing what they were capable of!"

"You're nothing but a reminder of the torment I suffered." Her face turns to stone. "I only had one goal, and that was to create an army from nothing to take them down. The Mafia falls today."

I stare at the two monsters who created me in hate, and it strips my soul bare.

Would this have been my future if I had been forced to marry Dante?

Part of me understands my mother's pain, and I try to reason with her. "Lucian saved me from suffering the same fate as you. I love him."

"There's no such thing as love," she spits out.

"Did you kill Cabello?" my father suddenly asks.

My mother laughs. "He was the easiest to get to. I drowned him in a tub of acid."

He levels her with an enraged look, and it earns him another blow to the head. Then my mother holds her hand out to Zeus, and he moves to place a knife in her hand.

Without giving it another thought, I jump up and run out of the room, moving as fast as I can.

"Get her!" my mother screams.

My heart explodes into a rampant beat as I dart down the stairs. Knowing my mother's men are outside, I turn into the living room, but then Zeus' fingers claw at my shoulder, and I'm yanked back against his body. Instantly the cold steel of a gun presses against my head.

My eyes dart around wildly, looking for a weapon I can use, while I struggle against his hold, and then there's a loud explosion at the front of the property.

"Gamo!" Zeus mutters in Greek as he drags me out of the living room.

Gunfire erupts with more explosions vibrating the air.

Lucian.

Roars of pain come from upstairs, and I try to elbow and head-butt Zeus like I did with Dante, but nothing I do helps. I'm thrown into the study, landing on my hands and knees. When I lift my head, I'm sickened by what I see.

My mother's stabbing my father in his groin area. He begins to convulse with shock, and it makes hysterical laughter bust from my mother.

"They're coming," Zeus shouts at her.

"Let them," she screams, looking completely insane.

Zeus leaves the study, and then it's just my mother and me. I scramble to my feet and knowing it's either me or her, I run for her. Plowing into her body, we tumble to the floor. My breath explodes from me, strands of my hair sticking to my face as I try to reach for the gun.

She pushes hard against me with her whole body, flipping us over so she's on top. I grab hold of her arms, the knife in her right hand and the gun in her left, my eyes darting between the two.

Our strained breaths mix with the gunfire outside. My heart thunders harder than it ever has.

Fight Elena.

For Lucian.

For yourself.

I let out a snarl, and using every drop of strength I have, I let go of her right arm, and pushing myself up, I grab hold of the gun and try to pry it out of her grip.

Her right arm comes down, and she plunges the knife into me. Then there's a deafening bang as she pulls the trigger.

Chapter 28

LUCIAN

(Ten minutes earlier...)

Nearing Valentino's villa, I order into the mic, "Blow the gates."

Seconds later, there's an explosion up ahead as the rocket hits the target.

Thank God for rocket launchers.

"Franco, you stay with me."

"Always," he bites the words out, and then he steers the G Wagon through smoke and debris.

Instantly we take fire, and halfway to the house, the tires are blown out, bringing us to a halt.

"Go!" Alexei orders, and we move.

As I throw the door open, my heart slows to hard beats. I only have one goal – getting to Elena.

The second I'm out of the vehicle, Franco falls in behind me, and we start to return fire as we make our way to the back so we can get the grenades.

Alexei and Demitri come from the left side of the car as my men pour onto the villa's grounds. They provide us with cover while Franco and I pull the pins and throw grenades at the fuckers shooting at us.

It's hell, fire, and death as we begin to move forward.

A bullet slams into my back, making me stagger, but I catch my balance, despite the pain spreading through my upper body from the impact to the armored vest.

My arms don't lower, and I don't stop firing, taking down one man after the other.

I'm vengeance.

I'm rage.

I'm fucking death.

I load another clip, slamming it into the Glock.

Then my eyes land on the Greek coming out of the front door.

The fucker.

He opens fire, and I return the fucking favor, hitting him in the side of his neck and lower abdomen. He ducks behind a pillar.

Letting out a growl, I run for him, letting one bullet after the other hit the pillar. I reload the clip in my Glock while Franco targets the Greek, and not having enough time to aim, I take a bullet to the chest, and then I slam the hilt of my gun into his face. Pain vibrates through my chest, the bulletproof vest having taken the bullet, but I ignore it as I begin to beat the shit out of the fucker.

I see the last time my father smiled at me. His body on that cold slab of steel. His funeral.

I keep crushing the hilt of my gun against his face, his head, any fucking piece of flesh I can find. Merciless and seeking only one thing – death.

My breaths are roars. My blood demanding revenge.

A gunshot rings from inside the house, grabbing my attention, and it gives the Greek a split second to punch me in the side of my neck. The blow jars me for a moment and needing to get to Elena, I bring my gun to his head. He grabs hold of my forearm, and our strengths clash – his will to survive and my will to end him.

A deep growl rips from me as I use everything I have, forcing the barrel of the Glock closer to his head, and then I take the shot.

The Greek slumps back against the ground, his eyes lifeless. I'm filled with immense satisfaction, but not having time to savor the kill, I dart up and run into the house.

"No!" I hear Elena scream, her voice filled with the same anger pulsing through me. It propels me up the stairs, and when I storm into the study, all sanity drains from my mind.

My heart stops.

My breathing falters.

My whole fucking world comes to a standstill.

Umbria has an arm around Elena's neck and a gun pressed to her head. A Ka-bar has been plunged into Elena's left shoulder.

Raising my arm, I train the barrel of my Glock on the woman. My eyes snap between Umbria and Elena, and the uncanny similarities I see make my lips part with shock. They're identical, Umbria's just older.

Christ Almighty.

I can feel Franco behind me, and it offers me some comfort knowing if I fail, he will be able to take revenge for me.

Umbria begins to chuckle, the sound filled with madness. "Finally, you're a hard man to kill."

"Umbria? Who the fuck are you?" I spit the question out, even though I already know the answer.

"Eva Lucas, your father's trash."

Her words make me frown. "My father? What does he have to do with you?"

"I'm the one he threw aside for your mother. I was fed to Valentino."

My finger flexes around the trigger, but I can't take the shot without risking Elena.

"All Cotroni men are the same. All liars. I'm doing Elena a favor by killing you, just like I killed your father."

My eyes lock on my wife's, and then Elena grabs the knife from her shoulder, and pulling it out with an infuriated cry, she buries it in her mother's side.

Elena rips out of Eva's hold, and without hesitating, I take the shot. Eva stumbles back from the bullet hitting her chest, and as I stalk toward her, I bury another one in her throat.

Eva falls to the floor, gurgling through the blood building in her throat. As I come to stand next to her, I lock eyes with her. "This is for my father." Training the barrel on her head, I pull the trigger.

I watch as she stops breathing, her eyes dulling as death creeps in.

I savor this moment, wanting to never forget it.

Satisfaction fills me, and the sorrow of losing my father loosens its grip on my heart.

I've avenged you, Papà. Now you can rest in peace with Mamma.

Elena takes hold of my arm. "I'm so sorry," she says as she presses her body to mine, looking for refuge from the death surrounding us.

It was a fucking bloodbath.

I lift my right arm, still gripping my Glock, and wrap it around her.

She raises her face to mine, her mouth slowly curving up with relief. "Angelo mio."

"I told you I'd go to the depths of hell for you," I say, still fucking processing everything that's happened today but wanting my wife to know I will always come for her.

I push Elena away from me, my eyes roving over her to make sure she didn't get shot. Not finding any other wounds besides the cut on her arm and the stab wound to her shoulder eases the merciless grip panic had on my heart.

It takes a moment for me to realize Elena's okay, then I press my mouth to her forehead and take a deep breath of her scent. My sanity returns, and slipping my arms beneath her body, I lift her to my chest and bark an order at Franco, "Let's get out of here."

My eyes scan over the room. Valentino's mutilated, dead body is strapped to a chair.

Eva Lucas. *Umbria.* Finally fucking dead.

With Franco in front of us, we head out of the study and down the hallway. Random gunshots still ring in the air, and then it grows quiet.

All my men gather our wounded and dead, and then we head back toward the remaining vehicles, knowing we have to haul ass. It's going to cost me a fuck-ton of money to silence law enforcement, but I'll pay whatever I have to.

Alexei and Demitri get into an SUV with us. As Franco floors the gas and we speed away from Tino's destroyed kingdom, we all glance at each other.

These men. They went to war for me. For Elena.

Alexei's eyes lower to the blood staining Elena's shirt. "Demitri will take care of the wounds."

"Thank you," Elena whispers, and then she burrows against my chest.

I press my lips to her forehead, just needing to feel her warmth.

Knowing my wife is safely in my arms where she belongs, my mind turns to Eva. How does Nick Cabello fit into it, and where the fuck is he?

Remembering Valentino's mutilated body, I feel nothing. He deserved the death he got. You live hard, you die hard. It's just the way it is.

But he's dead. Dante's dead. Umbria, aka Eva Lucas, is dead.

My eyes caress Elena's face.

Amore mio, I've defeated your demons.

ELENA

After Demitri is done stitching up my wounds, I lift my gaze to Lucian's. He hasn't left my side for a second, gripping my hand tightly where he's sitting next to me on the couch.

I lower my eyes and whisper, "I'm sorry. I was so stupid."

He shakes his head. "You're okay. It's all that matters."

"I put your life in danger," the words shudder from me.

If Lucian had died today, it would've been my fault. I'll never forgive myself.

"Tell me what happened," he demands, residual anger tightening his features.

"My mother called and said she had you," I admit the biggest mistake I've ever made. "I didn't think and just wanted to get to you."

His face softens with love, but then he says, "You never do that again. Even if they have me, you don't come. They'll make me watch you die and then kill me. There is no way you can save me."

"I had to try," I squeeze the words out, all the emotions from the day flooding me.

Lucian shakes his head hard. "Never again, Elena."

Hearing my name from his lips, I know this is not negotiable. "Who will save you then?"

His mouth curves up again. "I will. No matter the circumstances, I'll always find a way to come back to you."

Lifting my right arm, I place my palm against his jaw. "Promise?"

"I swear this, amore mio," he says, and then he presses a tender kiss to my lips. Pulling back, he asks, "How do you feel?"

I move a little, and even though there's a sharp ache in my left shoulder, I reply, "I'm okay." I can't feel the cut on my arm, so at least there's that.

Lucian didn't show pain when he got shot, so I won't. I have to become stronger. For him. For our love.

"It was a clean wound," Demitri says. "It should heal quickly."

"Thank you," I reply to Demitri.

Then Lucian's face turns to stone again. "What was Eva talking about? What did my father have to do with all of this?"

My eyes close for a moment at the sharp ache it causes to know my mother was the cause of Lucian's grief.

I begin to tell him everything I know. About her love for his father and how she felt betrayed when he chose Lucian's mother over mine. How she suffered at my father's hands and swore revenge on the Mafia.

Lucian processes the information, nodding here and there, and then he asks, "Did she say anything about Nick Cabello?"

"Just that she killed him."

Lucian nods again. "Anything about who else she might've worked with?" he asks.

I shake my head. "Just Zeus. I don't know what happened to him."

"The Greek guy?" Lucian asks. When I nod, he says, "He's dead."

"Is it over?" I ask, hopeful we can find some peace in our lives.

Lucian gives me a tender smile, and then he leans into me and presses a kiss on my forehead. "It's over, amore mio."

When he pulls back, our eyes meet, and for a moment, we just stare, soaking in the fact that we both survived the attack.

All because of Lucian's strength.

"You need to rest," Lucian says.

I shake my head. "I'm fine." I've had worse, and never wanting to be in that position again, I ask, "Will you teach me how to fight and fire a gun?"

Lucian nods. "As soon as your shoulder has healed."

I lean against Lucian's chest. "Thank you."

For changing my life. For loving me. For saving me.

Lifting my head, I press my mouth to his, and I pour everything I feel into the kiss. I don't care that Alexei, Demitri, and the guards are moving around us. I just need to feel my husband's lips on mine.

Eventually, Lucian pulls back and asks, "What was that for?"

"For saving me from suffering the same fate as my mother."

Her death brings me only relief. She's finally free from the demons that haunted her. It's weird. I can't completely hate her, knowing the hell she must've gone through.

Some monsters are made, and she was one of them.

Lucian's fingers brush over my cheek. "I would've saved you sooner had I known you existed."

God, this man.

Can I love him any more than I already do?

"I would've run to you," I admit.

"Instead of running from me like I was some monster?" he teases me.

I nod. "I was right, though, it takes a bigger monster to keep the others at bay. But you're my monster."

He's a killer. A bad man to the bone. But that's what it took to survive the hell that followed me.

My avenging angel.

"Ti amo," I whisper, fusing our mouths together again.

I thank the heavens for hearing my prayers and sending Lucian to me.

Epilogue

LUCIAN

(Two weeks later…)

Standing at the VIP bar with Alexei, Demitri, Franco, and Leo, we all enjoy a drink while music fills the air.

We're having a celebratory party at Vizioso.

The Mafia did not fall. I came face to face with my enemies, and their deaths have sent out the message to not fuck with me and mine.

Out of the blood bath, I've raised a new empire. One, entirely under my control.

My eyes move between Franco and Leo, then I say, "Franco."

His attention focuses on me. "Boss?"

"You're being promoted. I need a man I can trust to take charge of Cabello's arms and customers. What do you say?"

Franco stares at me, first with surprise, and then a huge-ass smile spreads over his face. "I'd be honored to work alongside you."

"Good. It wasn't actually negotiable," I joke with him.

He lets out a bark of laughter.

"Matteo will take over the guards from you," I inform him.

Franco nods, and then I level my gaze on Leo.

Leo lifts his chin, his eyes locking with mine.

"You were willing to die for my wife." Leo nods, and I know without a doubt he would do it again if her life was in danger. "I need you to take over Tino's arms and customers."

The bear of a man begins to look emotional, and it catches me off guard. Then he gets up and fucking hugs the shit out of me.

"Thank you," he says as he steps away, then he lifts his chin again. "I won't let you down."

"I know."

"You'll each get forty percent of the sales, and the rest comes to me."

Without hesitating, they nod their agreements.

"And just like that, the Mafia is one big family again," Alexei mutters.

I smile, thinking my father would be proud of all I've achieved.

We drink to our future success, and with business taken care of, my gaze searches for Elena. I find her talking with Leo's wife, Maria, and the sight brings me comfort, knowing she's making a friend.

I nudge my arm against Leo's and gesture at our women. "They seem to get along."

Leo smiles. "That's good."

Aunt Ursula didn't want to know anything about coming to the club, so I left Marcello to watch over her at home.

"We're leaving tonight," Alexei suddenly says.

I turn to the man who's become like a brother to me. "You'll be missed."

He grins at me. "If I didn't have another job, I'd stay."

Letting out a chuckle, I shake my head. "I'd be bankrupt then. You're fucking expensive."

We all laugh, and then Alexei lifts his tumbler in a toast. "To living, fucking, and killing."

We all take a drink, and then I turn my gaze back to where Elena is. Not finding her and Maria at their table, I keep scanning the area until I see them dancing with the exclusive crowd.

I relax as I watch Elena have fun – just being a typical twenty-one-year-old woman enjoying life, and it mesmerizes me.

Her body moves sensually to the music, her ass perfect in the tight jeans she's wearing. She lifts her arms, a contented smile curving her lips, and I take in the sight of her breasts pushing against the silk top.

"Instead of eye-fucking your wife, go dance with her," Alexei mutters, drawing a chuckle from me.

I set down my drink and walk toward Elena. Her eyes lock on me, and as I close the distance between us, she draws her bottom lip between her teeth.

Fucking bewitching.

Reaching her, I wrap my left arm around her waist and yank her tightly to me. I begin to move with her, our hips instantly finding the same sensual pace.

We're only focused on each other as the need to be one builds between us.

Elena's changed so much from the first time I met her. Where she was skittish and afraid of her own goddamn shadow, she walked into the bowels of hell because she thought I was in danger. It was wrong of her to do it, but I can't ignore the fact she didn't cower before my greatest enemy to date, but instead, she faced Eva head-on.

With the training we started three days ago, she'll be a true Mafia queen soon.

"Are you happy, amore mio?"

She wraps her arms around my neck. "Indescribably happy." The corner of my mouth lifts, then she says, "But..."

"But?"

Elena pushes up against me, and her teeth tug at my bottom lip. Against my mouth, she says, "I'd be so much happier if your cock was buried deep inside me right now."

Christ.

This woman.

She pulls back with an alluring smile on her face.

"What my wife wants, my wife gets," I say, and taking hold of her hand, I pull her off the dance floor. I walk to the office I rarely use, and tugging Elena inside, I shut the door behind us and lock it so we won't be disturbed.

I switch on the light and then walk to the sofa to take a seat. "Strip for me," I order.

Elena doesn't hesitate, and with the music drifting from the dance floor, I watch as she takes hold of her top, slowly pulling it over her head.

Her hips begin to move as she unbuttons her jeans, and once she steps out of the fabric, my wife dances only for me in nothing but black lace.

Fucking perfect.

When Elena's naked, my eyes feast on every inch of her skin. Unbuckling my belt, I pull the zip of my suit pants down.

"Come show me those moves on my lap," I say as I push the fabric down, exposing my hard-as-fuck cock to her.

Elena's lips curve higher, and she closes the distance between us. Taking hold of my shoulders, she climbs on top of me, straddling my lap.

She reaches down between us, and positioning my cock at her entrance, she sinks down until I feel her ass resting against my balls.

Her lips part, and her eyes drift shut from how good it feels to take my cock deep inside her.

"Show me how you fuck," I demand, my cock needing her to move.

Elena opens her eyes, and digging her nails into my shoulders, she begins to swivel her hips, driving me wild.

My hands find her breasts, and leaning forward, I suck on her nipples until I can't hold back anymore. Grabbing hold of her hips, I take control, and I begin to thrust hard, my cock stroking her inner walls until we're both on fire.

My lips pull back from my teeth as a roar builds, and then my wife begins to moan as her pleasure increases.

My fingers bite into her soft skin. Our lips parting. Our eyes hooded with lust.

Knowing I'm about to come, I growl, "Come on my cock, amore mio."

Her head falls back, and as I take in her neck, her breasts, her snow-white skin, I begin to hammer into her. The roar tears from me, and when I empty myself inside her, I yank her to me and sink my teeth into her nipple.

Elena takes over, chasing the last of her pleasure by sensually swiveling her hips again, her pussy rubbing against me. She weaves her fingers into my hair, and when she stills, she holds me to her breast. I feel her press a kiss on my hair. "Angelo mio." She lets out a satisfied sigh. "Ti Amo."

Pulling back, I grin at her. "You love my cock more."

She shrugs and gives me a playful smile, and it has me slapping her ass. When her pussy tightens around my cock, my eyebrow shoots up. "You like me spanking you?"

Her cheeks flush, and it gives me a glimpse of the girl I fell in love with.

The woman on my lap leans in, and then her teeth nip at my earlobe. "Yes."

I harden for her again and slowly begin to thrust inside her, and then I slap her ass again.

Her pussy grips me tightly. "Again," she moans as she begins to move up and down my cock.

My palm meets her ass, and then my fingers dig into her skin, and I fuck her until she's screaming my name.

ELENA

(Three months later…)

On my knees by one of the flower beds, the sound of the fountain keeping me company, I pull weeds from between the tulips.

There's a permanent smile etched on my face.

"Cara," Aunt Ursula calls from the veranda. "Take a break. You've been out in the sun all morning."

I pull out the last weed and then climb to my feet. Pulling the garden gloves off my hands, I drop them on the grass and walk to Aunt Ursula.

A cool glass of orange juice waits for me as I take a seat at the table.

"Look at your cheeks," she fusses. "You need to wear sunscreen."

"I'll put some on," I say, my smile widening.

Aunt Ursula's become the mother I never had. With time, I opened up to her about my past, and talking with her helped me shut the door on those memories.

Aunt Ursula's smile grows, and then I feel a kiss on the top of my head. Tilting my head back, I grin at Lucian. "You're home early."

He presses another kiss to my lips then comes to take a seat at the table.

Aunt Ursula pours him a glass of orange juice, and after he's taken a sip, he says, "I had some time off between meetings and wanted to spend it with my family."

My eyes rest lovingly on my husband. "How would you feel about that family growing?"

Lucian's eyes snap to mine, and Aunt Ursula slaps a hand to her mouth.

I let out a giggle. "We're pregnant."

Lucian's face tightens with emotion, and then he darts up and sweeps me into a hug. His arms envelop me as he spins me in a circle, laughter bursting from him.

"Dio. Dio. Dio," Aunt Ursula chants excitedly.

Lucian sets my feet back on the ground, and fusing his mouth with mine, I taste his happiness, and it multiplies my own.

Then he lifts his head, and his eyes meet mine. "You're having our baby?"

Nodding, I say, "I did a test this morning, and it's positive."

"I want to see it," he demands.

Letting out a chuckle, I take hold of his hand and pull him into the house. Once we're in our bedroom, I take the test from my bedside drawer and show it to Lucian.

A proud smile forms around his lips, and then his eyes meet mine. "I'm going to be a father."

"A wonderful father just like yours was."

My words make emotion stir on his face, then he places a hand behind my head and pulls me to him for a kiss that's slow and filled with love.

Pulling apart, we go back downstairs, only to find Aunt Ursula in the kitchen, getting ready to cook up a storm.

I gesture to the sliding doors. "I want to show you what I got done in the garden this morning."

Lucian follows me outside, and as I sweep my hand over the flower bed, his arms wrap around me from behind and his hands settle on my abdomen. Resting his chin on my shoulder, he says, "You've been busy. It looks beautiful."

Pulling free from his hold, I walk to the next flower bed. "The St. Joseph lilies are flowering."

I planted them because they were Lucian's mother's favorite.

Lucian stares at them, then he smiles at me. "My parents would've loved you."

I wrap my arms around his waist and stare up at him. "And you, Mr. Cotroni?"

A loving grin begins to tug at the corner of his mouth. "You're my obsession, amore mio. The more I want you, the more I love you, and I'll never stop wanting you."

I lift on my toes and press a kiss to his jaw, and then I hug him. With my gaze on the ocean, I soak in the feel of my husband's strong arms around me, his undying love wrapping me up in a bubble of safety.

"You're my life, Lucian," I whisper.

My husband is one of the biggest villains in the world.

But he's my hero.

My avenging angel.

The man I would follow to the bottomless pits of hell because, by his side, I will live and die.

Lucian pulls a little back and tilts his head, just staring at me.

"We'll have more than one child, right?" he asks.

"As many as you want."

He lifts an eyebrow at me. "In that case, we better get to work."

"I'm already pregnant," I laugh as he pulls me back to the house.

"Practice makes perfect."

Not that Lucian could get any more perfect in bed. "I like the sound of that."

When we head toward the stairs, Aunt Ursula sighs happily, "To be young and in love."

The moment we're alone in our room, Lucian shows me how much he loves me, and in return, I worship him.

When I lie spent in his arms, drawing lazy patterns on his chest, I ask, "Will you show our children how to be strong like their father?"

Lucian presses a kiss to my hair. "I will." He turns me onto my back and stares down at me. "And you'll show them how to never give up."

I lift my hand to Lucian's face and cup his jaw. "I will."

Together we'll show our children what love is.

The End

Published Books

STANDALONE MAFIA NOVELS
Mafia / Organized Crime / Suspense Romance

MERCILESS SAINTS
Damien Vetrov

CRUEL SAINTS
Lucian Cotroni

RUTHLESS SAINTS
Carson Koslov

TEARS OF BETRAYAL
Demitri Vetrov

TEARS OF SALVATION
Alexei Koslov
A Standalone spin-off from St. Monarch's Academy for
The Underworld Kings Collaboration.

Enemies To Lovers

College Romance / New Adult / Billionaire Romance

Heartless
Reckless
Careless
Ruthless
Shameless
False Perceptions

Trinity Academy

College Romance / New Adult / Billionaire Romance

Falcon
Mason
Lake
Julian
The Epilogue

The Heirs

College Romance / New Adult / Billionaire Romance

Coldhearted Heir

Arrogant Heir
Defiant Heir
Loyal Heir
Callous Heir
Sinful Heir
Tempted Heir
Forbidden Heir

Not My Hero
Young Adult / High School Romance

The Southern Heroes Series

Suspense Romance / Contemporary Romance /
Police Officers & Detectives

The Ocean Between Us
The Girl In The Closet
The Lies We Tell Ourselves
All The Wasted Time
We Were Lost

Connect with me

Newsletter

FaceBook

Amazon

GoodReads

BookBub

Instagram

About the author

Michelle Heard is a Wall Street Journal, USA Today, and Amazon Bestselling Author of suspense, new adult, romance novels. She loves creating stories her readers can get lost in. She resides in South Africa with her son, daughter-in-law, and cat, who always wakes her at the crack of dawn.

Want to be up to date with what's happening in Michelle's world? Sign up to receive the latest news on her alpha hero releases → <u>NEWSLETTER</u>

If you enjoyed this book or any book, please consider leaving a review. It's appreciated by authors.

Acknowledgments

Holy crap, this one was hard, but I got it done with the help and encouragement of so many amazing authors and readers. Monica, thank you for talking me off the ledge. Harloe, you're a wonderful friend. And my book bestie, Victoria, it feels like we're soul-sistas! Dylan and Lauren, gah, my fangirl went crazy when you reached out to offer me advice. I feel so loved.

To my alpha and beta readers – Leeann, Sheena, Sherrie, Kelly & Sarah, thank you for being the godparents of my paper-baby.

Candi Kane PR - Thank you for being patient with me and my bad habit of missing deadlines.

Yoly, Cormar Covers – Thank you for giving my paper-babies the perfect look.

To my readers, thank you for loving these characters as much as I do.

My street team, thank you for promoting my books. It means the world to me!

A special thank you to every blogger and reader who took the time to take part in the cover reveal and release day.

Love ya all tons ;)

Made in the USA
Las Vegas, NV
24 September 2024

95703150R10212